Fulfillment City

E.M. Arons

Second paperback edition June 2025

ISBN: 979-8-9919389-2-1 (paperback)
ISBN: 979-8-9919389-3-8 (ebook)

For Michael and Darlene

I

AT THE END of a phone conversation, she liked to say, very breezily, *Call again on Calligan*. Not all the time, not like a rule; more like a pat on the back, a friendly goodbye, especially if the call was pleasant. Hail-fellow-well-met and all. At the other end of the spectrum was the story she often told of a call that went memorably wrong. It was a potential client, this guy who had been arrogant and abrasive from the get-go. She was on speaker at her office, alone, he on speaker at his, with what sounded like a roomful of chortling sycophants. While she tried to remain courteous, the guy just wouldn't quit; first he said her ideas were lousy, then he said she didn't understand the business, then he said her rates were too high. When she held fast, he disparaged her credibility. After they said their goodbyes, he hit a button on his phone to end the call, but not the right one. "Jesus, what a bitch," he said to the group in his office. "Yeah," she said, "I didn't like you either"—followed by furious banging on his end to cut it off.

Her agency had come to be known as LC Advertising. Unclear when the name became official; at first she simply typed *Lydia Calligan Advertising* at the top of the invoices, and the address on Post Street in San Francisco. Just herself and enough billable hours to support one income. Her ads were clever, often very funny, and people began to notice. She hired an assistant, then two, then an account executive, and from there, the agency was born. Somewhere along the line, some clever illustrator sketched the face of a smiling, sultry cow with a wink. It was so light and airy, she asked him to make it a logo. "We can't co-opt the cow, but I like the wink and the smile. Can you cut it down to those?" In an interview with an industry magazine, once her agency had become known as one of the city's sleekest boutique shops, she said, in response to the interviewer's question, "No, I don't mind being associated with a smiling cow at all. She's happy and healthy, making something valuable and nutritious. And she does it with good humor and a wink that lets you know she's in on the joke. So what's not to like?"

She specialized in advertising for consumer products, specifically food and beverage, restaurants, and on occasion, government relations. What made Lydia particularly good to work with was her easy folksiness. You could sit and chat with her like a buddy at the neighborhood bar—a really great broad, described by some; by others, a sage, wise elder, with experience to offer if you needed handholding; for account executives who preferred locker room banter, a teller of raunchy and racy stories; and of course, the efficient gal Friday, the woman who's quick with the wit and the pen, ready to handle the client's doubts, questions and inspiration any time of the day or night. So her reputation as a stalwart, no-nonsense wordsmith got around, and LC was the agency often recommended when you wanted to reach a sophisticated audience. And sometimes, when something went wrong and you needed a dignified way of cleaning it up. Your four-star restaurant gave everyone e-coli on the same night? Well, we are sorry. We're beyond sorry, we're mortified. We let you down and we hope we can win back your trust. So, it's not just a free dessert with every meal, it's a free dinner for a whole party, awarded to a lucky winner at each sitting, a thank you to the loyal diners who trusted us for so long.

When she proposed the dinner giveaway and the client exploded, she convinced him he had to do it; and of course, business took off like never before. LC had a way of persuading that was funny, warm, charming and idiosyncratic, the kind of advertising you could only find in San Francisco. And everything went gangbusters, decade after decade, until the berry debacle.

It was an old campaign, one she developed early in her career that made her reputation. It got recycled periodically, dusted off like a vintage suit, cited by agencies and journals, the campaign of campaigns. It was for the California Wildberry Association, one of her first clients. The challenge: how do you make berries even more appealing and irresistible than they already are? With a kid, of course. A cute kid. And not just any kid, but a perky kid with an adorable speech impediment. The only problem with kids is they grow up. And if you want to recycle the campaign, you either use vintage versions of the original footage—hoping the kid hasn't become famously addicted or litigious or otherwise problematic—or you recast with a new kid for the current generation. And the most recent kid had been Levon Charles, a Black 8-year-old with the cutest lisp any advertising director could have asked for. A far better lisp, in fact, than little Tommy Harrison, the first tow-haired, freckle-faced blond to utter the tagline, *When you want de berry vest!* And to emphasize the cute, the kid wears a vest festooned with all the berries represented by the CWA. A veritable cornucopia of cute that exploded in popularity every time the campaign was revived.

But something happened this time. The world that was charmed by lisping children seemed to have slipped away, and no one in charge of CWA's image caught it. Now there was an internet. Now there was social media. And people grumbled they didn't like a lisping Black kid being used to sell berries. It was disrespectful—to people with speech impediments for one, and although not inherently racist, for another, seemed to cast a vague shadow of something undignified and troublesome. But the decades of success—and the slight eye problem that necessitated Lydia having to use tinted lenses in thick, chunky frames—seemed to render her insensitive to the undertow of displeasure surrounding the latest incarnation of de berry vest.

First were social media posts, likening the spot to demeaning portrayals of the past. She ignored those, advising CWA, headquartered in Fresno and far from the simmering cities of discontent, that Levon served as the ideal representative of diversity for a trade group that had long been accused of the opposite. It'll blow over, she told them. Then the protests. First at supermarkets carrying CWA produce, then at CWA-contracted growing facilities, where the actual backbreaking work of picking and collecting those wonderful berries took place. Various groups uncovered cruel and unsanitary conditions at many of the farms, and an even greater hue and cry was thrown. Now, not just a racist organization, but one that mistreated its labor. The protests began in San Francisco and spread to Los Angeles, then to Fresno. The CWA called an emergency meeting, while shouting and screaming took place in front of the Association's nondescript 1950s office building. Irritated at Lydia, the director of marketing, with the president on the call, ordered Lydia to withdraw all the spots featuring Levon, and come up with a replacement immediately. This was only out of respect, he said, for their long-term relationship; without that, any other agency would be fired on the spot. Lydia agreed, but with a sensation forming at the bottom of her feet and moving slowly upward, like frostbite, that it was already too late. Because at that moment, outside the CWA office, another group of counter-protestors began their own battle cry. This group, the Friends of California Berries, had been popping up at CWA protests, asserting that complaints about Levon were politically motivated, organized by left-wing radicals and other socialist/communist rabblerousers of that ilk. They seemed outraged and resentful that anti-CWA protestors were politicizing something as wholesome and inoffensive as berries. In fact, this was something CWA had been concerned about from the start. One of the Association's founders, Colonel William "Jed" Heinecke, a Central Valley landowner of the 1920s, had been a hardcore Birch Society leader, well-known enemy of organized labor, and likely Klan member. CWA had been eager to bury that legacy, and was accordingly very pleased with Levon as the current, smiling face of the organization.

As the anti-CWA and FCB protestors became more animated, the director of marketing held his phone out the open window so Lydia could hear. Over the raised voices, angry bullhorns and sirens, she shouted, Yes, OK, we'll do it, but no one had the phone to their ear because of the shots and screams. One of the anti-CWA protestors, holding a poster of Levon with a red X over his face—*Racist Stereotype* scrawled across the image—flew backward. A scuffle ensued, and a man wearing a ski-mask was grabbed. With twisting, rapid strength, he broke free and took off behind the building. Others rushed to the young woman, now flat on her back on the pavement, blood gurgling from her chest. She held the poster on its wooden stick a moment longer, and one of the photographers on the scene got the photo that got picked up across the world: the image of Levon's X-out faced over the young woman holding the poster, on her back, convulsing. The imagery could not have been more brilliantly composed.

At Lydia's office, the phone went dead. By now the cold had crept into her chest and shoulders. Directing everyone in the office to call their media contacts to find out what happened in Fresno, she got the story not much later than everyone else. The young protestor's name was Darilyn Cogswell and she was dead. The shooter was still on the loose, but not a member of the FCB, they were adamant to point out. They released a statement decrying the violence and their horror at the cold-blooded murder. But further protests against CWA were unnecessary. The organization cut all ties with LC Advertising, repudiating the Levon campaign, and it quickly disintegrated as its member farms were exposed for everything from abusive treatment to falsifying tax returns.

In San Francisco, the phones stopped ringing entirely. Within days, almost every client terminated their relationship with LC. By the end of the week, the company was dead. Lydia paid out everything in the coffers for severance, ignoring advice to leave a reserve to rebuild. With an emptiness in her eyes behind the tinted lenses, she liquidated all the company's assets. And that, according to her friends, was the week it happened. Lydia withdrew from her own body. Something had broken. After she disposed of all the property and signed every paper, she sat alone on the floor of the empty office. Then she put on her trench coat, tightened the belt, and walked out into the bright sunlight. And it was this Lydia Calligan who began to haunt the streets of San Francisco.

Friends and ex-colleagues would see her, buttoned trench coat and sunglasses, moving alone down the sidewalk; into a delicatessen and eating alone; walking down Market Street, through North Beach, across Union Square. Always one hand on her abdomen—not far from where the bullet hit Darilyn—the other on top of her head, holding a nonexistent hat in place, bent slightly forward, as if into a headwind that also wasn't there. And she roamed the city like that, for a year, maybe two, a specter that wouldn't acknowledge old friends' hellos or nods; just wandering, always dressed in the same coat, a ghost moving silently through a city of living human beings.

2

CLARKE'S BODY WAS beautiful. Whether standing up or lying down, in repose, as it was now, on the bed next to Paul, half covered by a white cotton sheet. Paul's eyes moved over the rounded, sleek muscles, the shine and glow of the tan over his dark skin. The smell of his sweat—perspiration mixed with curry from the Indian dinner last night. Performing in clubs kept Clarke lean and tight; without all that cardio, someone as tall and muscular would simply be stolid. But the slenderness revealed the care and diligence Clarke put into everything: his body, his music, his relationship to the world. Clarke was handsome and smart and kind, only a few of the reasons Paul fell for him. And also why he pissed Paul off as much as he did. Paul felt in equal measure the desire to love him and slap him. So far, he'd been able to keep the slapping in check, while Clarke seemed to accept any wise-ass remark with the same wide, wonderful smile.

Unsure how he was feeling about Clarke this morning, Paul rose, went to the kitchenette at the far end of his one-room apartment and made coffee. Soon enough Clarke was roused by the aroma, sat up on his elbows. The beauty in the contours of his face was almost too much for Paul to bear. So he said, "You farted chickpeas all night."

Clarke wiped his eyes and smiled. Gazing at Paul, Clarke took his own inventory. Slim as a waif, not as tall as Clarke, Paul possessed something he couldn't articulate, the same thing everyone felt, and which he was warned about. Paul knew it, and used it. He wasn't sure what it was either, but it still seemed to work, even as he moved into his late thirties.

Stepping out of bed naked, stretching, Clarke's expressive hands almost touched the ceiling. Some part of Paul felt maybe he didn't deserve all this, that he was living on borrowed time. The real-life Dorian Gray. "Jesus, put on some shorts," he said. "If the neighbors see that ding-dong, they'll call the fire department." Clarke smiled, shook his hips. Then went to him, stood behind and wrapped his thick arms around Paul's slender frame, smelled the nutty smell of his soft blonde hair.

In truth, Clarke felt guilty about wanting Paul too. Lean and wiry, his skin white as lined paper, Paul was confusing: a mature man with the tight ass of a 16-year-old skateboarder, the crinkly smile of Peter O'Toole in middle-aged prime, and the clipped vowels of his modest midwest upbringing. Clarke felt guilty that he lusted after that ass too, that he liked the feel of Paul's wiry body inside his arms. And he supposed the guilt was why he ignored the variously boorish, insulting, cranky and sometimes outright racist things that spewed out of Paul's mouth. Clarke found himself laughing and brushing over things he would never tolerate from anyone else.

"Coffee for me too?" Clarke said.

"Well, there's the machine, bub," Paul said, his smile so bashful and charming.

Clarke approached, poured it himself, into an antique porcelain cup. This one Paul found at an estate sale, another of his charms—an encyclopedic knowledge of antiques and their value. He had the ability to spot quality among the heaps of junk at flea markets and house sales; this set, he pointed out, was 18th century British, discovered among a pile of crusty Tupperwares at a house in Bernal Heights. The old lady died and her greedy nephew was selling every-thing for fast cash. Recognizing how desperate he seemed, Paul asked about the chandelier over the hallway. The nephew hadn't noticed it and told Paul he could have it for fifty bucks if he took it down himself. Which he did, and now it hung in the center of his tiny apartment, French crystal and bronze, his friend at Sotheby's valuing it at somewhere between four and six thousand dollars. "What a *maroon*," Paul said, in his best Bugs Bunny, when he told Clarke how he got it.

"I think your bed is too small for me," Clarke said, unkinking a crick in his neck. The bed was another antique picked up at a yard sale. A white cast-iron frame somewhere between a modern twin and queen, it was too small for two people, especially one as large as Clarke. To fit the small mattress, Paul laid a piece of plywood over the frame, and the mattress over the plywood, and the wood and the frame creaked and groaned when they fucked or rolled around at night.

"It is what it is," Paul said, sipping his coffee. He watched the birds pick at seeds in the clear plastic feeder suction-cupped to the outside of the window.

"What is it?" Clarke asked, his trusting eyes searching.

"What?"

"You seem prickly this morning. Like nothing I say is right."

Paul shrugged, not disagreeing.

"Do you want to talk about it?" Clarke asked.

"There is nothing on earth I want to do less."

"Well, if I did something wrong ..."

"How could you do something wrong?" Paul said, laughing. "You're perfect."

Clarke flushed, not sure if he'd been praised or insulted.

"Well, it's true, isn't it?" Paul asked.

"I'm just a person."

"People like you don't know."

"People like me?" and he chuckled. "What are people like me?"

"You know. Young, beautiful. Everyone wants you. You walk down the street and people stare at you."

"I'm here with you," Clarke said. "You're no ugly duckling yourself."

Paul shrugged again, kept his eyes on the window.

They had been together for two months. While not a couple, at least officially, Clarke felt there might be enough to commit to, so he was dating no one else. Paul seemed like marriage material, which in San Francisco, especially among the party boys Clarke attracted, was something to consider. Paul said he had worked in advertising, his boss having closed the shop a few years earlier. Now he was casting about for something new, but with his tiny bachelor apartment—filled though it was with beautiful antiques, still, a walk-up more appropriate for a kid out of college than a man approaching forty—his expenses were low and he had all the free time to pick up cute DJs at coffee houses and meander the streets for garage sales. Though he'd asked several times, Clarke couldn't gauge where Paul was in all of this. He tended to look out the window and shrug in his bashful way when anything important was asked or mentioned. "Couldn't tell ya, bub," he'd say, in his clipped twang.

"Well, it's gonna be a busy week," Clarke said. "Two private parties and that big club on Friday. Atlas, I think. You want to come?"

Paul laughed. "Are you kidding? Can you see me in a place like that, with all those kiddies jumping around and sweating all over each other?"

"You'd still get pinched, if that's what you're worried about." Clarke flashed the beautiful smile. "And I'll pinch ya if no one else will."

And now Paul felt contempt for that smile. So full of hope and optimism. He couldn't let it stand. "No," he said, "I don't want to listen to all that ooga-booga music anymore. It hurts my ears."

Clarke felt his smile fade. A feeling of wrong washing over him, pulling something down and within. Sitting on this rickety antique chair next to this tiny antique table, there being only enough room in the kitchen for the table and two chairs, Clarke realized he was too big for the chair, for the table, for the bed. He felt himself sit upright, draw his arms and legs closer. There was nothing else on offer here besides the coffee; Paul's attention was focused only on the bird feeder.

"Well, okay," Clarke said, an effort now to keep the smile pasted on. Then the ritual gathering of clothes, dressing, looking around the room but trying not to, looking for anything he might regret not taking. At the door, he said, "I'll talk to you before Friday, okay?" Paul shrugged, standing at the counter. Couldn't look at him. Clarke thought he looked ashamed, unsure of what he was doing or why. But Paul was older, and confident, and seemed not to care at all. So Clarke withdrew slowly and closed the door behind him.

3

PAUL HAD AN interesting way of walking. Sort of like a crab moving down the street, his legs were so slender, his hips so small, he seemed to travel at an angle even if he was going straight. He held his shoulders high, a permanent shrug, as though constantly apologizing. His attraction was something he couldn't fathom. The hot guys—the body boys—never looked at him, he didn't register on their radar. But others, the ones with a more refined sensibility, noticed the delicate lashes, the crystal blue eyes—a boy in a man's swell suit. Those were the ones who struck up conversations. On the street, in coffee houses, at the gym. And his wry self-deprecation drew them in like moths to a pheromone trap.

On this particular afternoon though, less interested in a hookup than finding plastic drawer liners, he was moving slowly up Columbus when the mid-day fatigue caught up and called for an espresso. As he approached one of his regular spots, the flash of a tan, wrinkled coat behind the front window caught his eye. He back peddled—a Gene Kelly move for an absent audience—to confirm what he thought he saw. He debated the wisdom of the detour, wishing to complete the errand; but at the same time, perhaps this was the chance to capture a moment that eluded everyone else.

"Dr. Livingston, I presume?" he said, standing at the edge of the table. Lydia sat with the trench coat buttoned and the belt secure, her half-dunked biscotti sitting sadly on the plate like a capsized battleship. She looked up at him with no reaction. "Oh no, I couldn't," he said, "I'm far too busy. Busy, busy, busy, so many places to be." Still no reaction. "But if you insist, I *suppose* I could give you a minute, dear." He sat and nodded to the teenage girl behind the counter. After he ordered his own espresso, he picked up the half-eaten biscotti, chewed it with fast, tiny bites at the corner of his mouth. "*Ehhhhh*, what's up, doc?"

No reaction from her.

"Well, you know it *was*," he went on, launching into his impression of clenched-jaw society matrons she used to laugh at. "We got to the club at seven when they'd begun serving drinks at *six!* Can you imagine? We were overcome, let me tell you, *overcome* with embarrassment! I had to say to Winthorp, I said, Winthorp, have you ever seen a duller crowd in your life?" Lydia wouldn't focus her eyes on him. "It got to the point where I had to get down on the ground and just *blow* every one of them. On my knees, don't you know!"

The girl brought Paul's espresso, her brow wrinkled.

"Thank you dear," he said, and brushed her off. "Mmmm, refreshing," he said, after a sip. "Thtimulating!" She still wouldn't look.

They sat like that for a while, Paul drinking his coffee and watching her over the top of the cup, tossing off a non-sequitur, something she would have laughed at in the past. He tried a Lucy Ricardo routine, laughing and chatting silently. He tried some faces, some nasty hand gestures. A straw up his nose. She sat in isolation, refused to make eye contact.

"Well," he said, after he finished his espresso, "it's been grand catching up with you dear, but no, no matter how much you ask, I simply *must* peel myself away." He stood. "No, I mean it. I mustn't hesitate a moment longer. No matter how much you beg and plead. It's out of the question!"

He stared down at her; she stared at the buttons on his shirt. He let out one long, final breath, shrugged, headed for the door. The girl behind the counter followed him with her eyes. "Oh, she insisted," Paul said, nodding at Lydia, "it's on her," and walked out.

⊶⊷

The ironic thing was that nobody liked Paul much in the advertising community. Even though he looked so much the part—the handsome blond in the crisp poplin suit—in practice, he was so cranky and short-tempered that anyone who hired him regretted it immediately. Only Lydia seemed able to tap his best qualities, and he had worked for her as account executive for more than ten years. Invariably, their relationship would come to a head, followed by an explosive argument, after which he would apologize, come slinking back and she always took him back with an eye-roll. Not just because of their friendship, but because he sold. His looks, his midwest demeanor, his charm and baby blues.

Women were helpless, especially when he played the shy kid. Hiring LC was a joy, if only to see him sliding into the office from time to time for flirty chats. Which he specialized in, sitting on the edge of a desk and drawing the dreamy account manager into long, involved conversations. Their eyes scanned his face; even though he seemed older, with his lines and beginnings of silver hair at the temple, something about his boyishness, the saucy glint in the eye, made their entire day. He had celebrity magic, and along with that, came Lydia Calligan's quality and wit. What's not to love?

And other clients as well.

Lydia called him into her office once, the grand Palladian window behind her desk overlooking Ghirardelli Square. "There's a piece of business at the Chamber of Commerce I would really love," she said, "managing communications for the winter conference. Can I send you on a sales call? One of the new VPs, who makes the decisions on that, is a charming *single* gentleman I met at the Oyster Bar the other night. Neither I nor the oysters seemed to be his cup of tea."

"Package or ass?"

She thought a moment, pursed lips. "Neither, I think. Let his fingers do the walking."

"Got it," he said, and he did, and the account, and a nice Thursday night regular for the duration of the job. Even when it was done, there was, miraculously, never any rancor or bad will. Paul had usually been able to separate the cleanliness of his work sex from the messiness of personal sex, in which every relationship ended with a door slamming, some variation of *"You're an asshole!"* shouted at him from the hallway, him shouting back, *"I know you are but what am I!"* from inside the apartment. His neighbors shook their heads when they passed him in the hallway, unwilling to speak. Most of the other tenants in his sad, four-story walkup were elderly widows, many having lived there since they were newly married. Only his apartment—actually the kitchen of a much larger unit carved into pieces—had been on the market in the last fifty years. One of his older tricks, the owner of an antique shop who traded discounted merchandise for an occasional suck on the south pole, knew about it and steered it Paul's way.

The point was, Paul's career was largely determined—wholly in fact—by Lydia's, and the fact that LC, and Lydia, were out of business, was no good for his friendship or his bottom line. So it was a surprise one night, dining with a friend at Zuni, that Arthur something-or-other, who had been one of Lydia's closest friends, actually stopped at Paul's table to ask about her.

"I see her every once in a while," Arthur said, "just wandering like a zombie. I've tried to catch up to her and catch her eye, but she skitters away."

"She's like that with everyone," Paul said. "I've tried to talk to her a few times. She won't even look at me."

"What a tragedy. Well, if you see her again, tell her I said hello. My God, we could use her soft touch with one of our new clients. I'm sure I could find a shell or something to pay her through so no one would know it was her."

Paul said nothing, just stared at the man, knowing Lydia would be unable and unwilling to even receive such a suggestion.

"Well, nice to see you Paul," Arthur said, not meaning it at all, and moved on with his dinner partner out the door.

"Who was that?" Paul's friend asked.

"Some asshole Lydia used to like."

But as Paul's bank balance continued to sink, and he was alerted of the occasional Lydia sighting, he started to think of it as a challenge or a puzzle: over here, a piece of cash-paying business from a rich guy with a big company; and over there, this sort of spectral presence, floating around the city like a character in an old video game. Lydia's appearance had become almost comical, the outfit something out of a 1940s screwball comedy—tall woman with dark hair pulled into a bun, the same trench coat all the time, ridiculously large sunglasses, bent forward and walking determinedly up and down the city's hills, across parks, down sidewalks, never stopping, never seeing anything, unclear where she came from or where she was going. It was, Paul decided, too silly to go on this way.

She might have been wandering the panhandle because the next time he saw her, she walked passed the front window of Zazi while he was eating lunch in Cole Valley. She was moving briskly down the sidewalk, her shoes soaked with mud and wet grass. He jumped up and out the door and followed her. Today she was wearing a clear plastic rain bonnet, tied under her chin, shoulders hunched as always, making her way nowhere in the afternoon drizzle. He grabbed her from behind by the coat's belt.

"Just hold it there, buddy," he said, and she stopped. Didn't look at him. "This is idiotic," he said. "You're acting like a fucking moron." She stood, shivering slightly, though it wasn't that cold. "Come with me," he said, and tried something new, moving her bodily with two hands on her shoulders. She went without protest, back to the restaurant, to the seat opposite him at the table. "Sit," he said, and she did. The waitress raised her eyebrows. "One more?" Paul nodded and sat as well. Stared at her a moment. Once again, her gaze went only as far as the buttons on his shirt.

"Okay, I've had it with you," he said, the anger rising so suddenly he nearly sneered it through gritted teeth. "You have been making a fool of yourself. Which wouldn't be so bad if you disappeared or jumped off a bridge or something sensible. But walking around like the ghost of gloom and doom, you obviously want everyone to see you. What kind of bullshit game are you playing?"

No reaction.

"And this is the *stupidest* thing I have ever seen," he snapped, and yanked the plastic bonnet off her head. "You look like a fuckin' retard."

She smoothed the hair he messed up. The waitress brought a menu. "What'll we …"

"Chicken sandwich," he said. "Coffee. Two sugars and nonfat milk. Side of cottage cheese."

"I'm not sure we …"

"Find some," Paul said, his gaze fixed on Lydia.

"Right on it," and she stepped away quietly.

"Now, you're going to sit here and eat and I'm going to watch you," he said. "I know that's crap you like, and it looks like you haven't eaten anything healthy in a while. What are you living on, cat food?"

Her eyes on his buttons.

"If you don't talk to me, I'm gonna kick you in the cunt. I swear to God. I will take those fucking glasses off your head and break them into tiny pieces and spit each piece in your face until you speak."

She sighed. "It's Livingstone."

He shook his head.

"Dr. Living*stone*, not Livingston," she said. "Everyone gets it wrong."

"You must be kidding."

"Don't use such nasty language." She still wouldn't meet his eyes.

"You made me do it."

"No excuse," she said. "Language is important. The words we use have meaning."

"Oh, thank you Henry Higgins, for that observation. Let me jot that right down."

The waitress brought the coffee and milk, set them down gently. "Sandwich is coming," she whispered.

"This is such bullshit," he said to Lydia. "Obviously, you want everyone to know how much you're suffering. Ok, we get it. Walking around like some kind of ghost. You've ruined whatever remained of your reputation, you know. Everyone just thinks you're just insane now. Is that what you wanted?"

She shrugged.

"Well, if it is, it's working. So, what am I supposed to do? Wave at you every time I see you? Hi there, don't know ya! What is anyone who knows you supposed to do? And look what you've done. You've got the whole city acting like they don't see you, like we're all in on whatever *farce* you're playing with us."

"It isn't that," she said.

"Then what is it? Tell me."

"You wouldn't understand, Paul. You're a kid."

"I am not a kid. And don't condescend to me."

She took a long breath, and the sandwich came, and she took her time cutting it, in fourths, salting it, moving it around on the plate until it was positioned correctly for her fork to lift it.

"You eat a sandwich with your hands," he said, angry. She ignored him, continued to move the parts around.

"It's more than that," she said, and for the first time, looked at him. It felt like such a long time since he had seen her sad eyes. Now they seemed filtered, still the deep brown, but dimmer and frightened. "More than just the berry thing. It was everything. It all had to come down."

"What did?"

"I can't ... put it all together," she said. "It was all wrong."

She sighed again, took a sip of the coffee.

"Thank you," she said, and pulled something out of a pocket. A twenty-dollar bill, wrinkled and bunched up. She dropped it on the table, and stood. He opened his mouth to speak, but she looked at him, raised her hand. It was enough.

"You ripped my hat," she said, looking sadly at the crumpled plastic on the table.

"Good. You looked like an idiot."

She laughed, slightly. "Thank you," she said again. Tightened the belt around the coat, got up and left. He didn't follow. He noticed she had eaten everything on her plate.

4

ONE OF PAUL'S favorite things to collect was tableware from famous old cruise ships. The good vintage stores often had whole sets of dishes and serving pieces from the *Queen Elizabeth*, the *Homeric*, the *Normandie*. It impressed boyfriends no end to sit at his wobbly table and eat off stoneware from the *Ile de France*. He decorated the apartment with vintage travel posters too, and when he was in his 20s, with long, hippy-boy hair, and older men friends paid for international travel, he got around; now, it seemed aspirational but not imminent. Still, though, the narrow apartment, the smell of the bay in the morning, the seagoing dishware, gave him the sense of fine oceangoing travel. When he imagined it, he imagined it in luxury cabins on the top deck.

As he sat drinking his morning coffee, his thoughts returned to that guy Arthur from the other night and the mention of work he had for Lydia. Which would be work for him as well. Something about a new client and paying through a shell. Whatever that meant, it was money, and it was waiting to be had. And Paul's days of leisure living would not last forever. Probably not even three more months. The problem with that job—and he could smell it already—was desperation. Guys like Arthur have a problem, and they need someone to solve it. And they know when someone talented like Lydia is on the skids, they can get that talent for cheap. It would be dirty, crappy work that Lydia wouldn't have given a thought to in the past, and it wouldn't pay as much as it would be demeaning. It would certainly not be all expenses paid and it wouldn't be top deck, but it was a real thing. He didn't know what to do, so as usual when he felt overwhelmed, he decided to forget everything and jerk off, his solution to all problems.

Later in the day, his phone rang. He looked at the number—a San Francisco area code—and answered cautiously.

"Is it Paul Swenson there?" some man asked.

"Yes?"

"Paul, this is Richard Morris at Coleman Pressman, how are you?" A firm they used to work with. Vague recollection of this guy—silver hair, ruddy cheeks, too many lunchtime cocktails—another back-slapping friend of Lydia's.

"I'm well thanks, Richard, how are you?"

"Paul, I'm sorry to call you out of the blue. I fished your number from one of our associates. I hope I'm not intruding." He was, but what's the point? "I am just so concerned about Lydia. My wife and I ran into her outside the Civic Center the other night. She looked so disheveled and not herself. You know, I've seen her every once in a while the last year or so but I never had the occasion to stop and actually talk. My lord, it was disturbing. She's been such a good friend for so many years and seeing her like this was really upsetting. My wife was in shock. She begged me to do something. I'm wondering if you'd been in touch with her. I could barely get her to acknowledge us at all."

"That's just how she is," Paul said. "I caught up with her a few days ago and made her talk to me. She's in there, she just won't come out."

"Is it mental illness or something? Should we call in a healthcare professional? It's painful to see her like this."

"I know."

"I've spoken to some other friends and we feel … that is, if there's not some sort of institutionalization necessary to get her back on her feet … that we can't just let this go on. It's inhuman. I've come across a job she could take on, something perfectly respectable that's right up her alley. Not terrible demanding and it's out of the way. No one who knows her at all. Arthur Koretz mentioned it to me, and it seemed like a good possibility."

"I saw him a few weeks ago. If it's the same thing, he said something about it to me too."

"Well Paul, the problem is, no one knows how to get in touch with her. She disconnected all her numbers and she won't answer emails. We remembered how close you were and we thought if anyone could reach her, it might be you."

He thought about it. Thought about doing what he had avoided for the past two years because he just didn't want to do it.

"Yes," he said. "I know where she lives. I can go and see if she'll open the door."

"Well, that's a *wonderful* idea, Paul, if you wouldn't mind." Even though this guy's grand manner of going way up and then down nearly guided you to the exact place he wanted you to be, Paul let himself be guided. "I can give you all the details so you can discuss it with her. Perhaps this might be something that could shake her out of this funk."

It seemed a strange conversation after he clicked off. He remembered these guys, these big, beefy business guys who barely noticed him as they passed his desk, on their way into or out of Lydia's office. They regarded him like a fussy cat Lydia kept around. It was interesting that anyone remembered his name and took the time to actually recall it and search for his number. Whatever the reason, or the motivation, it did seem to him that he had spent too long not doing the thing he knew he should have done, which was go to her door and knock.

⋅⊷══◉◉══⊶⋅

Once on the street, he realized he didn't know it. In all the years he worked for her, all the years spent lying on the floor while she talked on the phone, all the years of coffee and chat, he never wrote down the address. He found his way there because he had to, and once he stopped having to, he forgot. Now, he tried to recall it from memory.

What he remembered was the view—which wasn't too helpful, since a lot of apartments at the crest of San Francisco hills have the same view. He tried recalling landmarks like weird hydrants or old police call boxes, but again, so many looked the same. Streets with cable car clanking didn't help either, because he couldn't recall which street you cross and which you follow. But after an hour of walking, scrutinizing, finding several buildings that looked like what he remembered—a creamy 1920s façade with Spanish curlicues over the doorway—he found the right one, at the corner of Green and Leavenworth. Now, only having to find the button. This would be a process of deduction: there were thirty apartments, the tenants listed in no particular order—none of them Calligan or LC—and only one blank, the name on the old strip of cardboard scraped off with a fingernail. So, press.

Of course, nothing. The electronic gurgle. Press again, more gurgle. He kept pressing, in every jingle he could imagine. Fifteen minutes in, at *Camptown Races*, he gave up. She wasn't there, or so calcified that nothing would rouse her. But he was too lazy to jot down the address and return, so it had to be now. I'm not climbin' this fuckin' hill again, he grumbled to himself.

It wasn't long before a good target arrived. Middle-aged woman, small, stylish. Bright Hermes scarf, crisp jade jacket, mesh shopping bag with fresh vegetables. It was amazing how his aw-shucks smile and blue eyes could unlock any door. "My friend is up there and all her friends are worried and I was sent to check on her. Could you let me in?" A line any rapist or maniac would use and any San Franciscan would ignore; but from Paul, a radiant smile, a helping hand, and asking if she could do anything for him. "Who is your friend?" she asked, on their way up in the elevator. He told her, and she gave a quiet nod. "Give her my regards, would you? We used to chat all the time. My name is Avis, from the tenth floor. Tell her hello from me." He said he would, and continued up to the floor just below the penthouse level. "Got to save something for the future," Lydia had said, when asked why, at the height of her success and income, she hadn't sprung for the top.

The door at the end of the hall in the right corner. Name removed from the slot below the peephole. Black plastic button rings the bell inside the door, that clunky dong you know they hear inside. He put his ear to the door after ringing a few times; some movement echoing off the parquet floor.

"I can hear you," he yelled into the peephole, "I know you're in there." But nothing more. So he started with *Oh, What a Beautiful Mornin'*, and by the time he got to *The Farmers and the Cowhands Should be Friends*—one neighbor opened his door and Paul pointed to Lydia's; the neighbor nodded and went back inside— scuffling came up behind the door and the deadbolt unlocked. The scuffling moved away, and Paul turned the knob, opened the door.

It wasn't the hoarder horror he feared. The place was tidy, if dusty. No trace of the life that once filled the space. Sheets should have been over the furniture. But someone had been living here, moving, it seemed, from a dining room chair turned to face the window, to the bedroom, to the kitchen. Nothing in the kitchen at all except a coffee cup, clean, upside down on a paper towel next to the sink.

"Not a single cat food can?" he asked. "Well, I am disappointed."

She moved ahead of him into the livingroom, her back to him, and sat on the sofa against the wall. Not looking at him, not looking at anything. Aware, just not looking. She wore a drab skirt, a drab blouse, apparently the uniform under the trenchcoat.

The lonely chair facing the picture window seemed to be where she spent her time. He turned it to face the coffee table and the sofa, and sat in it. Stared at her a moment.

"Thanks," he said. "I'll have an Americano. Two shots, almond milk."

She didn't move, didn't look up.

"You know, climbing this hill is a fuckin' chore, and I had to walk. Offering a refreshment is kind of good manners, you know?"

A look at him, a disappointed scowl.

"Now, there's that pretty face we've all been missing." Then, in his best cockney, "'Ere now, give us a smile then, gov'ner." And she did, a tiny one.

He sighed, got a glass of water from the tap. Came back and sat down.

"What are you gonna do? Wait til the bill collectors cart off the furniture? You really want to be a homeless bag lady? Well, you keep sitting up here, staring out the window, that's what's gonna happen." Her eyes met his and she sighed. "So what's the plan?" he asked. "You're the one who's always ten steps ahead of everyone else. I'm the one you yell at to get my hands out of the cookie jar. You really want someone like *me* telling someone like *you* what to do?"

"I'm tired of talking," she said.

"You haven't said a word in two years."

"All of it. All the bullshit."

"Then get out of town. Get lost. Otherwise, everyone is watching you and it's painful. If you think you're invisible, you're not. You're making everybody uncomfortable, and that's why I came. I was sent on a mission. By someone who doesn't even like me."

Her eyes rose to his. The first reaction to something he said.

"You remember Richard Morris? He called me. He said he and his wife ran into you and it freaked them the fuck out. You're freaking a lot of people out. Everyone's talking about you, and if you ask me, that's worse than being invisible."

"What do I do?" she said. "I have no idea what to do. I'm at the bottom of the well."

"Well, to start with, how about something instead of nothing? Morris told me he had a job. Well, actually, it came from, whats-his-name, Arthur Kornitz …"

"Koretz."

"… and he said he has a project you'd be perfect for. It's something out of town, away from everything …"

"I couldn't."

"… and he and Morris and a bunch of other people are worried about you. Maybe they really care about you. I mean, they called me, and you think any of those assholes really wants to talk to *me?*"

"I'm not ready."

"Well, I am. And maybe you need to think about something other than yourself. I got about twenty-five dollars left, cookie, and I'm a little old to make a living on Polk Street these days. Or Scruffy or Instafans or whatever it is these kids make their money on now. I need to eat, and a job sounds pretty good to me."

"There's no company left."

"They don't care. They want your brain and that's all."

She sighed. He knew from the sigh she would listen to more.

"Good," he said, and got up. "I'll tell them you're interested. And I'll let you know what they say. Will you pick up the phone if I call? Because I'm not walkin' up that fuckin' hill again, bub."

She nodded.

"Good. And put on some makeup, would you? You look like a boiled raccoon."

For the first time, an echo of a laugh.

5

PAUL AND LYDIA flew to Denver on a Monday, picked up the rental car, then drove east, out of the city and its surroundings.

"There's nothing here," she said, as Paul drove. The dire emptiness of the landscape reflected across her dark lenses.

"Peace and solitude," Paul said. "What could be nicer?"

"How do people live out here?" she whispered, mostly to herself.

"West Coast elitist. Speak for yourself."

"Don't try to tell me you really like this?"

"Maybe Saltair Springs has a spring we can lie in and watch the stars. Chew peyote and have visions. Like them Injuns."

She took in a long breath, let it out slowly. "I can't believe we're here. I can't believe I let you convince me to do this."

"I didn't convince you of anything. This is all your doing. Big advertising genius. *Call again on Calligan*, isn't that it?"

"I'm not ready."

"We never are, bub."

After what seemed like hours of driving, the desperate emptiness of the landscape gave way to a graceful rise, and coming over it, they beheld their destination for the unspecified future in the valley below. "Oh my God," Lydia gasped. "How could this be here?"

--◦═◦═◦--

The trip had been arranged quickly. Only one face-to-face meeting, Paul assumed, so they could get a gander at Lydia to be sure they weren't sending someone totally incompetent or babbling incoherently.

She had shown up at Arthur's office in the same trenchcoat as always, belt tight, bun in place, sunglasses. The only concession to the smiling, concerned people in the meeting was the legal pad and the pen Paul shoved in her hand before they walked into the conference room. She stared at them around the table like they were blinding lights.

"So it's a local focus but with national ramifications," Arthur said. "The point being we don't want there to be any. There's a lot of bad press around these kinds of communities and Carl doesn't want any of that on this one. The community needs to appear to be normal, friendly, natural ..."

"Organic," said a young woman on one side of the table.

"... *organic*," Arthur said, pointing her way, "... a community that just happens to have this one big employer. We don't want the people to think it was built by the client. We want to give the impression it was always there, and the client simply came in as a boon to the existing economy. Helping rural families make ends meet, and so forth."

"A heartening story about the American heartland," Lydia said slowly.

"Precisely," said Arthur.

They went on, with slides and a video showing the town being built, maps of where neighborhoods would be laid out, the central shopping mall, the parklets, and of course, the warehouse. *Fulfillment center*, the woman from the client corrected Arthur. Of course, said his authoritative nod. Arthur could nod with more authority than anyone. Paul watched, barely contained himself from snorting.

At the end of the meeting, and questions, Lydia had only one.

"Do you really need a campaign for this? It looks like there's nobody and nothing around for miles, except gophers and prairie dogs."

All the people at the meeting were friends or associates who knew Lydia or had worked with her, except one, the young woman from the client—officious in her dark blue suit, skirt, and open-collared shirt, the uniform of the executive trainee. At least that's what Paul guessed, and why they had sent her. She had probably been briefed this was an agency on the rocks, and they were getting this expensive professional cheap. That Lydia's friends would prop her up and promise to stand behind her. The young woman had been skeptical the entire meeting and looked at Lydia like a rash that wouldn't clear up.

"It's not for the community, Ms. Calligan," she said, "it's to make sure no bad press is generated. We'd like it to be positive messaging about the town and the new center. Mr. Hausen wants it to be good news."

"And is it?" Lydia asked.

The young women squinted.

"Is there something we're trying to deflect here?" Lydia asked.

"No."

"So that's the long and the short of it," Arthur said. "Thank you all for attending ..." and they finished with the pleasantries, the men shaking Paul's hand but looking toward the door, toward Lydia, to be sure she wasn't talking to herself or doing something peculiar in the corner. But she had rallied; stood when she needed, shook the hands presented, looked into the eyes that needed looking into. She'd done nothing wrong or worrisome, and they all hoped the young executive would bring that message back to old Carl, and the assignment would be accepted. Which it had been, and now here they were, in rural Colorado, rounding the rise and descending slowly on this newly paved highway.

"You better believe it," Paul said. "That's 'Merica, honey. You been stuck in the big city too long."

"How could they have done this?"

Looking down from the top of the hill, the flat floor of the plains seemed to reach east toward Kansas, the emptiness wide and expected. But smack in front of them, at the bottom of the hill, was something so foreign and strange, it looked like a bad special effect, something pasted over the scenery that made no sense. A vast city of large two-story houses, each one squat and square, with the same rust-colored sides, the same light-colored tile rooves, crammed together, for miles in all directions. And at the edge of the housing city, a sharp delineation where the dry, empty plains began again. It was a confusing spectacle: the houses themselves so big and solid, with two-car garages, driveways, yards and fences—a suburban world, conjured instantly and completely, with a genie's magic wand; but so many, mashed together, facing each other, backing into each other. It almost seemed to hum, the houses mumbling and grumbling inside the corral they'd been confined in. As though it had not registered yet there were too many in too small a space, and a dire, empty nothingness all around. Except for one thing: at the far end, a huge white building. The warehouse—the fulfillment center—the nucleus of this world. Taller than the homes, a stark box with a flat roof, it sat on one side of the town—soon to be filled in, like grandchildren on all sides—while the shopping center, with its immaculately laid-out parking lot and strip mall and super-center, lay on the other.

"I've never seen anything like this," Lydia said.

"You've been staring at your navel too long, honey. This is the world now."

They arrived at the hotel, a pleasant, upscale chain—not too fancy, not too shabby—designed solely for businesspeople like Paul and Lydia, coming to do a job servicing the great center. Everyone in the hotel smiled the same smile. Happy to have this town, this hotel, this job here, at last, but just out of high school and not sure how wide you're supposed to smile in a hotel, having never been in one.

A young man standing behind the desk shouted as they entered the lobby. *"Welcometomidwaysaltairspringsdoyouhaveareservation?"*

"Hold on a second there, bub," Paul mumbled, approaching the desk, fumbling for a folded paper in his pocket.

"Or the email associated with the reservation!" Still almost yelling.

"It's Calligan," Lydia said, placing her arms over the reception desk and leaning forward, like a midtown hotel in 1958. The young man pulled slightly back, unsure of this person with a wrinkled trench coat, smelling of mothball.

"Unclean," Paul whispered to her, "unclean. Move back, they don't know from names."

"Maybe you have it under Swensen," she continued.

The young man maintained his smile but didn't understand the language.

"Here," Paul said, and tossed the folded paper at him. He scanned it, then beeps and the sound of a printer.

"Thank you, Miss, uh … Calgan … and Mr. Swenson. I found your reservations here." He squinted at the screen. "Oh. I see you're here … indefinitely … for Hausen?"

Lydia sighed, almost groaned. *Indefinitely.* "Yes," she said.

"Very good," the young man said, impressed. These were reservations from on high. Cheerfully, he gave them the spiel and the folded card with the Wifi, pool hours, cleaning schedule. "You have … uhm … adjoining rooms," he said, working out in his mind what that meant, "… will that be ok?"

"Ok with you?" Paul said to Lydia. "You won't mind me bursting in in my skivvies now, will ya?"

She ignored him, the young man squinting again.

When they were sorted, card keys in pockets and rising in the new-smelling elevator to the second floor, Lydia let out a long breath. "What am I doing here?"

"You're makin' the American dream a reality for thousands a' crazy, hopeful kids, ya nutty dame, that's what."

"What a nightmare," she said.

"That too."

⊷▰▰◯▰▰⊷

Lydia knew some of the story already. Everyone in business did. She read up the week before they came out to Denver so she'd know how much of the story, and what angle, to inject into the work they would be doing here.

It was archetypal: Karl Hausen, the great-great grandfather, the industrious young immigrant from Sweden. Arrived in America as the gold rush exploded, opened a hard goods store and did good. Expanded to several, then hundreds, up and down the west coast and western United States. Hausen Hardware became the trusted name in everything from padlocks to shovels to paint. Then, authentic nineteenth-century brand transitioned to twentieth-century needs, expanding into home goods and furniture, washing its hands of the saddle soap and gear lubricant of its industrial revolution roots. Hausen Home Goods was the place for young brides to buy their first apartment furnishings—smart, cost-effective, long-lasting—plus, later on, dinnerware, tablecloths, then baby furniture and everything for the toddlers when they came along. As Americans expanded to the suburbs, so did Hausen—lawn and outdoor furniture, grills, fertilizer, you name it. Today it was Carl Hausen, the grandson, running things. Carrying on family tradition, he and his team made another smart transition, staking their claim among the big-box giants of the twenty-first century; and now, with a sleek new branding—removing the space between the two names—a new logo, and one of the best online fulfillment operations in the country, *HausenHome* was surging. And Saltair Springs was a key link in its cheerful, relentless march of expansion to own the home goods market across America. Or so said the brochure Lydia put down at 10pm, her eyes straining.

Paul came back in through the adjoining door, opened now on both sides, his tie loosened and top shirt button undone.

"This stuff is really awful, you sure you don't want some?" He held up a clear plastic cup filled with pale yellow liquid and read from the bottle. "It's not wine, it's wine *product*. There's a whole bunch of other stuff in there, too." Lydia shook her head, perusing a sheet of notes. "Wine product," Paul said. "I haven't checked the mini-bar. Maybe they have food product. It's like food, but not."

"I'd rather not be fuzzy tomorrow. That looks like it's guaranteed to make you fuzzy."

"Darn tootin,'" he said, lifting his cup. "I'm just the emotional support animal here. I want to be as fuzzy as possible."

"Yes, well, you're still expected to walk and talk and help me with these people. You saw the look on that kid's face at the desk. We're here at the behest of big old Carl. We're supposed to look like we know what we're doing."

"It doesn't make a difference," he said, finishing the cup, already slightly toasted. "This is a handholding gig anyway. Look, it's a park! Look, the kids are smiling! Look, Carl Hausen loves you, he lets kids sell lemonade! What a wonderful, happy, Nazi little town it is!"

She looked at him over the thick frames, shook her pencil. "Be good. They're the client."

"Yecch."

"Look, I'm as shocked as you are to find myself here. And I'm still trying to figure out their angle. Arthur called me before we left and gave me a little background."

Paul raised his eyebrows.

"Out in the middle of nowhere, they need these towns badly," she said. "Fulfillment center towns. It's cheaper to build a whole community around it than it is to locate them in a city that already exists … for taxes, local regulations, that kind of stuff. It brings jobs to places where there's no chance of anything else. And there has to be housing around the center to stash the employees. Hausen needs these centers to compete with the big boxes and online giants. Saltair Springs is their biggest test so far. Arthur's company is dealing with Hausen corporate on government relations. Our piece is making this fulfillment center look good. This is their lynchpin town. If this one works, then others around the country will too."

"So, big whoop. Happyland in the middle of the Colorado plains. That doesn't sound very hard."

"Well, there's an undercurrent of pushback on this one. Some of the other towns aren't crazy about all the tax breaks handed out to build all this. And on-line news sites with cranky reporters are looking for misdeeds to expose. They've been crawling around, trying to interview the kids who work at the center, looking for bad stories. A couple of them published videos about what a hellhole it is, and they generated a lot of bad publicity. The company wants to wrangle it all, get the message tightened up."

"So what are we doing here, patching the Titanic?"

"I don't know. I don't think so. There's some low-level chatter on the internet about bad management, but that's pretty typical stuff. I can't get a clear picture yet. It could just be that old Carl wants to avoid being blindsided."

"Do we get to meet old Carl?"

"Unlikely. He lives on a ranch in Idaho, shooting things and staying under the radar. That's one fellow who does *not* want publicity. But don't think he isn't keeping a close eye on everything we're doing."

Paul put the empty cup on the table and it fell over with a plastic clang.

"Did you drink the entire bottle?" Lydia asked, incredulous.

He mouthed at her again: wine *product*. He thought it might get another laugh, but she took off her glasses, rubbed her eyes—dark circles beneath, darker than he remembered, and probably one reason for the dark lenses—and the familiar haze seemed to slip back, like fog, the light behind her eyes dimming.

"Hello?" he asked. "You still here?"

Without looking at him, she said, "How about retiring to your lair, or your coffin, or where ever it is you go to keep yourself fresh. I need my sleep now. I've run out of energy to be in this world."

He stood up like he did, a toy soldier, gave her the loose limbed, stiff salute, and retreated to his room behind the connecting door. Lydia's eyes returned to the pile of papers and brochures and reports on the coffee table.

What were they doing here?

6

SHE LIKED TO watch him sleep. Sometimes he woke up but kept his eyes closed. He'd lean up and kiss her, then lay back and sleep some more. Most of the time he was asleep though, and he was a heavy sleeper, so she could watch him freely and trace the lines of his face and his hair with her eyes, feel the sense of contentment just from looking at him.

This morning he was sound asleep. She watched him in the dim light of the early sun through the curtains. She loved the shape of his eyes. Large and brown, they seemed to be drawn by some graceful hand that sketched angles and curves no human could match. She'd known him for a full year now, and for every moment of this year, when she looked at him, she looked first at the eyes. Even under stress, the eyes remained calm. Someone described them as almond shaped, but she thought that was inadequate. Another word, a better one she came across, was aquiline. Sounds like a line of water, something as smooth and fluid. His whole face was aquiline, in fact. The plane of his eyes ceding to the gentle rise of wide, flat nose; the high cheekbones and beautiful lips. It could never get ugly, she thought, when she imagined his face old, the two of them as old people; it would still be exquisite, and he was her exquisite, and even still, it wasn't only his beautiful face she loved. That was just the surface, the suggestion—the reminder—of the person he was beneath.

Cherise herself leaned toward the dramatic. She was slender, thin as a reed, her mother's friends said, and told she had a knife-edge temperament. She could feel one moment easygoing and calm, then someone would pull in front of her on the road, cut her off at the frozen food case, and out came the temper. *Fuck you, man!* Middle finger deployed too freely on the highway; her mother warned her, someone's going to pull a gun on you sweetheart, you keep blowing up like that. So now, while she might still think it, she wouldn't say it. High school guidance counselors and visits to a therapist helped with impulse control. And that learned behavior probably kicked in when she first spotted this tall man with the beautiful eyes at Taffy's, the only sit-down restaurant in the new center of Saltair Springs. Alone in a new town, a new state, she wanted to put Atlanta behind and begin her adulthood fresh. She had friends who worked at the HausenHome retail store at home, and when they told her about the opportunities opening up with the online side of the company, she jumped. But she hadn't expected rural Colorado to be so cold, so empty, and so white. So when she spotted this tall, easygoing Black man with the upswept brows, watched how still he sat while his friends fooled around like kids, she felt his sense of calm seem to reach out and envelop her. She was sitting alone with her basket of soggy fried calamari, trying to overcome the twin anxieties of being in a new world and out in a restaurant by herself. She spotted this guy and tried not to be caught looking; but as if detecting an interruption in the force field, he turned and looked right at her. He wasn't smiling, he didn't need to. His face, his composure, said it all.

It took him halfway through the dinner to get up and go to the restroom, and when he returned, it was by her table. He simply stopped and asked. Was she by herself? Had she come to work in the center? How long had she been here? All he had to do was nod to his friends at the other table—they gave him high signs and winks, but he ignored them—and sit with her. She wasn't even shy, didn't play games. A couple of times she heard herself jump in too fast, make some sarcastic comment. He smiled and took her in, like sunlight. He even seemed to like her snappishness, and she liked that he liked it. Finally, he asked if she'd like to join his friends, but they looked like a bunch of irritating twenty-somethings. She said maybe next time, and itched to get back to the studio apartment—her first own place—and get some rest before her long shift tomorrow. But that was it. They saw each other the next night, and now, a year later, she gazed at his sleeping face and realized every minute of that year had been the most wonderful one. How strange, she thought, in the middle of this bizarre town, this bizarre state, to find the real thing, when up to that time, in her entire life, it had eluded her. Maybe he was the missing piece she needed all along to become whole, to calm down to normal speed.

His name was Darnell.

7

WALT DROPPED THE gob of toilet paper into the toilet and held the lever until the water sucked it down. Held a moment longer to be sure it wouldn't burp back up after he left the bathroom for Kathy to find the next time she came in. Like a floating white lily pad: *Hi there, here's another load your husband blew into something that isn't you! Have a nice day!*

She'd caught him several times when she came home from work early to retrieve something she forgot. He'd be in the upstairs office at the computer, pants at his ankles, pounding away. When he heard the keys in the front door, he knew he'd have only thirty seconds. Despite his size, he could yank his pants up fast, careful not to zip the dick, button his shirt, and rearrange everything on the desk. "That you, hon?"

Soon enough she stood in the doorway. Smiling, saying nothing. Did she hear the sudden rifling of clothes, the belt smacking the chair legs? Did he look too sweaty to have been pricing Toyota hybrids? She only held a moment then answered. "Yeah, I left my keycard in the tray and I couldn't get into the storage locker without it. You're home early." And he had some excuse, some reason, which of course, was true. The reason he'd arranged the time off, for an hour or two, for some relief.

Walt and Kathy ate dinner together, and as usual, discussed their day: the new software Walt had to learn, the online training sessions, the challenges Kathy faced as produce manager at the new Winchester's Supermarket. Everything they talked about every night was all true, and interesting, and Walt was happy he could surrender so honestly to the conversation. Because, in truth, he felt bad about their diminished relations, and the confusing, confounding fact that he got a greater satisfaction from porn than the woman he was married to. How much she guessed he didn't know; but she was as smart, if not smarter than him, so he guessed she guessed it all. But still, their home, the massive three-bedroom

Tudor floorplan they selected, was warm, and warmly furnished, mostly with HausenHome furniture, except for a few antiques Kathy brought from before they were married. Walt had been happy to throw out everything from his own studio apartment while they were dating in Eugene—all junk he picked up at garage sales—and let her design their new home, create the world they wanted, and which he now felt lucky enough to inhabit. If Walt ever gave it a thought, and he didn't very often, he might have thought Kathy went in for kitschy Americana too much, the modern colonial line from Hausen a little too grandmotherly for his taste. But faced with the alternative, he was pleased every night to come home to the solid kitchen table surrounded by captain's chairs, furnishings that would last a lifetime, if they so desired.

"So, what about Panamax?" Kathy asked, chewing the meat off a hot wing she'd microwaved for appetizers.

"There's so much to learn," he said. "The rollout won't be complete until the end of the month, and they haven't finished the training modules. I got through most of the ones I'm supposed to."

"And they still want you to be team leader?"

"I think so. At least I haven't heard anything different."

He noticed that Kathy had a habit of asking things, of saying things, while doing something else. Like chewing a chicken wing so it obscured the tenor of her voice asking the question. Like this. Did she mean she wondered if they were considering someone else to be team leader, or, she couldn't believe they would have selected him as team leader? Walt knew that asking what she meant would just provoke that look—staring, irritated—and he'd rather not get into it. So he learned to let those ambiguities float away like clouds in a windy sky.

For the most part, she was his cheerleader and rock of support. Walt had a long career in logistics, starting at Fedex years earlier. When warehousing and distribution exploded, he was an easy fit. The industry had moved at dizzying speed, and he found it exhilarating to try and keep up. HausenHome was a plum company to be part of, and everyone had been told how important Saltair Springs was, not just to the company, but to the industry as a whole. There was a David-and-Goliath sense of excitement about it, trying to mold Carl Hausen's modest business into a powerhouse that could compete with the giants and keep its own identity. That was the challenge, it had been made clear to Walt during his interviews: HausenHome wanted to own its own business, from start to finish. They didn't want to sell out to a conglomerate. The HausenHome brand was still its own, and old Carl wanted to keep the manufacturing, the distribution and the retail in-house. He wanted HausenHome products handled by HausenHome people. Was that a challenge Walt was willing to meet, the interviewer asked? He felt a rush of excitement and purpose. You bet, he said, with genuine enthusiasm, just the kind of energy they wanted.

So now, after a rocky start managing the loading dock, Walt was the presumptive head of picking, though still on probation, like all the department heads. Panamax was the project name for the rollout of the latest robotic automation. Each phase was given a name of its own, something exciting and thriller-like, and they had successfully completed Eiger, Whipsaw and Ganymede. Walt's response under pressure and his leadership in those rollouts brought him to executive leadership attention, and when the departmental lead for picking opened up, it was offered to him.

As impressive a position as it was, along with the salary and prestige, came the headaches. The facility, of course, was data driven. Performance was calculated in real-time, and reports of the day, week and month were generated automatically. Software made it clear where inefficiencies existed, and it was Walt's job to close those gaps. For example: the company set the benchmark that eighty items need to be picked per picker per hour. A picker is the person who stands at a station and reads a monitor that tells them the items requested in the online order. With Panamax, a platform on wheels brings a tall shelf of items to the picker's station. The monitor tells the picker which shelf the item is on, along with the name; the picker grabs the item and scans it—the software confirms it's the right one—and the picker drops it in another bin on the other side of their station to be whisked away to collating and distribution. So that's what a picker does. All day, all shift. Then there are floating pickers, people sent out into the vast landscape of four- and five-story shelves of inventory to find items that the robots are unable to locate. They call these fringe items, and the goal is to reduce fringe as much as possible. Only the very intrepid, and limber, can be floaters. You have to be able to climb ladders to the top shelf, avoid any robotic arms that might come your way—although they have sensors and are supposed to avoid people and unknown objects—and have a keen sense of observation to find the object, which is usually mislabeled or the barcode incorrect, and know it by sight to grab it. Floaters are the cowboys of Walt's operation—scrappy kids who, without this facility and this job in this town, might get into trouble. And it gave him a sense of purpose to know these young people were employed and trained for a long and satisfying career. There were a couple of girls on the squad as well, slender and nubile, who had been high school athletes. He tried to deal with them the same as the boys, avoiding any sexism, but sometimes one of them creeped into a masturbatory fantasy. When that happened—while at work, if he was talking with them—he felt his face flush, then the employee's face would flush, and though neither would say or do anything, he felt ashamed, sure that the girl knew what he was thinking and would tell her friends, and maybe a supervisor, what a perv he was, even though he hadn't done anything at all. And it weighed on him.

Right now, as he pondered the tight breasts of a floater named Annabelle, he looked up to see the staring face of Kathy, the chewed wing in one hand. "Where are you? I asked you twice."

"I'm sorry. What?"

"You said they have new benchmarks?"

"Yeah. I don't know what it is yet but I'm pretty sure they want to increase the pick rate."

"What are you gonna do?"

"I have to check operations and HR. To find out what I can do. I mean, I can't just yell at them to work faster."

"Why not?"

"Well, they're kids. This is their first job. And you got old people like Terry and that guy with the gimpy leg. They can only move so fast."

"You're too nice," she said, and went back to the kitchen to start the main course. From in there, over her shoulder, she spoke louder. "You're a softie, honey, and you won't put the screws where the screws need putting. I see the same kids you do at the store. They're lazy and spoiled, that's their problem. They'll do as much as you tell them. And they'll surprise themselves if you put the pressure on 'em. Don't be so nice. Otherwise, it's *your* promotion you're giving away."

"I guess," he said, considering how he would even phrase such a blatant command. Work faster. It sounded so mean.

"You're not going to, are you?" she said from in there, her voice echoing off the tiles.

"Yeah, I'll … you know, I'll figure it out."

"No you won't," she said, and her voice lost the hard echo as she came toward him and leaned against the doorway, wiping her hand on a cloth. "You'll sit in your office, too afraid to make any waves, and you'll *diddle* yourself into not doing anything. That's why you don't move ahead like you should. Those kids get paid good money, just like you. If you don't push them, guess who absorbs the pressure? Those kids and those gimpy old people can get off their lazy asses and earn that money. And you too. Do you hear me, Walter Mulbacher?"

He nodded, in the confident and loving way he knew she meant these things as support and encouragement. The way one loving spouse speaks to another. Though he wasn't sure why these lectures, in that tone of voice, sometimes made him feel small and uncertain.

She turned back and opened the fridge, pulled out the Tupperware with the burgers. He had bought her the new George Foreman Grill, the one that could do four burgers at once. She loved that thing, and kept it at arm's reach on the counter, near the sink, where he could see it now from his chair in the dining room. He watched as she placed the burgers on the hot, nonstick plates, lowered the cover, and pressed gently but firmly. The sound of sizzling juices filled the air. A miracle of efficiency and entrepreneurship, he thought. Not unlike himself. His eyes transfixed on the burgers, as Kathy's hand pressed down, being grilled to perfection by the magical feat of heat coming from both sides.

8

ALONE IN HIS room, Paul had been watching videos on his phone—tonight, statuesque, bored-looking Czechoslovakian guys bonking each other, groaning *yaw yaw yaw*—but by 7pm, realized he was hungry for actual food.

He asked the cheerful young woman at the front desk if the hotel had a dining room—it did not—and she told him the nearest place would be Taffy's, a couple of blocks away. He walked it, still in the crisp suit pants, shirt, and loosened tie, moving as always at an angle down the sidewalk. While he waited for a table to be cleared, he looked around. The place was decorated with a combination of street signs and photographs of old Saltair Springs—or what this empty patch of land must have looked like before—and folksy home decorations one might find at HausenHome: woodcut plaques with 19th-century typeface and pointing fingers indicating Ladies and Gents; large replicas of buoys floating from the ceiling, suspended by netting; enlarged antique photos of college rowing teams, the men standing at attention with big oars, large mustaches and comically old fashioned one-piece bathing suits. Paul noticed some of the guys had quite astonishing packages that apparently no one caught or thought to blur out. So—nostalgia, seafood, vintage sausage—this place just couldn't pick a motif and stick to it.

When the hostess led him to a table, he grunted, flopped into the seat, gazed at the menu and tossed it aside. "Anything in here not out of a can or a micro-wave?" The waiter was an older man who looked like he'd be more at home in a hardware store.

"Uh, everything is fresh and delicious."

Not looking up, Paul grunted. "Tuna salad sandwich, ice tea, chips. And no celery in the tuna."

The waiter jotted it down. "It might be mixed in," he said.

"Well find out!" Paul shouted, sending the man scurrying. "Shithole," Paul said to himself, slouched further into the chair, and drank from the sweating glass of ice water. Looking around the room, he was depressed by the predict-ability of it all, and still couldn't believe he was here.

He had had dreams, and was smart enough to have had sophisticated ones. When he was young, his looks and charm opened doors that matched the dreams: a fabulous New York life with parties and famous artists laughing over dinner at Elaine's. He planned on a wealthy boyfriend with houses in Europe and the US, jet-setting from one splendid residence to another. Wit, charm and glamour would be all he'd need, since the partner would have the money. He'd be from an old New York family—one of the Dutch ones—and they'd spend their time in the company of playwrights, directors, and actors.

But after his twenties, when no magical boyfriend had stuck, he left the east coast and settled in San Francisco; bounced around a few agencies, then was in-troduced to Lydia, who found his peculiar blend of sweet and sour to her liking. Somehow, he let his twenties slip into his thirties, and thirties into late thirties, and the dream of laughing uproariously over a bottle of champagne in the back of a limo on the way to his partner's Broadway premiere had failed to material-ize. And now here he was, staring at a pile of limp, fried mozzarella sticks in a plastic basket on a greasy napkin. This is what he had come to.

"I'm sorry, it is all mixed in," the waiter said, behind him.

"Yecch," Paul grunted. "Fine, whatever." The waiter slipped away quickly.

The table tent advertised desserts. Ice cream sundaes, bomb blasts of choco-late and caramel that could kill a steer. He flipped the cards on the tent, nothing else to do in this godforsaken hellhole. He became aware of giggling and tittering from the next table. Several girls, they looked like high school girls, whispering, looking over at him. He'd seen this happen before. Something about his boyish face, his broad forehead and shiny hair made him still, despite his age, weirdly appealing to girls. To this one in particular, a tall blond with curly hair piled high, colored ribbons and scrunchies holding it up, her outfit a hobnob of styles: torn jeans, a vest, baubles and spangles. Clearly the adventurer of the group. She stared at him, and though he looked away, he could feel when she stood up, the other girls giggling *No, no,* and made her way over. She took a flirty posture next to him, provocative and nervous. Not quite a finger in the mouth, but almost.

"Are you working for the center?" she asked.

"Uhm, yeah," he said, studying the plastic-coated menu.

"Are you, uhm, like a manager or something?"

"Yeah."

"Are you from New York?"

Interactions like this made Paul nervous. Old as he was, with all the experience, he should be able to brush these kids away easily. But it bugged him, made him as tense and anxious as the kid—maybe more—and set off the viper that lurked inside.

"How old are you?" the girl asked, turning the flirtiness up a notch.

"Thirty-eight," Paul growled, and turned and stared her in the face. "Is that what you wanted to know?" She barely nodded, flushed, and retreated to her table. The other girls weren't laughing anymore. They huddled and finished their desserts quietly, not looking his way again.

He felt bad, of course. He didn't like lashing out like that. But it came out, beyond his control, and the worst part of it was that it didn't seem to get him anything aside from the bad reputation.

He ate his sandwich and chips alone.

By about 8:30, Taffy's had nearly emptied out when a shadow moved behind him.

"Not out painting the town?" Lydia asked, taking the seat next to him. Trenchcoat on, dark glasses in place.

"Nuthin' to paint," he said, hunched over his plate, finishing the last of the sandwich.

"Eat the crust," she said.

"Shut up," he said, through a mouthful: "Shuh ... up."

"You look like a child. What do you want, someone to cut the crusts off for you?"

"I don't like them."

"Well, give them here, it's perfectly good ..."

He slapped her hand as she reached for it. "It's my dinner. Don't be a pig." She shook her head. "Call the waitron over," he said, "get your own crusts."

She did catch his attention and ordered a cup of decaf and a slice of pie. "They always have good pie in places like this," she said.

"Don't bet on it. The whole place is fake. Thrown together and made up to look like a real town, but it's not."

"Well, whatever it is, we start on it tomorrow. I have the schedule here." She pulled a folded paper from her coat pocket and put it on the table. "We'll do the interviews first. Key players in the morning, floor workers in the afternoon."

He scanned the paper, moved it around with his forefinger.

"I'm thinking we should find some nice faces to put in a spot," she said. "Real people with real stories. How working at the center paid for college, got them into their own home, stuff like that. If we can zero in on four or five characters, we'll use them as case studies in video and print."

"Any directives from on high? Anyone we're supposed to highlight?"

"They gave some general demographics but mostly, I was told, a happy crowd saying how happy the center has happily made them. And happy, if I didn't mention it already."

"Gives me the creeps," he said. "Phony town in the middle of nowhere. Big factory in the middle of it all, belching out smoke."

"There is no factory and there is no smoke. This is one of those … triple E something … environmentally A plus operations. You can eat off the floor. We have to fit that in somewhere."

"Clean and dandy," he said. "Antiseptic."

She had finished her pie and half the coffee when they were done talking.

"So, you'll be bright-eyed and bushy tailed for tomorrow?"

"This is as bushy as my tail gets," he said, and shook it in the chair.

She sighed. "I wish I still smoked."

"You gave it up for lent?"

"One of the things I let go during the last two years. I just didn't care anymore."

"Well, that's good, isn't it?"

"In theory," she said. "I just wonder what else went."

"You want to say more about that? You still haven't offered much of an explanation."

"Not really," she said, her eyes starting to tire. "I don't mind it, honestly, doing a puff piece for a glorified furniture factory. It is a nice assignment. I need to thank Arthur for throwing it my way."

"You're welcome."

"*Our* way," she said. "Well." Stood up. "I'm going to bed. Don't get in trouble."

"You think I could?" he asked optimistically.

"Just be careful out here in the hinterlands, with that prickly humor of yours."

"I hear ya, Tex. Y'all get on your horse and ride off to the hitchin' post now."

She shook her head and left him. He had still not eaten the crusts.

9

THE COMPANY SET them up in one of the conference rooms with large windows facing the main floor. There were several others as well, with lights off and doors locked. Those were for business purposes, not relaxation. For that, there was a break room, which was one of the first things Adele told them as she gave the walking tour of the facility. A break room for associates was always available, to relax, unwind, take a load off their feet, when their breaks come.

"And when *do* their breaks come?" Paul asked, as they moved across the polished concrete floor, the constant sound of motors, moving shelves, platforms, forklifts, ventilation systems over and around them.

The fulfillment center was basically a single, huge room that seemed to cover acres of land. Lydia had watched the videos of the center under construction. It was built exactly the way it looked, with nothing hidden, no clever architectural or support members obscured: a giant room to enclose a giant amount of space. First, the narrowest of steel skeletons was thrown up to create the box—the walls and roof—then flat slabs that looked like concrete were brought in on trucks, in stacks, and laid against the steel frame, like a skin, to enclose the space. Huge, UFO-like dome-shaped lamps hung from the ceiling, casting a pure white light that illuminated everything, leaving no shadow or unlit corner. The result was a landscape of unsettling alertness, the visibility startling. In the time-lapse videos, the shelves are shown being brought in, then boxes of inventory, then machines moving the boxes around in fast motion, onto fork-lifts, into trucks and the trucks departing comically fast. Although the videos were designed to show the center's construction quickly, inside it felt like things were attuned to moving in fast motion as well.

Guests were required to wear orange safety vests with ID badges and reflectors; employees seemed to be wearing a variety of outfits based on their position: forklift drivers, pickers, managers, supervisors, office personnel. Paul and Lydia were told to wear white hard hats in addition to the orange vests, which they dutifully donned, knowing it was for show and liability, or perhaps to alert others of an outsider's presence, interlopers in the hive.

"At varying, appropriate intervals, depending upon the associates' position," Adele said, smiling, after she had recalled, or prepared, the proper answer to Paul's question.

"Because we heard they don't get breaks as much as they should," he went on, speaking loudly over the sound. Lydia casually observed something to her right, but put her hand on Paul's arm.

"Breaks are mandated and made available according to, and exceeding, industry standards," Adele replied. Lydia kept her hand on Paul to restrain him from the snotty reply she knew was coming; he shook his arm free but didn't say it.

After the tour, they arrived at the interview room. This was not one of the rooms with a broad window onto the floor, but a conference room with no windows at all. Only a large table, eight cushy, vinyl-upholstered chairs, a space in the wall where a TV might fit, and on the table, a tray with a jug of water and glasses. An orange extension cord lay curled on the floor like a fluorescent snake.

Lydia took the seat at one side of the table next to the head. Her idea was to put each interviewee there, and she and Paul would ask their questions from either side. She put her briefcase on the floor and pulled out stacks of folders and papers. Paul pulled a laptop from his briefcase and sat across from Lydia's setup.

"I hope this will do," Adele said.

"Hell, it's the nicest sarcophagus I ever saw," Paul said.

Adele smiled, ignoring him. "We'll bring in your interviews as you scheduled them, starting at ten. Will that work?"

Lydia said it would, and thanked her.

"They sent us here to die," Paul said when she left. "This place has no oxygen."

"Be quiet. It's a room. That's all we need."

"Seriously. You could expire in this place and no one would find you."

"Shush."

They set up for the first interview of the morning, a man named Lester Kenworthy. Lydia checked his stats: floor manager, age 41, white, been at

HausenHome for eleven years; five in floor sales, five in distribution, one in fulfillment. Married for six years, wife named Louise, two children, lives in a 3-bedroom *Victory* floorplan. Paul had just finished positioning the camera on a small tripod on the table when Lester knocked.

"Come in, please," Lydia said, using a voice Paul hadn't heard in a long time: the confident, mellifluous announcer's voice she learned from her father, Uncle Marty, the biggest star of golden-age television comedy. Jesters always have the most comforting tones and Lydia learned hers from the master. "Please make yourself comfortable."

Lydia had a general idea of the personnel the company wanted profiled, so she and Paul dug through piles of resumes to find the people they would interview to narrow down the finalists. This one, in Paul's shorthand, was the old white guy, and Lester looked the part. He seemed equally flattered and flustered, pleased anyone took notice of him and unsure of what to do. He stood near the corner of the table; if he had a hat, it would be in his hand.

"Sit down, please," Lydia said, and extended her own hand. He took it, turned to shake Paul's, but he was fooling with the camera and just grunted. Lester pulled his hand back, sat down quickly in the chair at the head.

"Now Lester," Lydia said, "today we're just going to ask you some questions about your experience at HausenHome. We're going to speak to a number of others as well. From those initial interviews, we'll be selecting several individuals to profile for some national and regional marketing campaigns. Will that be alright with you?"

He nodded.

"State your name," Paul said, flat and hard. Lydia glared at him.

"Tell us your name, if you wouldn't mind," she said, in the mellow tone, "and how long you've been with HausenHome." And he answered, and all the other questions she had prepared. Only a few times Paul had to adjust the camera position, or interject—"Look at the camera, Jesus!"—before the first half hour was complete. The next interviewee was just as smooth, with the answers rolling out like they had been rehearsed and polished. And the third.

"What's going on here?" Paul asked, during their lunch break. "These people are all happy idiots. Why isn't anyone saying anything bad?"

"I know. It does seem a bit automated."

"Someone always has something nasty to say. You opened the door, like ten times, and not even a flicker. What's wrong with these people?"

She shrugged, checked the list for the next interview. "Maybe our big city cynicism is out of place in happy valley." He stared at her. "Who's next?" she asked.

Paul handed her the one-page summary. "Cherise Watson." She glanced at it, lowered her chin and read over the glasses. "Do you really need those?" he asked.

She kept her eyes on the page. "Protection," she said, then the knock on the door.

-→⇒ ⇐←-

Cherise was seated and given the standard intro. She smiled, made herself comfortable on the cushy chair. Lydia had remained distant and professional, nodding to each participant and asking her questions; not too cool, not too warm, but there was something about Cherise she liked. She seemed bright and alert, her smile sincere, the eagerness genuine. *Good kid*, Lydia penciled next to her name. She had a self-assuredness beyond her years, so Lydia asked her age again—the sheet said 22 but she wanted to confirm. "And what is your role at HausenHome Saltair Springs?"

"Right now, floating picker," Cherise said.

Paul snorted. Cherise snapped a look at him; Lydia gave him her professional *shut the fuck up* smile.

"And what does that mean?" Lydia asked evenly.

"That means I do everything no one else can figure out how to do," Cherise said with a laugh.

"Such as?"

"Well, to start with, finding the stuff the robots can't. Everything is supposed to be where it is so the klingons can find them ..."

"Klingons?"

"That's what we call the robots. I guess because they're big and scary and they seem to cling to you. When something isn't where it's supposed to be, the system gives an error message and the floaters get a notification ..." Cherise pulled out a device, an orange plastic tool with a small screen and a keypad. The shape of a small axe, it was one of the items hanging on the leather belt around her waist, along with clear plastic bottles of transparent liquid, sharp-looking metal tools, utility gloves, a hammer, and a white container of baby powder. "It tells us which row and shelf the item is supposed to be on." She showed Lydia the message on the tiny screen. "So we climb up and see if the item is there, if it's stuck, or if it's not there at all. Then we have to report it to inventory and then sometimes they just tell us to go and look for it."

"I see," Lydia said. "And what else do you do?"

"Well, a lot of times the klingons malfunction or get stuck on something, and operations asks us to fix it."

"That sounds like a job for an engineer."

"Yeah, if it's serious, you know, that you can't see right off. But a lot of the time it's something stupid like some object stuck in the wheels or it got caught on a piece of wrapping plastic. Then you can just see it and yank it out."

"And what else do you do?"

"What else don't we do? Sometimes, on the night shift, they don't have enough loaders, so they call us onto loading. Then that's a lot of physical work, you know, just getting stuff onto dispatch."

"You load trucks?"

She nodded pleasantly.

"And how often do you do that?"

"I don't know, it depends. Maybe two, three times a week."

"Uh huh. And what's your schedule usually like?"

"My official schedule or my real schedule?"

"What you're supposed to be doing."

"That doesn't exceed forty-five hours, and it's floating. But while they're ramping up operations and bringing on more associates, they need help in other divisions so they add on my hours. I'm supposed to work the six-to-two slot, but I end up getting called in earlier and stuff happens so I stay later. It's more like seventy to eighty hours."

"*A week?*" Paul blurted.

She shrugged.

"Some people like to work," Lydia said, evenly. "But that does sound like an ambitious schedule. You're paid for all those hours of course?"

"Usually."

"When isn't it usual?" Paul asked. He'd lifted his head from the viewfinder.

"Oh, I don't know. I check my hours every week, mostly it comes through. But they're struggling, you know. We're trying to compete with the big boxes, so, you know, everyone has to pitch in and help now and then."

Paul and Lydia exchanged glances; Lydia resumed the questions. "Tell us, what sort of skills or abilities does your work call upon?"

"Well, you have to be athletic, that's for sure. I mean, you climb a ladder and you get on the shelf, and those things are big, let me tell you. Not enough room to stand up, so you have to crawl around with a flashlight. Then you always come across something weird, like stuff out of place, or some broken machine part or a dead rat …" She stopped, the broad smile hesitating for a moment. "Hey, that was only once, don't say I said that. That happened and they took care of it right away. Can you delete it?"

"Of course. Go on."

"So you kind of have to crawl around on your stomach and fix things. And you have to watch out the klingons see you because sometimes they come into the same shelf looking for something and you're there, and if it doesn't see you, you can get whacked. Then other times, you have to run, and I mean run across the floor to another part of the facility if they need a floater, because we have the clock and you're gauged how quickly you respond to the call. So, yeah, I ran track in high school and it helps me now. And then, you know, loading is loading, so you have to be strong enough to lift the boxes and get them in the truck."

"They sell a lot of furniture, don't they?" Lydia asked.

"Yeah, and those boxes are big. I mean, if you're strong you can move some of the stuff yourself. But if it's a sofa or a sectional, then you have to get other people to help."

"And do they?"

"Oh yeah. I mean, that's the place you get injured mostly. Broken bones, joints coming out of sockets, stuff blowing out."

"That happens?"

Again she nodded like it was ordinary and expected.

"And then what happens?"

"They send you to Care and look you over."

"Care?"

"You know, the nurse, whatever you call it."

"Have you been to Care?"

"Me? Yeah once," she said, and laughed. "There was this dining room table ... this huge wood thing. It was so heavy, and we were all lifting it, and it was like three in the morning, and we were kind of tired. I let it slip and it fell on my foot, and all the guys busted out laughing so hard. I did too, but I knew I had to have it looked at. But there wasn't anyone there at that time so I went back in the morning and they said I did the right thing."

"What did you do?"

"One of my toes wasn't in the right place. Kind of cranked in the wrong direction. It didn't hurt, it was just weird looking. I Scotch taped it to the toe next to it and went home. They said it's hard to set toe bones and I did it right, so the next day they just wrapped it up better and said it was ok to go back to work. It's all healed now, but that toe is sticks up more than the others. They said toes don't have the same sensory nerves as other parts of the body so they don't hurt as much."

"They told you that?" Paul asked.

"Yeah?"

"What do you think you've learned on your job?" Lydia asked. "What skills have you acquired while working at HausenHome?"

"Oh, lots. I mean, it teaches you to be independent. How to solve problems. It keeps you in good shape. And mostly, it pays. I mean, the pay is decent. And they help you with a place to live."

Lydia checked her briefing sheet. "You live in the Sundown Gardens complex, in a Starling suite?"

"Yeah, it's nice. New appliances, hardwood floors ... well, engineered wood, technically, but they're nice. And the whole place is modern. Except when the plumbing backs up or the trash catches fire."

"What?" Paul asked.

"That was actually hilarious. I went to dump my trash in the chute, and when I opened it, my hair blew back and this blast of flame shot out. I was with ... I had a friend, and he pulled me back, and slammed the door shut. It singed my eyebrows a little. I reported it and they said that happened a couple of times.

The alarm goes off in the middle of the night sometimes and everyone has to go outside."

"Does that bother you?" Lydia asked.

Cherise shrugged. "I don't care. The rent is decent and I got a car and a nice place to live. I mean, I think that's pretty good, especially compared to Atlanta. This is all new, what we're doing. It's the future."

Lydia and Paul exchanged glances again.

"Cherise," Lydia said, "we're looking for several people to profile in a series of spots, to be used for a national ad campaign ... TV, online, billboards and so forth. Would you be interested in participating?"

Her eyes widened. "Of course! Sign me up!"

"That's great," Lydia said, and drew a star on the corner of her sheet.

Cherise stood, smiled again, shook Lydia's hand. "Thanks," she said. "That was fun."

When she had left, and they were alone, Lydia began organizing her papers for the lunch break, looking down at the table. "I just don't know about you," she said to Paul.

10

OUTSIDE SALTAIR SPRINGS, in the empty grass and prairie, the highway was scattered with billboards advertising the town at the edge of the future. *New Homes! 3 and 4-bedroom, 3000+ s/f! From the low 200s!* The photos showed the striking architecture, the clean, boxy lines, bright and optimistic, like real estate sales signs have always been: your opportunity for the dream of home ownership. What was different about Saltair Springs was the fact there was only one opportunity, and that was working for HausenHome—which would work with you to arrange generous financing for that dream. If you didn't work for the center, monthly payments would be hard. Retail positions in stores and restaurants didn't qualify for company assistance, and minimum wage wouldn't cover the mortgage. For those who didn't opt for home ownership, the company offered new apartments, with area-appropriate rent; and that's where Cherise found herself, having realized, once she arrived in Colorado, that no cities or towns within a reasonable driving distance with lower rents existed. She slept in her car for three nights before she found Sundown Gardens. And as the sun came up this morning, she got up, exhausted from yesterday's 14-hour shift, and went into the kitchen to make coffee. When she was fully awake, and the sun was higher, Darnell lumbered in, his dark T-shirt damp from the warmth of the bed and the fact that he slept so hot.

"Jeez-*us*," she said, "you must have sweat off ten pounds last night."

He smiled, wiped his hand over his face and made his way to the coffee machine. "What time you due in?"

"Nine-thirty," she said. "Walt gave me a half hour grace." She leapt up like she did, quick, her hand on his forehead. "You are still hot. I don't know, baby, maybe you're coming down with something." He shrugged, spooned coffee into the filter. Looked down. Spooned more in. "That's an ass blaster," she said.

"Got to be more awake. They're upping the benchmark. I missed a couple last week and got written up."

He made a large Thermos of coffee every morning and drank as much as he could on the way to work. At break, he went outside to the car, drank more, then did the same on the next break. They didn't let you bring anything inside, your own water bottle or coffee, so you had to keep all your stuff in the car. Technically you weren't supposed to bring cell phones in either, but a lot of people did, just woe to anyone who got caught using it. What bothered Darnell was the fatigue that had been slowly creeping up the last few months. He needed more and more coffee to stay at the same level of alertness it used to only take one cup in the morning. With the increase in caffeine came the headaches, which now seemed to plague him many hours of every day. So then the ibuprofen, which controlled the headaches.

"You ought to go to Care again," Cherise said.

"I did, I told you. They said it was from standing still too long. They said to get orthopedic shoes. Or expensive Nikes. And I'm not doing either of those. My shoes are fine."

Cherise had seen it too, the onset of the various aches and pains. She knew what it was like. Darnell had been fine when they met, maybe a couple of pounds extra, but now, working stiffs, they already started getting working stiff diseases; in her case, she was smart enough to score the floating gig, so her athletic training and muscles stayed in play. Darnell, though, stood in one place all day, with a monitor blaring orders at him, klingons throwing items at him. He said it felt like being trapped in a phone booth with the phone ringing inside and people hammering on the glass outside. Unspoken, they both relied on their secret weapon, their youth. When you're young, you can absorb any abuse, any pressure, any injury, and it'll heal and you'll be fine. It wouldn't last forever, of course; they both figured by thirty, they'd have worn out the youth and assumed they would be in better, more secure jobs by then. But for 22 and 23, this was the world as it was now.

"Well, if you get a headache or dizzy again, will you go to Care, please?"

He grunted. A crybaby he was not. The fact that she knew Care was basically useless was one problem she kept running into, like the corner of a room, and each time her mind followed the same pattern: go to Care, they don't fix the problem, we're young and it'll go away, forget about it.

"Hey guess what?" she said. "You know those people from the ad agency? They might use me in a campaign. I think they liked me."

"You're gonna be a spokesmodel?"

"May be," she said, and did a little shake. "I mean, who else are they gonna use around here?"

"When do you find out?"

"I just saw them yesterday. They're still talking to other people."

He smiled, leaned down, kissed her. "The superstar. They pay extra for that?"

She pointed at him. "Now, *that* was gonna be my very next question."

They were reminded to wear the white hardhats every time they crossed the main floor.

"This is such bullshit," Paul said, "I swear, tomorrow I'm coming in buck naked except the hat."

"All the girlies will love that," Lydia said, a half step in front of him.

"What girlies?"

"I've seen 'em. The same old gigglers. I have to admit, you've still got it. Good thing too, we may need it when we start conducting the interviews."

He reared back at her. "Oy don't know what you're tawkin' 'bout, missus, oym a proppah girl, oy am."

Adele walked up quickly to greet them, hand outstretched. "They would like for you two to meet with the foreman this morning. Do you have time?"

"Of course," Lydia said. "That would be wonderful."

"What's a foreman?" Paul whispered.

Reuben Gallardo had a small office off the main floor. It looked like he had just moved in, only a computer and two monitors on his desk; on the monitors, views of the facility from many angles. He stood when they arrived and Adele introduced them and left.

"So, what do you think of our little operation?" he asked, smiling. He looked mostly at Lydia, his eyes darting only briefly to Paul. Which Paul knew how to interpret. His own eyes went up and down, made sure Reuben saw them graze his package, heavy and well supported by some nice-fitting khakis. The mustache and dark hair channeled a 70s porn vibe; intentional, Paul wondered, or unaware?

"It's very impressive," Lydia said.

"It certainly is," Paul said, raising his eyes. Reuben flushed.

Lydia said, "We're selecting people to use in the campaign this week. We'll have the final list by the end of the day. From there, we start crafting the messaging."

"Great," Reuben said. "Can you share the names you have so far?"

Lydia pulled a sheet from her briefcase and handed it to him; he scanned it, nodding, grunting once or twice.

"Cherise," he said.

"What about her?"

"She's a firecracker."

"What does that mean?" Paul asked.

"She's one of our best floor operators. Fast as lightning. Bit of a loose cannon. Not sure what's gonna come out of her mouth next."

"Well, they're looking for optimism and energy," Lydia said, "and she seemed to fit the bill. Besides, that's what editing is for. We'll present everyone in a good light."

"Suits me," Reuben said. "Show me your final list tomorrow?"

"Absolutely."

As they walked back to the conference room, Paul said, "That's interesting. I didn't know there was another decisionmaker in the loop. What do they need the foreman in on this for?"

"Everyone wants to keep their eyes on it. We're probably the only ones he doesn't have on one of those fancy monitors in his office."

"Or maybe they do. You think the conference room is bugged?"

She thought for a moment: those black plastic beetle eyes in the ceiling corners. They probably even tracked heartbeat and respiration.

"Well," she said, irritated, "from now on, let's keep the small talk to a minimum."

In the afternoon, they got approval for the five employees to profile: one each from picking, logistics, packing, operations and distribution. Meanwhile, in the conference room next door, Walt was meeting with the other department heads to review the numbers from the previous week. They had their marching orders from on high, and for each of them, those translated into specific actions for the coming weeks. Walt crunched the numbers in his head and knew what it meant for him: he would have to increase his team's hourly pick rate from eighty to eighty-five. At these meetings, you were expected not to raise any doubts, and instead, smile and nod assertively with a results-oriented, get-it-done attitude. That was in a lot of manuals. And he thought of the word he had heard, from Kathy and HR and several of the online courses: *linchpin*. The success of any operation comes down to its weakest point, the spot of least resistance. You have to fortify that point, harden it. He was that point, and what he chose to do would have direct effect on the success of the whole operation, possibly the whole company.

When he met with his day shift and told them about the new pick rate, one of the guys, a recent high school graduate named Schuyler, asked how they were supposed to do it. Walt started with a light touch and a wink. "Work faster!" But Schuyler moaned. "We're already working fast. You said that a month ago, and that was seventy-five. So now it's eighty-five? Jeez Walt, I barely have a minute to take a piss." The others nodded in agreement.

But Walt was prepared. One of the sections in the manual said these were the questions he would be asked. In HR, she had a three-ring binder and when she opened it—Walt remembered those binders from school, how sharp and scary the rings were, snapping open, ready to snap shut into your fingers—she pulled out a pamphlet and handed it to him: *Motivational Strategies*, published by Supply Chain Management Today. Among the top three: gather suggestions from your employees to show them you value their input.

"Well," Walt said, smiling at the semicircle around him, "why don't we all think about it a moment and come up with suggestions? I want to hear from you. Your opinion is valued, and your contributions make this company the success that it is."

"Are you gonna ask us to hold hands and chant?" Shelley asked. She had blond and grey-streaked that hair swept up like stiff peaks of meringue. Walt was quietly annoyed at Shelley, always complaining about being tired when she clearly had enough energy to wake up and blow-dry these waves into acrobatic configurations before her shift at 7am. He laughed her off breezily. "Cassie?" Now here was a good one. She took pride in energy and drive, wore her work goggles at all times, even though they weren't required for pickers, demonstrating for everyone the tremendous amount of danger she was apparently exposed to at all times. Walt guessed she might be a lesbian, but didn't take the fantasy any farther, not wanting to imagine her without clothes.

"Well," she said, "toughen up," and flexed her arm, grabbed the bicep with her other hand. "Just speed it up, people. Haul ass."

Walt pointed at her: excellent suggestion. "How about you, Jed?"

A tall guy, slender in his overalls, a bag covering a frame that was hard to locate. "I don't know, Walt. I mean … we're working as fast as we can. You can't get blood from a stone."

"Aw, come on, you can do better than that, I know it. I have faith in you guys. Aren't we the number-one team three months in a row?" They nodded warily. "So, come on, give it a try. What do you think, Jed? Just one idea."

He stared at Walt like a slice of stale toast. "Well, I mean … maybe concentrate more?" Walt raised his eyebrows, waited. "… I mean, sometimes I know my mind wanders. I space out after a couple of hours. Maybe we could, I don't know, concentrate harder?"

"Ah, now *there's* a suggestion, Jed, thank you! How about you, uh …" he scanned the new guy's badge, "Mah-ham-mood, am I pronouncing it correctly?" He nodded. "What do you think? You must have a lot of good suggestions."

"No, I don't know. I'm just learning everything."

"Come on. Off the top of your head?"

"Just maybe, I don't know … use both hands instead of one?"

"Yeah, like an octopus," Shelley said. They all laughed.

"Well yeah," said another man, "if you want to get your hands caught in a klingon and get your arm ripped off. You can't just grab everything like a kid for eight hours at a stretch. You'll get tired. I already have repetitive shoulder injury. And Walt, I asked you …"

"You know, let's try putting it another way," he said. "Two hands is a good idea. Let's think about our dexterity, what we're doing with our hands. Maybe we can be more deliberate in our movements to produce greater results if we're using both our hands to their maximum potential."

Linchpin, he reminded himself. Have an impactful effect on your outcomes.

"What about you, Darnell? You're always so quiet, but I know you're very observant."

He shrugged. "I don't care. Whatever you want, we'll do. I mean, we have to, right? If it's a benchmark."

Darnell watched with his even-tempered gaze; Walt paused a long, uncomfortable moment before he replied.

"Well, that's right, Darnell, I think you hit the nail on the head," he said. And decided this would be the doorway to end the meeting. "That's the best suggestion we've heard. It *is* a new benchmark, and since this is your company as well as mine, it's a goal we know we're strong enough to achieve. Is that right, team?" They nodded, groaned. "Right!" he said, and clapped, alone, as though some performance had just been completed. They realized they had to do the clapping-at-nothing too, so they all clapped, like wet clams. "Then let's get out there," Walt shouted, revving them up, "and make things happen, people!"

When he got back to his office, he felt so stressed, he couldn't contain it. He stared at the monitors with their ticking, demanding graphs. Looked at the clock. Fifteen minutes unscheduled. There was time. His office had the plastic blinds that fold closed when you rotate the wand. Sometimes he turned on a video. It all worked out, except for the thing that time. But he had to: Kathy told him to toughen up. HR told him to toughen up. He was a manager of people now, not just systems on a flowchart, and in management you have to push. But still, the anxiety from pushing people the way he was supposed to. There was no other satisfaction, no other way. He got up and turned the wand, locked the door, and unzipped his pants, hungry for relief.

II

THEY PLANNED TO feature the five employees performing their daily activities first. After that, they would conduct the interviews and edit the whole package into modules that could be used for different media. Over the past two weeks, they had completed three sets of interviews; Lydia scheduled Cherise Watson as the fourth, giving it only the briefest consideration. She did this, she later realized, because she liked Cherise and wanted her in the schedule as something to look forward to, but not so obvious as to place her last. Fourth position seemed a reasonable obfuscation.

"This is where we're supposed to start," Cherise was saying, turning from Paul's camera to Lydia, not sure who to look at. "But we never really have a home base. Before you even clock in, there's messages and emergencies you have to deal with."

They were standing on the main floor, near the managers' offices, where a large box was drawn on the ground with yellow tape, the word *Float* in more tape, worn down from shoes and fork-lift tires. "Like now," she said, and showed Paul's camera the device on her belt. "We call them scammers, 'cause they're scanners, for bar codes and stuff, but they're also communication devices. We can send and receive messages about where we need to be and where there's a problem." She showed them lines of text on the small screen. "This says there's an error on row twenty-six, shelf nine, section two. Want to check it out?"

They scrambled after her. Paul kept up with his spindly walk, Lydia leaning forward, huffing slightly. "You know, you might want to take that off in here," Cherise said, nodding at Lydia's trenchcoat. "You can get caught on stuff really easily." Lydia nodded, waved it off. When they arrived at the row, Cherise grabbed the steel rungs on the four-story-high shelving and scrambled quickly to the third level. "You wanna see?" she shouted down.

"That's you, Sabu," Lydia said. Paul sighed, reached for the rung and hauled himself up, much slower. When he arrived, he and Cherise crawled toward the problem. The wooden leg of a table lodged between the floor and ceiling of the shelf, which was only four feet high. It was jammed in tight. She tried to kick it, push it, pull it, until eventually she asked Paul to help push with his foot while she kicked from the other side.

"How do you do all this yourself?" he asked, winded, after they knocked it down.

"You just do. I mean, what choice is there? If you don't perform they fire you or put you on loading. And that's a one-way ticket to the boneyard."

"Is it?"

"Well, yeah." She took a moment to catch her breath, stowing the chair leg in her belt for the journey down. Trying to remember what she had already said. "You're not gonna use this if I tell you?" He said no. She took a moment to consider. Not sure why she took Paul into her confidence now—maybe she was winded too, maybe she needed to tell someone—either way, she said, quietly, "That's kind of how they get rid of the dead wood. It's supposed to be a good deal, you know, just moving things from the dock to a truck. But honestly, a lot of people break something or sprain something."

"Like your toe?" Paul said.

She nodded. "But really ... they put everyone who gets moved off some other job onto loading, and if you get moved there, you don't come back."

"Do they pay for the healthcare? The hospital or something?"

"None of my business. All I know is, don't get moved to loading." As they wriggled along the shelf back to the ladder, Cherise said, "Hey, is your lady friend okay? She looks kind of shell shocked. Why does she wear the overcoat and shades all the time?"

"That's just ... her professional attire for the time being."

"She's not gonna flip out or do something weird, is she? I mean, I'm letting her use me in the ads. I don't want to come out looking like a fool."

"You won't. She'll do a good job. She just had some business problems a couple of years ago, and this is kind of a comeback gig."

"So you know her pretty well?"

"Yeah, we worked together for a long time. This isn't … just … don't worry, it'll be fine."

"Okay," Cherise said, at the edge of the shelf. She turned around to place her foot on the rung, stared at Paul full-face. "I don't want to say the wrong thing. I mean, if she lost her mind or something." She could tell he was about to say something but didn't, so she descended, and he followed, slowly and carefully.

"Well?" Lydia asked when he got to the bottom.

"Good footage," he said. "I can't believe they do this all day."

"Even better."

With Cherise out of earshot, he said, "She took me into her confidence a little. Things aren't as rosy as they would have us believe."

"Aha."

"And she's worried you're going to crack up on her."

"And did you reassure her?"

"Of course. I told her you'd probably have a meltdown and rip all your clothes off, screaming."

"Oh, good. What would I do without you?"

They followed Cherise through the rest of her morning tasks until break. Usually twenty minutes, where, she said, you run to your car, chow down what you prepared for lunch, squeeze in a bathroom break or piss in a jar, then run back. The clock marks the first second of the first minute you're late. But since Cherise was participating in the campaign, Lydia got her a half-hour break, and permission to use the management cafeteria. They were one of five or six couples sitting at round plastic tables, the same antiseptic white as the conference room. Only vending machines with candy and soda, so you had to bring your own lunch. Lydia had sandwiches, sodas and chips for them both.

"Oh, I love tuna salad," Cherise said, biting in. Lydia watched her gusto diving into it. An energy Lydia couldn't remember; the ability to gain pleasure from something so small and insignificant. "Don't choke," she said.

"Ha," Cherise said, through the mouthful, "I could eat ten."

Lydia ate hers slower, dabbing the corners of her mouth with a napkin. She noticed Cherise sneaking looks at her, sizing up this odd individual, huddled in the trenchcoat.

"Now, you're from Atlanta, is that right?" Lydia asked. Cherise nodded. "Is this a big change for you?"

She took a big, dry swallow, followed by a long Coke gulp. "Yeah. But good. I didn't want to stay there. All my friends from high school got married and moved into an apartment a mile from where we grew up. And got fat and had babies. Not for me. At least not yet."

"You have other goals?"

"Well, life is supposed to be interesting, right? It's supposed to be an adventure."

"Once I thought so."

"And I didn't like school. I'm not academic, I wasn't getting any scholarships. And I was never out of Georgia, so when I heard about this, I grabbed it."

"Interesting. What drew you *here*?"

"Well, my mom works for the phone company, my dad's a contractor. They have a good life, but they never left the city they grew up in. There's so many new things now, all kinds of new businesses and opportunities. I wanted to try something totally new, not just sitting at a desk your whole life. And I think I frustrated my parents anyway. Too much energy." She laughed in between bites.

"It's tough when you have more skill and ambition than the people around you," Lydia said.

Cherise considered that.

"Is Colorado the place for you?" Lydia asked. She gave Lydia a look: *Are you fucking kidding me?* "So, no," Lydia said.

"I look at it like a first job. And it pays. And I have my own apartment, and a car ..."

Lydia waited. "And?"

Cherise smiled. "And a guy. A good guy."

"So Colorado *has* worked out for you. At least in one respect." Cherise gave a wide, tight smile. "You like him very much." She nodded. "Well, that's a gift in itself. At least it seems to be, in this world."

"So, *you* married?" Cherise asked, popping the bag of chips. She pushed it gently against the table, applying the right amount of pressure without crushing the chips or blowing them out the hole.

"No. I've never been that lucky. Or misfortunate. Lots of boyfriends, though. Back when that was important."

"And now you own this ad agency?"

"I used to. Before."

"Before what?"

She hesitated a moment. "I made a mistake," Lydia said. "I wasn't on top of things and they got away from me. And something upsetting happened. That, and some other things. Just life catching up with me, I suppose. One day you wake up and realize you're old and out of date, and you don't know how it happened."

"You don't look that old. What are you, fifty?"

"I'll take it."

"So, that's what this job is about? You had to come out to the sticks to get your career back?"

Lydia laughed. "Something like that."

"Sorry. Where you from, San Francisco?"

"Yes."

"I always wanted to go there. Seems like a really cool city."

"It is."

"Better than here."

"It's different."

"Better. But that's ok. I got lots of time." She had finished the sandwich and started munching on the chips.

Lydia watched her, admiringly. "You know, Cherise, you have this optimistic outlook that's very appealing. I hope you don't mind me saying that. It's one of the reasons I wanted you for the spots. Tell me, how does that come about?"

She shrugged. "I don't know. I'm just me."

"Well, it's nice. I think I may be a bit jealous of you."

"Of me? Hell, girl, I got nothing on you. Advertising agency and all."

Lydia smiled. "Don't be so sure. When you get to a place where you look back and see what you really have … and it's not what you thought. You have a lot, Cherise. Where it counts. Does your, uhm, young man work at the center too?"

"Yeah. He's in picking."

"And you're a … floater, right? Do you work together?"

"No, I'm always on the move. He's in one of the stations where all you do is pull orders. I want him to get into something different."

"Can he ask for another assignment?"

"Well, that's a problem. He's real easygoing. Too easygoing. He's fine with anything they throw at him. I'm the one who wants him out of there. And anyway, it's not so easy to get reassigned. And we don't want to make a lot of waves. Just make some money, build some savings and move someplace interesting. Like San Francisco."

Lydia lifted her soda can and they toasted. "But you're committed to this for now? I mean … you'll be here for a while?" Lydia wondered why she asked. She was genuinely curious, but also, she had to be sure the employees they spotlighted wouldn't bolt next month. The campaign needed a year shelf life, at least.

"Yeah, we are," Cherise said, guessing whatever lay behind the question.

"And what do you think of the place so far?"

"It's fascinating," she said. "It's a great opportunity and a privilege to help achieve the company's mission and goals."

They both ate in a silence a few moments, then Lydia asked, "You have to memorize that verbatim or did they give you leeway to make it your own?"

Through a mouthful, Cherise said, "Verbatim."

Lydia smiled. "The world looks very promising to you, doesn't it? You have such confidence that everything will work out."

Now Cherise did look at her. This older woman who seemed bogged down with disappointment, her eyes dark behind the chunky glasses. Huh, she thought. She's looking for something from me. Which seems strange, because she's the kind of person who should have it all, someone who built her own business in a big, fancy city.

"You just have to believe it's all for the good," Cherise said, and put her hand on Lydia's. It startled her and she pulled away. "But what do I know?" Cherise said, unbothered. "I'm just some kid, right?"

Lydia nodded, then steered the conversation back to safer waters. Where she knew who she was and what information she needed for the job at hand.

12

PAUL WAS IRRITATED because he knew why he did it, even though he didn't want to give the motivation a second thought. It was the weight of the package in Reuben's khakis. The image kept entering his mind as he tried to drift off to sleep. He imagined opening the package, what it looked like, what it felt like. "Pig," he grumbled to himself. But it wouldn't leave him alone. So, when he found himself standing at the doorway of Reuben's office the next day, lounging like the high school girl with a finger in the mouth, he was irritated at himself. But he did it anyway.

"So, what is it you need exactly?" Reuben asked, squinting.

"Just, you know, for verification purposes," Paul said. "We'd like to run some of the stories by you before we submit them. To be sure they're accurate."

"Is that really something you need *me* to do?"

"Yeah. Just to pass the stories by. You know, just, verbally." Paul knew it made no sense either, but he often got his way simply by not leaving and waiting for the other person to give up. And so Reuben shrugged, watching Paul without expression.

"Thanks," Paul said. "By the way, would you know any good places for dinner? We've been going to Taffy's every night, and we're looking for something different."

Reuben thought. "You might try Kubla Khan's, near the container place off Sunrise. It's Hawaiian."

"That's where you would go? I mean, if you wanted someplace ... different?"

"I guess."

Paul thanked him, and as he walked away, caught a reflection in the window of Reuben's tilted head. He seemed to be thinking.

So it was not unexpected, the feeling of something you know but don't quite know, when Paul went to Kubla Khan's two nights later, that after half an hour

Reuben walked in. Staring up at the menu on the wall, looking too preoccupied to notice Paul at one of the four tiny tables in front of the counter.

"Ah yes, very busy," Paul said. "Busy, busy, busy. Late for your train at Grand Central?" Reuben looked half caught, half confused. "Never mind," Paul said. "While you're waiting for your very important order, why don't you join me?" And after he got his seared tuna poke bowl and Kamehameha Kola, he did.

They spoke professionally for the first bit, Paul being careful to ask the predictable questions and letting the poor guy answer. After a while, Reuben started to loosen up, smile, charmed and delighted to find Paul smiling back, flushing red himself when he answered something Reuben asked. Paul caught Reuben's eyes jumping to his throat, where the shirt was unbuttoned one button too many, a few blond hairs poking out invitingly. Paul could tell Reuben wanted to put his tongue right there.

In an hour or so, he let him.

"No, it's pretty quiet," Reuben said later, in Paul's bed at the hotel. "Houston is great, it's a really nice town. I figured this wasn't going to be that big, but I didn't expect this. Like ... nothing."

"So, no adventures for the super burrito?" Paul said, and grabbed Reuben under the sheets. That strange, non-reaction Paul often got when he said something he thought was funny. But then Reuben laughed, shook his head. "Wow," Paul said. "Poor guy."

"Well, not until now."

Paul sat up on his elbow. "Wait, are you telling me this is the first bang you've had since you moved here? Like, a year ago?"

"No, no. I went to Denver a couple of times and I met some guys there. But those were just, you know, fucking around. There's like, nothing here. It's all married couples and straight kids right out of school. You've seen them. They're nice people, but you know. Nobody."

"So this is all for me?" Paul asked, disappearing under the sheet.

"Oh, yes."

Paul surfaced again, doing a squirrel. Reuben laughed. It *was* all for him. Paul liked him. He liked his brown eyes, he liked his sweet disposition—the efficient foreman routine had been what he thought, nerves and anxiety, which melted once what he wanted to happen had happened. Maybe hanging around a little longer in the death spiral of American culture might not be so horrific after all.

⊷═◐ ◑═⊷

In the morning, in their antiseptic conference room, Lydia sipped coffee while Paul unpacked the camera and files from his briefcase.

"And how are we today?" she asked.

"Very well, thanks." He didn't look up. "How are *we* today?"

"Well, *we* didn't have a cacophony of moans and groans coming from our room all night long, so *we're* rested and ready for work. Do any of us have anything we'd like to tell any of us about anything?"

"I think we're all just fine," he said, "And we have nothing to share. As of yet."

"Well, let's all of us remember discretion. City slickers have been known to break hearts out in the provinces. And the rules."

Paul grunted, said nothing more, as he screwed the camera onto the tripod, and they began their work for the day. And the day's work went well, and the next day's and the next. And as they followed their subjects with the camera throughout their duties, conducting interviews in the conference room after the day's work, building storylines around each person, Paul noticed he had almost no need to goose Lydia to take action; she had begun to return to herself, to fill her own space again. On occasion, he even caught flashes of her old, sharp humor and even-handed command of situations. She still wouldn't take the trench coat off, but hey, he thought, some progress is better than none.

⊷═◐ ◑═⊷

Walt knew how good it would taste, the beef stew, but for some reason, the mechanics of how she prepared it bothered him. Sitting at the dining room table, looking over the latest status reports, he could hear the squeaking from the top of the instant pot Kathy used—sometimes she had a hard time getting the tabs aligned and had to struggle to twist the top, cursing under her breath—until she had it latched tight and the settings put into the keypad, the steam beginning to escape.

"So?" she said, wiping her hands on a towel as she came in. "How does it look?"

He shook his head slightly.

"Eighty-one."

"That's two weeks, honey," she said. "You gotta get that number up. They want eighty-five."

"I know."

It felt that she was about to get harsh with him again, but something entered her head, and she finished wiping her hands, sat down next to him. Sighed. "Talk to management. You can't carry all of this by yourself. They can't assign *all* the blame to you."

He wasn't sure there was blame involved yet, but he answered. "I did. They said there's nothing wrong with it. It's a best practice. We should be able to do it."

"Well, it's up to you. I mean, if you want to put it in concrete terms, that's a new car payment. And a vacation. And the boat you said you wanted. And who knows? Maybe you don't stay head of the team. Maybe they find someone else. I don't know what not hitting a benchmark means. Seems to me you're taking an awful big risk."

Kathy liked this new approach. Instead of tough love, this strategy was based on information and facts. She'd read about it earlier in the week, in her ongoing search for ways to improve herself as a supportive spouse. It was from a blog she liked, a woman who specialized in motivational marriage strategies for greater love, productivity and joy. Lay out the facts, it said. Put things in clear, quantitative terms. Motivate by *objective* persuasion and let your spouse make the choices himself.

"Well, they just gave it to us," he said. "I mean, it might take a few weeks to ramp up to the target. That's reasonable, isn't it?"

She smiled, furrowed her brows the way she did; empathizing, perhaps, or the assent one gives a child who doesn't understand grown-up things yet. She wiped her hands one last time on the dishcloth and stood.

"Well," she said, "if you don't get anywhere with Reuben, talk to HR. Maybe she'll have some ideas."

He watched the instant pot over her shoulder. Full with steam now, shooting out the vent in the top the label instructs you're not supposed to cover. Amazing, he thought, since people use those things to make bombs, that more of them don't explode in kitchens every day.

13

SOMETIMES A FOOT massage helped the swelling go down. Tonight it didn't, so she made an ice pack of frozen meatball packages wrapped in towels she then wrapped around both feet.

"*You'll* be eating those, not me," Cherise said. Darnell smiled, wincing only slightly as she closed the cold around him and lifted his feet onto the bed. Then got the ibuprofen and gave him two.

"Don't even say it," he said. "No sick days left."

Cherise felt guilty because she'd been so focused on the ad agency project that she let the situation get worse without realizing it. Now it seemed more serious, and her delayed reaction, sending him to Care twice last week and once this week, struck her as trying to make up for something she should have been on top of before.

"*Ibuprofen?*" she shouted after the second time. "That's all they said? You showed them your feet?" He did. But by the time he'd stood for half his shift, some of the swelling went down. "Did they do tests or something?" They didn't, he said. They don't have equipment to do testing. It was suggested he make an appointment with his own doctor for that. "You told them we don't have a doctor, right?" she snapped. "Like, we're in the middle of nowhere? And we don't have health insurance? You told them all that?" He said he did. She sat back in frustration.

Up to this point in life, she had been able to solve anything with speed, guile, agility, and when all else failed, a short temper. But now, watching Darnell with closed eyes, his feet swollen, was like watching a cloud encircle them and not knowing how to get out from under it. Health was not one of the things she worried about when she moved to Saltair Springs. The lack of care from a department called Care seemed mystifying. But then, she rationalized, this is work in the modern world. This is how business runs.

Everyone told her, everything you read about says it. They want you for your labor, for what you can do for them, not the other way around. It wasn't like in her parents' day.

She put her hand on his forehead. Still hot. She already called her mother, who suggested the cold compresses. And going to a doctor's office. "Fine, you want to find me one?" she snapped. Her mother countered with all the reasonable questions and suggestions, how you need a primary care physician and getting tests and second opinions. But her mother wasn't there, and didn't understand what it was like living in this town in the middle of a prairie. Cherise got frustrated, as she usually did, and ended the call, as she usually did, with, "Yes, fine, *bye*," and threw the phone at the wall.

Darnell had begun to snore. The sound of him sleeping peacefully gave her a moment of temporary relief.

⋆⟞◉ ◉⟝⋆

"I think the drones should attack from the west," Paul said.

Lydia squinted, trying to imagine their view on approach.

They were in the middle of scoping out the shooting schedule, standing outside the center. The previous week, Lydia had sent Arthur all the footage they shot over the past several weeks, and received a response she didn't expect: not good enough. This was spelled out on a call from Madeleine, the agency rep Arthur assigned to manage the job.

"I thought this was a low-key, guerrilla campaign," Lydia said.

"I did too," Madeleine said. "They looked at the footage and they liked it … what you captured was perfect … but they want a more professional look. We're sending you a crew to do it over."

Lydia and Paul looked at each other over the speakerphone. He made the slash across his throat; Lydia shook her head.

"Madeleine, are we still on the job?" Lydia asked.

"Oh, by all means yes. I didn't mean to imply anything was wrong. They love what you're doing. They just want to step it up in quality. The crew will be under your supervision, Lydia. No one's undermining your position, I promise."

"Do we believe her?" Paul asked after the call.

"What choice do we have? Maybe they thought it was a toss-off, but now they like it? We still seem to be employed."

"So we have to shoot everything again?"

"We'll find out. It does feel a bit odd, though. Suddenly paying attention to something that started out, honestly, as a mercy fuck for yours truly." Speaking in her low, mellifluous tone, the hardness of any individual word floated gently past like a lily pad on a Monet pond.

"I don't think they thought of it that way," Paul said, unconvincingly. She looked at him over her glasses.

And so, as discussed, two days later a crew showed up with serious equipment, including drones for exterior shots, which she and Paul were sketching out at that very moment, at the edge of the center's vast parking lot, when Paul tapped her shoulder. "Look."

Headed their way was Adele, and next to her, taking large strides in a tasteful business suit sans jacket, was Myron McAllister, general manager of all center operations—who, at the very outset, made it clear he wanted nothing to do with the ad people, and had deputized Adele to serve as buffer, insulation and decoy. But here he was, in person, moving toward them with a calm but assertive gait, Adele struggling to keep up, tablet under arm.

"Uh oh," Lydia mumbled, "this doesn't look good."

"Ms. Calligan!" Myron shouted, paces away, extending his hand to reach for hers, "it's a pleasure to meet you finally. And Mr. Swensen," he said, nearly pulling Paul's arm out of the socket. "I'm sorry we've been delayed welcoming you personally."

"No problem, we ..." was all Lydia got out, her glasses jostled by the force of his handshake. He continued: "I understand a crew was dispatched to support your efforts. I've heard very good reports about what you're doing, very impressive indeed."

"Thank you ..."

"I want you to know, right from the horse's mouth, how important this is. Quite a big deal, I'm being told." He spoke loud because the wind blew hard at the edge of the parking lot. This side faced east, where the rest of the city would be built some day; for now, the edge of the frontier, and here was a man with commanding silver hair and a demeanor not unlike the sheriff of the territory this once might have been.

"That's very nice," Lydia shouted back.

"Now, here's the development. Mister Hausen will be arriving first thing tomorrow to see for himself how the campaign is progressing."

"*Carl* Hausen?" Lydia lifted her chin to peer through the lower half of the lenses. He nodded. "Carl Hausen is coming here? In person?"

"Apparently there's more riding on this than we've been told. I wanted you to know as soon as possible so we can make arrangements. Why don't we speak in my office?" He took her by the arm, charming but firm, and led them to the Executive Level high above the main floor.

Paul and Lydia had not seen this yet. Adele brought in coffee and tea—better than the vending machines, so there must have been a real coffee machine around here somewhere—and Myron tried to keep his Executive Level demeanor in place, not entirely successfully, as he was clearly shaken by the news as well. Which was because Carl Hausen didn't visit places. He didn't go to meetings or talk to Wall Street or give press conferences. He was hardly photographed at all. It was one of the things the Hausen family was known for. The business they built, and handed down through generations, was kept solidly in the hands of the current president. And that president did not like coming out in public view. He exerted control over every aspect of the business and made strategic decisions from his lair in Idaho without fanfare or publicity. So the idea of old Carl showing up to oversee a pro-motional video struck them all as more than curious and just short of alarming.

"Have you ever met Mr. Hausen?" Lydia asked, seated now in front of McAllister's suitably impressive desk.

"No I haven't. He's a very private man."

"Have you ever heard of him coming to inspect one of his facilities?"

"Can't say that I have."

"So, this is unusual."

"I'd go out on a limb and call it that." He then outlined what he wanted them all to say, do, prepare and wear, and dismissed them to return to the conference room on the main floor to discuss and worry among themselves.

"I don't want to meet old Carl," Paul said, swinging his feet onto the table. "Rich old bastards who shoot varmints on ranches scare the bejesus out of me."

"What can I say? The client's the client. If he says meet, you meet."

"McAllister looked like he swallowed a porcupine."

"It certainly unnerved him. I don't think he knows any more than we do."

"What do you think is going on here?"

She sighed. "We shall find out tomorrow."

In the morning, they were all arranged in a receiving line outside the front entrance as a small convoy of large black SUVs pulled into the center's parking lot. The SUVs made the loop around and pulled up to the covered portico. As contractors, Paul and Lydia stood at the back of the line. Several large men wearing tweed jackets stepped out of the front vehicle, made their way to the third, and opened the back passenger door. Paul leaned forward, looking down the line. Behind the open door, someone slipped out, a flash of red, then McAllister stepped forward and blocked his view. McAllister's tall silver head nodded eagerly, the motion of arms pumping in handshake, then they stepped in front of the door and made their way down the line. As McAllister introduced each person and the man next to him surveyed them, Paul surveyed the man: shorter than expected, wearing a bright red sweater and gray pants. Pale white skin, dark nondescript hair, brushed back in a nondescript style. He looked like someone designed not to be noticed. Paul looked to Lydia, who didn't meet his gaze. She watched as the party approached. When they did and McAllister introduced them—McAllister four inches taller than Hausen, Lydia several inches taller, even Paul finding himself looking down—Carl stared, without words, an impassive gaze and white skin as soft and smooth as a child's.

"It's very nice to meet you, sir," Lydia said, shaking his hand. No reply. He moved on to Paul.

"Very nice," Paul said, and Carl seemed to observe him, peer into him with a studied non-reaction. McAllister moved Carl and his team down the line, into the lobby, and away from the welcoming committee. Lydia finally met Paul's eyes. *Creepy*, he mouthed.

The meeting was short, in another conference room decked out with a big monitor and video equipment, trays of cheeses, meats and baked goods. Carl, McAllister, and the center's senior staff at the head of the table, next to a group of people who also arrived in the SUVs. Paul and Lydia were positioned at the foot. They could only see the backs of heads. What they were all watching on the screen was a completed version of the video pieces Paul and Lydia had shot over the past several weeks, raw footage they thought was being sent to Arthur as a rough draft. Instead, it had been edited and worked on by unseen hands, and packaged into this sleek presentation. Carl nodded throughout, and when the lights came up, swiveled to face the whole group.

"Excellent job," he said. His voice measured, slightly soft, mild and plain as the unreadable face. "Very nice. Keep it up."

Then Paul and Lydia and most of the group were dismissed. They waited, in their own conference room, for questions or to be summoned back upstairs. But nothing happened until the phone on the table rang and they were asked to return to the front to bid farewell.

"What the fuck was that?" Paul asked, as they stood outside in the same formation as the morning, waving the SUVs off in style. Later that day, they found out; McAllister called Lydia to his office and she brought the whole story back down to Paul.

"It's a hostile takeover," she said. "Hausen is going after Country Goods. Smaller company in the south and west. They have a big presence in brick-and mortar stores but no online delivery. Hausen wants to gobble it up. He's anticipating a shareholder battle, so he wants fulfillment to be the selling point. And since Saltair Springs is the crown jewel in his fulfillment operation, it looks like we're the agency of record for his hostile takeover."

"What does he want from us?"

"More footage and better footage. They're going to use it in presentations to shareholders, funds, investment banks, all the big dogs. They want us to make this place look slicker than Disneyland."

"Is that good?"

She stared straight ahead. "It will be a lot of front-line work … that I didn't plan for. To be honest, I'd rather ride off into the sunset right about now."

"So what does that mean? Get out of Dodge?"

She considered a moment. "Can't. There'd be no coming back. If it was just us, I'd cut and run. But we're here on Arthur's word. And all his agency buddies are counting on a piece of this business. If we drop the ball now, we fuck them all."

"So, Carl wants to cannibalize this little old company and we're supposed to put a happy face on it?"

"That's about it," she said, and sighed. "And just the position I wanted to be in. Ear to the ground, ass in the air, right in front of an oncoming locomotive."

14

THE STORY BROKE in the press later in the day. Corporate waited until Friday afternoon to release it, guaranteeing weekend buzz and not having to answer questions until Monday. But Lydia's phone buzzed anyway, and rang and vibrated, and when she didn't answer fast enough, Paul's started. They fielded calls well into the night, the most important being Arthur's.

"And how are you?" she asked. "Quiet evening?"

"Didn't see that coming, did you?"

"Darlin', I don't think either of us would be on this call if I had."

"What do you think, Lydia? How are things looking out there?"

Paul leaned across the conference table to hear better.

"Well, I'm confident we can deliver the assets we promised," she said, "and with the camera crew, they'll look better than what you've seen. By the way, I didn't know old Carl was getting the footage directly. I thought that was only for internal purposes."

"I'm sorry, Lydia. That was a command, not a request. It all belongs to the client anyway."

"I know. I just … didn't expect to see our stuff shown to the big cheese himself."

"We didn't mean to blindside you. Besides, he's delighted. And from what I hear, that's not an easy thing to do. So, well done you. And Paul."

"Thank you. But anyway, yes, I don't see a problem delivering what we agreed upon. Unless that's changed."

Arthur sighed. Lydia looked at the ceiling. Paul leaned closer.

"Well, there you've touched on it," Arthur said. "The assignment had been to simply show stories of happy, smiling people shipping products to happy, smiling customers. Now we have to pivot a bit. We have to show the team out there in Saltair Springs infused with strength and determination. Show how HausenHome is best positioned to take control of Country Goods, and leave no doubt in any shareholder's mind. The work needs to say Saltair Springs is a powerhouse and Carl won't accept any hesitation. This has to be a steamroller and you're at the helm."

A moment of silence, Lydia thought, in memory of the blissful years she had spent wandering the streets with no responsibilities at all.

"This would be the moment, Lydia," Arthur said. "Can you deliver?"

She took a long, last breath.

"We'll stay on."

Paul sat back.

"I'm glad to hear that," Arthur said. "No need to reiterate the obvious. You know the business better than any of us. The stakes, my dear."

"Ah yes, the stakes. Right through the heart."

"Can you give us a revised proposal by Monday morning?"

Paul rolled his eyes. He had been planning to roll in bed the whole weekend.

"Of course," Lydia said, staring at him. He raised his middle finger. "In fact, Paul will send it to you Sunday afternoon." *Fuck you*, he mouthed.

"That would be wonderful," Arthur said. "Well, enjoy your weekend. As much as you can."

She held up her hand after the call. "I don't want any flack out of you. Just the answer. In or out?"

He stared at her, considered her. He really wanted out of there. Back to San Francisco, back to scaring up cute guys on foggy streetcorners, lazing in bed, grumbling about his lousy life. If he left, she'd have to scramble to find other ex-employees, people she could fly out on a moment's notice. And she might find them. But she didn't look to Paul as confident as she thought she was. Underneath was still the vast unsaid. He often felt like a heel and didn't mind feeling it too much, but he knew he would feel even more heel-like on a plane back to SF.

"You suck," he said, pouting.

"Such a baby."

On Monday morning, Myron called the first ever all-hands meeting at Saltair Springs. Everyone gathered on the main floor in front of a small riser set up with a podium. Paul and Lydia sat in the row of folding chairs behind the podium, next to several executives from HausenHome corporate who had accompanied Carl the week before. They had not introduced themselves and seemed instructed to remain nameless, dressed in serious dark blue suits and white shirts. Only sunglasses would have made them more ominous.

"So, that's about the long and the short of it," Myron said, concluding his remarks. "Because of the nature of the offer, that is, our company making an aggressive bid to take over another, every one of us needs to pitch in and row in the same direction at the same time, just as hard as we can. Like everything here at HausenHome, this is a team effort. The ultimate success will belong to all of us."

"Well, those of you with vested options," Paul whispered. Lydia pinched his arm, hard. "*Ow*. Bitch."

"Many of you have been involved with the team from our ad agency," Myron said. "They'll be extending their work a bit longer to capture additional footage. Please give them your cooperation, and work with your managers to secure the time needed to accommodate them." He thanked everyone, and they applauded courteously, most not sure what was happening; only that more hours would be needed, and the suspicion that output goals would be increased again.

Later that evening, Kathy sat across from Walt at the dining table, the suspended lamp above them the only light in the house.

"You look like you have a test you haven't studied for," Kathy said. The blog suggested starting from a place of levity.

"They want to hit ninety to a hundred now. Same equipment, same people. Nothing different."

"Well, this is serious," she sighed. "This is the biggest business story in America. They talked about it on the network news. And you're in the middle of it. You're the shit. You gotta rise to the occasion."

"I know," he said, hunching forward, feeling his belly slip over his belt. She had seen this look before. Collapsing in on himself. She wanted to continue being supportive, like the beautiful wife with the silky hair on the show about high school football. She wanted to lean that way, and she meant to; but something intruded. Contempt scrambled her concentration. The sudden rage at this disgusting blob in front of her felt so much more authentic than that fucking actress and her hair. His snoring and whining, his revolting whatever he did on the computer. The smell of his clothes, the yellow stains in his underwear.

"Will you goddamn man up please?" she said, with a sudden surge of relief. "You are such a pathetic excuse of a man. You just wallow in your own stink, all day and night, blubbering about what you can't do. I am so sick of hearing it. Do you know how much I sacrifice for you? How hard I work to keep our lifestyle maintained?" He seemed to sink deeper into his own belly. She thought he looked like a turd on a hot sidewalk. "A *lot*," she went on. "That's all I'll say. So, why don't you find some self-respect and stand up and do something on your own for once? You think I like carrying your dead weight on my back? I don't. So, you listen to me, Walter Mulbacher. If HausenHome drops the biggest business deal in the United States in your fat, fucking lap, then you pick it up and you run with it, do you hear me? This is a gift from God. So fucking do it." Then she got up from the table, walked out to the backyard, and slammed the door.

And he knew she was right. There was nowhere else to disappear to.

15

IT TOOK ONLY a few days for the new video crew to edit the old footage and the new footage together. They made one-minute packages, each one showing a different aspect of the center's operation: delivery, inventory management, software, picking, order fulfillment. Lydia worked with the editors to cut down the interviews and background into short videos. They sent the pieces to corporate, and heard that Carl was delighted, handing them off to the business guys in New York managing negotiations and crafting the deal. But, as Myron told his department heads, and Paul and Lydia, messaging wasn't enough. The center also had to increase volume, output and flowthrough in concrete terms.

"Jesus," Paul said, "sounds like it needs a good stool softener."

Myron continued: it would be up to Lydia and Paul to communicate the sheer force of the center's performance. Saltair Springs was the engine that would push the takeover bid to its successful conclusion. And if not—implied but not said—it would be their failure for not getting this message across.

A mood descended on the center, and the town, like a high pressure system of uncertain origin: nebulous and foggy, a cloud that made everyone nervous and edgy, the hairs on the arm standing up as ions charged the atmosphere. Indoors, the sound and feel of machinery picking up speed as more orders were redirected to Saltair Springs from other parts of the country; not because of supply problems, but to demonstrate to investors the number of items that could be fulfilled by this one magnificent facility. Only the executives knew this, and why it was being done. Lydia suspected, but was not involved in those discussions.

On the Monday following the announcement, news crews descended on the center, pushing for interviews, opinions, insight. Dirt. McAllister made the first blunder. Adele called his office from the parking lot. Reporters were buttonholing employees, asking what was going on, what they saw, what they thought.

"Oh, no no no," Myron said, panicked. "Jesus, stop them."

"How?"

"I'll call security."

"They talked to a bunch of people already. Do we want security out here on camera, roughing these people up?"

"Shit. Yes, alright, let me call Lydia, this is supposed to be her job."

And he did, and she answered, deep inside the insulated conference room.

"Reporters outside," she told Paul. "Myron needs someone to run interference. You up for it?"

He slid the knot of his tie up and buttoned the top button. And was surprised to see how easily Lydia slipped back into the easygoing press-friendly persona he hadn't seen in two years. In the parking lot, all he had to do was stand by her side, looking pretty, as she cooled the frenzy of reporters, microphones, cameras. Lydia knew how to give each reporter attention and courtesy while saying absolutely nothing. And she had it under control until the flash of dark suits appeared: the pack of corporate agents who arrived the week earlier, invisible but intent in one of the other conference rooms, now descending on the scene like bats. One man stepped in front of Lydia and took control; a woman herded the other reporters away with the aid of still more staffers, now in sunglasses.

"What was that?" Lydia asked Paul, as they stood to the side, spirited away by unseen hands.

"I think we done been put out to pasture," he said. "This here's the pasture," and pulled up a piece of long grass and chewed it, as they watched the MBA squad neutralize the journalists.

"Well, ok," Lydia said. "Message received. Stay in our lane." And they did. The suits, it was made clear, would handle the press from now on.

At least until Wednesday morning.

Lydia's phone rang so many times at 4 am, even the mind-numbing anti-anxieties couldn't keep her in sleep. She reached for the bedside light, tapping the table for glasses, searching for that annoying sound.

"We have a problem," the phone shouted.

"Hi. Ok. Yes. Who is this?"

"Lydia, it's Myron. We have a problem."

"So you said."

"I'm sending you a text now," and she tried to focus on what came up from the link in the message. Social media posts. Videos. Replies. Exclamation points, skulls and crossbones. Evil-looking icons she didn't know the meaning of.

"Apparently an ex-employee," Myron said. "An angry young woman who thinks she's some kind of whistleblower. I spoke to HR. We let her go a few months ago and she's making a lot of noise online. We need to do something, fast."

"You said you wanted the dark suits to handle this stuff."

"I spoke to them, Lydia. They're out of their depth. This girl lives outside of town somewhere. You have expertise in these matters." She wasn't sure what he meant by that. "You need to do something about this. I got called by corporate at 2am. They're very upset. Which means Mr. Hausen is very upset."

"Yes," Lydia said, swinging her feet onto the floor. "Of course. Send me everything you have."

Once awake, she scanned the pages he sent, made coffee and knocked on the adjoining door.

"The fuck?" Reuben grumbled, his damp hair under Paul's slow breathing chest.

"Sssshhhh," he said, his hand over Reuben's mouth. He got up, went to the door. "If you're a Jehovah's Witness, I'm sorry, we're all homosexuals here."

"Open up," she said, "we have a problem."

"Could I get back to you on that? The connection isn't very good. I'm going into a tunnel. Ssssssuuuhhhhhssss …"

"I don't care what's going on in there. Just be ready at seven. We have leg-work to do."

"Uh, copy that, red leader."

Lydia turned and flopped back onto the bed.

"Who is this girl?"

Paul drove the rental car as they sped, once again, through empty landscape away from the manufactured town. Lydia fished in her purse for something to apply, maybe a forgotten lipstick in some interior pocket. "Her name is Maria Carvey," she said. "She worked on the receiving dock for six months. They let her go a couple of months ago. Let go, not resigned. HR said it was for too many absences, bad attitude, blah blah. Since then, she's been posting videos and making a lot of noise online. The usual stuff. Long hours, no breaks, too much pressure. Everyone who ever worked at a fulfillment center posts the same stuff so no one paid any attention. Until the announcement. Now she's the oracle of everything awful about Saltair Springs. She's got reporters and interviews and a ton of traffic to her posts. She lives in a community outside of town."

"A community? What does that mean?"

"A trailer park."

"Ah," Paul said.

In the past, Lydia realized, she would have said it, shorthand in conversation with friends, as a pejorative, a joke. *Trailer trash.* Someone who is trash because they live in a trailer. She would have laughed about it too. But now she didn't find the humor. In the last two years, she had become used to talking with people who lived on the street, who had no homes to go to. From her demeanor and dress, they thought she was homeless too. Sometimes they would shout or threaten, and she would simply stare. Other times she fell into conversation, sometimes sharing a cigarette, sitting on a bench or a low concrete wall. She didn't remember their names, they simply started talking as if they were old friends; the lack of social rules, being outside of society, freed them from the anxiety of judgment, having to notice one's social position and adjust accordingly. They were just two people discussing the pain in their knees. Although she had a bed to sleep in, she was as broken as the people she met, and it felt alien now, entirely wrong, to fall into the pattern of judgments she used to make.

They pulled up to a collection of ten trailers, positioned next to each other with a road in front. A small wood fence with chicken wire around the property; rigged-up electric lines connected the houses to the main. Nothing else around, the yards neatly kept, each one with a car or an SUV. No trash to be seen.

"Odd," Paul said, at the starkness.

"The real world."

He stopped in front of the yard with the number they were given. The trailer door opened immediately, and a young girl came down the few steps, waving her hands no.

"I don't want to talk to you," she said. "I told you."

"Wait here," Lydia said, and slowly opened the door, stepped out. "Miss Carvey, hello," she said, in her most soothing tone.

"I'm not kidding. If you're from the center, I don't want you here."

"We're not from the center. Technically. I work for an ad agency the company retained. We're not here to harass you."

"Well you are. So please leave."

"I get it, I get it," she said. "But we drove a long time to speak with you. I'm wondering … I'm hoping … would you just hear me out? I won't come any closer."

The girl came up to the car. "I'm not afraid of you. I just don't want any trouble. I'm not doing anything wrong and all I'm saying is the truth."

Lydia regarded her. A small girl, white, about 25. Short jeans skirt, bold eye makeup, two short ponytails on either side, a tangle of wristbands.

"Who's that?" she said, nodding at the car.

"My associate, Paul. He's not an employee of the company either. I understand your position, Miss …"

"He looks like some kind of a business guy. Are you some business guy they sent to strongarm me?"

Paul laughed, delighted. "Honey, *I* don't even know what I'm doing here."

"Maria," Lydia said.

"I don't know you."

"Miss Carvey … I'll be totally honest. Yes, we've been sent by the company about your online postings. But we don't work for the company. The suggestion was made that a disinterested party like me might listen to your concerns, and if possible, work out a compromise you might find acceptable."

"What, they want to buy me off?"

"I think the idea is to find a way to address your legitimate concerns. If that's possible. And I'm probably talking out of school, but they're not exactly destitute. You might be able to leverage the situation to your advantage."

"Buy me off," she said, harder.

Lydia gave it her best comic shrug, the one they screamed at on Uncle Marty's show. It even got a laugh out of Maria Carvey. "I'm not getting bullied or muzzled," she said.

"Do we look like we're here to do that?"

Maria regarded Lydia, her sad eyes and rumpled trenchcoat, and Paul, this bashful-looking, skinny business guy. "Alright, whatever," she said.

Inside, the trailer looked like any young girl's hip apartment; handmade art, mobiles, rock and roll posters. A jumble, but not the home of a crazy or a hoarder or a drug addict. She made coffee, then sat with them at the compact table facing a window that faced the empty plain as far as they could see.

"So what's their problem?" she asked. "What are they gonna do, sue me for telling the truth?"

"I watched some of your videos," Lydia said, "though not all. Can you tell me, in a nutshell, the gist of what you're concerned about?"

"Just the *nut* and the *gist*, huh? That's what you want?"

Paul laughed into his coffee. Lydia nodded.

"Well … they work people to death there, that's what that's about. They came in here and promised they were bringing all this great stuff to the town and then they went and built that concentration camp … and didn't do the stuff they said they were going to. At least, not much of it."

Lydia tried to nod without agreement. "Tell me, are you a native? Were you born here?"

"Yeah, I'm from here. My house was under that town. My folks moved out to Fort Morgan."

"I see. So, you're angry about what they did to your home?"

"Actually no. There wasn't much of a town to begin with. I mean, this wasn't some beautiful paradise they paved over. It was pretty much a ghost town. We were all really happy when we heard they were building a center and putting in all these millions of dollars. I wanted to get in on it, I wanted to make some money. It's just that's … it turned out to be kind of a meat factory, and now everything goes into feeding the monster."

"I see how that would impact you. Could you tell me about your specific experience? I mean, anything you feel comfortable telling me. And again, I don't work for the company. I would keep anything you tell me to keep confidential from them."

"What about him?" she said, nodding at Paul. "You look like you're sitting there listening to everything."

"Honey," he laughed, "believe me, I'm with you when it comes to corporate goons and secret police ..."

"Please don't," Lydia said.

"... and their Nazi business suits."

Lydia closed her eyes, sighed. Maria regarded them a moment. "Well, all I'm saying," she continued, "is they work people too hard. And there's no one to watch out and make sure they're treating people right. You can see it in some of the videos I shot. I mean, people have to piss in jars because they don't give you bathroom breaks. People take dumps behind the center, behind the parking lot in the middle of the night. People pass out from not eating enough. It's fucked up. It's inhuman."

"Did you talk to the managers about it?"

"Of course, lots of times. But they're as scared as everyone else. They give you these goals they tell you you have to hit. And it's just, really, work faster. That's all it is. And is there a raise or a bonus or, what is it, stock options or something? No. You work and they make the rules and there's no discussion. And I know they picked our town to stick this thing in because there's no other work. You have to work at the center because you have no choice."

"I hear what you're saying, and I don't disagree. But just so I've said it, and I've earned my pay for the week ..." and she looked down at her hands, pondering what she could, should, had to say, "... there *are* jobs now where there didn't used to be. There *is* work and the chance to build a life where there wasn't before. Kids are growing up and going to school. The company provides assistance and a lot of people wouldn't be able to buy a home if not for the fulfillment center."

"Well, not me. They didn't pay enough and I don't want some four-bedroom monstrosity with a huge mortgage. I just wanted to pay my rent and have my weekends free to have a life, like a normal person. That place sucks you in, and if you don't take the shitty schedule they give you, then fuck you. And those managers, they all got suckered in with that house bullshit too, and now they can't quit either. You think they can sell that house and move someplace else? Forget that. They're chained to this place." She looked at Paul. He shrugged at Lydia: *she's right*.

"Be that all as it may," she said, "and I'm not disagreeing with you. But to get to the business at hand ... the company has a problem right now, and that's why they asked us to meet with you." Paul pointed at Lydia, mouthed *her*. "As you know, they're attempting this corporate maneuver to take over the Country Goods chain. It's a very delicate moment. They have some tough shareholder negotiations and government approvals and so forth. And I've been told you've done a yeoman's job of gumming up the works for them." Maria knitted her brows. "You've done an important thing by drawing attention to some very legitimate concerns," Lydia said. "And thrown a monkey wrench into their plans. You've done it and it worked and for that you should be applauded. So, at this point, the company would be happy to meet with you to discuss what you've brought up and consider reforms based on those concerns."

"What does that mean exactly?"

"Well, the gist of the nut is … you win. They want to hear what you have to say, and they're willing to implement changes to address your legitimate complaints."

"Oh," she said, the wind somewhat taken from her sails. She looked at Paul; he seemed just as confused. "So?"

"So," Lydia said, "what was your intention in making those videos and putting out the messages you put out?"

"Well. To tell people how bad the conditions are. What they're doing to the people who work there."

"And for what purpose? What did you hope would come from your putting those videos online?"

"Well … that they would stop … hurting people. Raise some awareness so someone would do something about it."

"And you've been very successful at that. You've done it. The company is over a barrel. They're willing to take what you have to say into consideration and adopt changes. Is that what you were hoping to accomplish?"

"Uhm, I guess."

"Okay. Well. There you are. And in addition, they feel there should be some compensation for your experience, given the way things turned out. They're certainly willing to offer you your job back. But if that's not of interest, then a package that would provide you with funds to cover your expenses, and a bit more, to get you settled in whatever career, or new location you might like to explore."

"So, they do want to buy me off."

"They want to make you whole. Compensate you for your inconvenience."

"And what would I have to do?" she asked, slowly.

"Well, to begin with, stop talking to the press. Take down your videos. At least for the time being. And for the duration of this merger going through its various hurdles."

She stared long and hard over her coffee cup. "This smells weird," she said.

"It does. But they're making the offer in good faith, and they'll follow through on it. They want this to stop, and they're willing to meet you halfway."

"I don't know. I don't like to just … what's the word …"

"Capitulate," Paul said. Lydia glared at him.

"I understand you," she said to Maria. "But in addition to the offer, there is one additional item they asked me to bring up."

"Which is?"

She looked down at her hands on the table. "They're extending this offer to settle your grievances in an amicable fashion. That would be to everyone's advantage. But they're also a big company, Maria, with effectively bottomless pockets. They have a lot of lawyers. If asked to do so, those lawyers will find creative ways of making your life unpleasant. It doesn't mean you wouldn't prevail, and it doesn't preclude you from rallying the troops to your cause. But as of this moment, it's David and Goliath. They're the ogre with the deep pockets and you're the one living in a little room on wheels."

"Are you threatening me?" she asked, quietly.

"Yeah," Paul said. "Are you threatening her?"

"No, I'm not. But it was made clear to me, I'll be honest, with a certain, sinister undertone, that taking a step like that was not beyond the realm of possibilities. They sent me here to wave a good-natured white flag. Failing that, they have other avenues to pursue that don't lead to such a genteel disposition."

Paul stared at Lydia.

"Look, I'm not an activist," Maria said. "I just want a job and a life. And to tell the truth. If I agree, they'll take my changes seriously?"

"They promised. I wouldn't lie."

"I'm the only one," she said, to herself, to no one in particular. "I mean, if this was some big city and people would help me and wave signs and protest and everything. But you see what there is out here. I guess if they're giving me what I want …"

"I think that would be a good choice," Lydia said, comfortingly. "If that's agreeable to you, may I let them know we spoke and get back to you later today with the details?"

She nodded.

"Great," Lydia said, and reached out to shake her hand.

On the way back, they didn't speak. Paul drove with the window open, his elbow resting on the sill. After miles of silence, he said, "Fancy footwork back there."

Lydia grunted, watching the highway in front of them, eyes glazed over.

"They bought you off to buy her off," he said. "And with a threat too. Was that their idea or did you throw that in for free?"

She turned away to look out her window. "Did you knock on my door to ask me to find you some charity work?" she asked. "Because if you did, there's a soup kitchen down at my church. They'd love a volunteer with your sparkling personality."

"You know what I'm talking about."

"They'll take what she has to say into consideration …"

"Bullshit."

"… and give her some money to put down some roots."

"Bribery."

"So, welcome to the U.S of A. Nobody got hurt and everybody wins."

"If that's what you tell yourself, bub."

Now she did turn to him. "Just to put it out there, Paul. Your opinions are not always welcome. I still sign the checks, at least for this job. Maria will get a hearing and a shitload of money, and you will get to keep your nocturnal visitors loaded up with booze and Toblerones from the minibar. Everyone gets what they want, so end of discussion."

Neither of them dwelt on it, but they both guessed it was Arthur who suggested they send Lydia to deal with Maria Carvey. He figured her low-key manner would be better suited than the suits to gain the trust of this troublesome young person. And she had done it, and Myron expressed his gratitude the next week after the online videos disappeared. Lydia shared the news with Paul, busy again in the conference room.

"And you got a raise," she said.

"Beg pardon?"

"They upped the contract. Four more weeks, higher rate. Congratulations."

"Uh, thank you?"

"I didn't have to tell you, by the way. You'd never have been the wiser. So, if you wouldn't mind not crapping on me when I try to make us both a living, I would appreciate it."

"You still sore about trailer park girl?"

"It was necessary."

"Oh, I don't think that's what you think. I think you regret it. I think you don't like it either, and you think giving me a few tuppence in my bag full of crumbs will make you feel better about what you did."

"I have a therapist, thanks."

He was about to say, *well he's not doing a very good job*, but even he knew that went too far.

"And by the way, Mary Poppins," she said, "when I met with Myron last week, he wanted me to go out there and flatten that girl. He told me to tell her to cease and desist, and if she didn't, they would destroy her with every lawsuit they could throw at her. I talked him out of that. The suggestion to listen to her concerns and take her seriously was mine."

He wanted to hit back with some smart remark, but couldn't come up with one. So there, she didn't have to say. And he knew it, and put his head down and went back to work. At least the end was in sight. Only four more weeks in purgatory, albeit at a higher hourly. But still, it would be a slog. Thank goodness, he reminded himself, for Reuben and his kind eyes and his warm, musky smell. He was sort of a puppy, so attached and in love so fast. Paul knew he would have this effect on him, a guy for whom a weekend in Denver was the highlight of the year. Paul knew he had bowled him over with his stories of famous conquests, adventures in New York and Europe. When the time came, Paul realized he would have to be quick and blunt: *It's been fun! Look me up when you get to California!* He was so good at it, the poor guy wouldn't see it coming. Nice people like him never imagine you can switch it off like that, become someone who doesn't care anymore. It was Paul's power and secret weapon. And he knew he'd have to use it soon.

16

WHEN CHERISE WAS a kid, her father took the family on a trip to Los Angeles. At the seaport, there was a huge, old ocean liner docked at a pier, and her father bought a tour that took you down into the hull of the ship, the bowels they called it, where the engine room and boilers used to be. They were pulled out long ago, and all that was left was a terrifyingly huge, yawning space, five or six stories high, with rusting metal walls and the echoes of water dripping from nowhere. A dark, airless horror. The whole time she felt they were sealed inside this iron coffin and she would never escape. It took all her strength not to run out in terror, especially since all the other kids seemed so thrilled and delighted. Sometimes she still got the feeling of being inside that ominous space, and just the thought of it made her heart race, made sweat break out on her forehead.

She had that feeling that night, and remembered it in the morning when she had what she called preemptive vomiting. It happened when she heard the sirens. She was working to move a stuck klingon next to a pump that had something to do with the HVAC system, and standing next to it was so loud, she had on the earmuffs she carried on her utility belt. She and two guys were rocking the robot back and forth to unstick it from the groove on the floor, and she heard this vague repetitive sound. No bother to her, she kept rocking, directing the others to rock it with hand signals, since they all had earmuffs on. After a while, it started to irritate her, this sound, and she pulled off one muff. Over the roar of the HVAC, it took a second to register as a siren, and judging from the volume it was right outside the walls of the building. Then, without warning, she puked all over the floor and the shoes of the two other guys.

"What the fuck?" one yelled, and she doubled-over, emptied her whole stomach, sank down on all fours.

They tried to help her up, but with the thick safety gloves, they looked like Minnie Mouse trying to get a grip. After a moment, she nodded, mouthed *I'm okay*, and they helped her to a box nearby. She sat, dizzy, legs shaking too much to stand. The siren continued. She leaned forward, put her hands on her knees, took deep breaths, and in a few minutes, shook her head, waved the guys off—standing around, unsure what to do—and she lumbered away from them, drawn toward the siren.

The center had developed a protocol for emergencies involving fire engines or ambulances: stay at your station and keep working. Supervisors walked around and reinforced the rule, waved you back if you came out to see the commotion. So, while the older people remained in their place, the new ones meandered out to the parking lot and watched. It was a body on a stretcher under a blanket, covered completely. The ambulance lights were still flashing, but the siren was silenced now. And the way everyone out there moved, without urgency, it was obvious this wasn't someone they had to rush to the hospital.

Cherise pushed her way past security, out the loading dock, and approached the group of officers milling around the ambulance. They turned to look. One stepped forward to move her back, but he could tell from the look on her face. From inside the building, people watched as the officer put one hand on her shoulder, pulled her gently toward them, toward the ambulance.

On the other side of the main floor, in the conference room, Paul pulled out an earbud. Lydia was studying a monitor, wearing headphones, but when she saw him, she took them off. They both listened.

"Another one bites the dust," he said.

"Don't joke. Go find out."

He did, and in a few minutes came back, ashen. "I was just kidding."

"Oh, please, tell me it was an injury," she said. He shook his head. "Oh, fuck," she said, and slumped into the chair, threw the headphones onto the table. "Mother. Fucker."

⊷══◉═══⊶

Among the angry, demanding, hysterical calls Lydia fielded over the next 24 hours was one from Maria Carvey. "If you think I'm taking your fucking money now, you can *go fuck yourself!*" she screamed. "You fucking murdering *bitch!*" and hung up.

Paul waited only a moment.

"But ya are, Blanche," he said. "Ya are."

She put her head in her hands. "Quicksand," she moaned. "I should have seen it before."

This was the second day of intense news coverage—helicopter flyovers, microwave trucks, reporters scrambling after employees at night, in the morning, at the supermarket, anywhere anyone who worked at the center might be cornered. As the details emerged, it couldn't have made a more perfect story: young, handsome guy dies inside a cage-like contraption deep within the confines of a facility churning out goods to feed corporate America's unquenchable thirst for expansion and conquest. And not just any facility, but the very one at the center of a hostile takeover, and about which a vocal and popular online critic had been waving a red flag—until she was mysteriously silenced.

Paul and Lydia sat in on the hourly briefings. Conference calls with HausenHome corporate and the ad agencies in San Francisco, that team being led by Arthur. They had retained Chandler/Perkins, a premiere crisis management firm, to gain control of the rapidly exploding situation. Other disgruntled employees had also come forward, joined forces with Maria, all of them now doing wall-to-wall interviews on cable, network and online news, sharing their every thought, gripe and opinion. Carl himself was not heard from; his deputies and assistants spoke for him. But the silence reinforced the impression that he was imploding with rage out on the range. The only message from his proxies: get this under control.

Even Arthur was demoted, placed under the authority of Chandler/Perkins. Their crisp British accents laid out the action plan for each company, team and individual, for each segment of each day. Paul and Lydia had been silent participants for the last 24 hours, nodding emphatically at meetings, but so far assigned nothing. By the end of the second 24-hour cycle, and not a peep, Paul asked, "What do you think, are we toast?" He sat at the table in the conference room, bouncing a rubber ball off a wooden paddle with the HausenHome logo, a promotional toy from the center's opening he found in a closet.

Lydia had reverted, unnervingly, to her San Francisco state of mind, wrapped up tightly in trench coat and sunglasses.

"I am in the dark," she said. "You've been in every meeting I have."

"You think anyone would notice if we just drove away?"

"How I'd love to do that. But I don't think the people who got us the gig would appreciate it. We have to sit here and take our lumps. The only thing worse than knowing nothing is finding out what's on the end of the next phone call."

And right on cue, the speakerphone rang. Paul nodded at it. "Your carriage awaits, Marie Antoinette."

In a few minutes, they sat across from Myron. Anxious, unsure what to do, he leaned forward, splayed his fingers on the desk.

"I just got off a call with senior management. Including Mr. Hausen. To say he's displeased would be an understatement. He doesn't feel he has a good grasp of the situation at all. The agencies are telling him they can't craft a credible response without more information."

"What do we know so far?" Lydia asked.

"We've been talking with the police but they still don't know much. The basics you've heard already. This young man," he scanned a page on his desk, "Darnell Spragg ... died at his station, as of now, cause unknown. They're waiting on toxicology, but initial reports find no suggestion of drugs ... no weapons found, no detectable injury at all. Obviously, the autopsy is ongoing. He was 23 ... worked in picking for just over a year. Lives in Sundown Gardens ... has ... had ... a girlfriend, Cherise Watson, they live together. She's also an employee, a floater. She's ... I believe she's one of your profile subjects, isn't she?" Lydia nodded. McAllister shook his head. "And that's all we know so far. But in the vacuum, the world out there is trying the case in public, making us the villain in every story."

"You have the best people money can buy," Lydia said. "Chandler/Perkins is the gold standard when it comes to spin."

"And they're working with what they know. But the story is spiraling out of control. We need the police to finish their investigation and come up with an answer. Until then, it's a free-for-all. And of course, the takeover has been put on hold."

"So we have to wait for the police report," she said.

"Yes ..."

"I sense a but."

He nodded. "We're dealing with a rural police force here. The county sheriff really. Everything has to go to Denver for analysis, and my sense is this is not a group of individuals with a great deal of experience."

"Hausen is concerned they'll mess up the investigation?"

"We're entirely transparent and working with law enforcement to the fullest extent possible." Lydia wondered if the room was bugged and he had to say that. "At the same time," he went on, quieter, "this is Mr. Hausen's business. His family legacy and future. This is our town, and my home, and home to all the people who work here. I'm sure the authorities will do their work to the best of their ability. But Mr. Hausen would like to know what happened to his own satisfaction."

"Oh … no," Paul groaned.

"Lydia," McAllister continued, "Mr. Hausen's been impressed by your tactfulness and diplomacy. As all the external messaging is being handled by the crisis managers, Mr. Hausen asked me if you, and your associate, would do a little … nosing around. You seem to have the trust of the employees you've worked with, and given that Cherise is already someone you know …"

"This sounds like a police matter," she said. "You have the unexplained death of a young man. They need to do their job."

"And they are," he said, defensively, "but Mr. Hausen would like another set of eyes on the matter. He simply wants to know what's happening in his own house. That's not unreasonable, is it?"

A long sigh from inside the trench coat. "Of course not."

"And Arthur Koretz seconded the idea. He thought it was a wonderful suggestion."

"Well, that doesn't give us much of a choice, does it?"

"It's up to you, of course. But as Mr. Hausen himself asked … I know he would appreciate it. Personally."

"Then that's what we'll do."

Paul had been sitting, slack-jawed. She stood, nodded, indicated he should stand.

"We'll start right away," and she reached across the desk and took Myron's hand, as much in agreement as to steady his nervous shaking.

17

PAUL SWIZZLED THE Manhattan he had to explain to the waitress to explain to the bartender how to make. Taffys' full bar meant only beer and wine product.

"Are you sure you want to be drinking in the middle of the day?" Lydia asked.

"Are you sure you *don't?* This whole thing sounds like a job for alcohol." He downed half in one gulp. "G'yuck, paint thinner." He wiped his mouth, lifted the glass and shook it at the waitress. "Another one, please?"

"I can't imagine what that young woman must be feeling," Lydia said. "This has to be awful."

"Who, Cherise? You haven't spoken with her?"

"I left messages."

"It doesn't seem like she has a ton of friends here. Maybe she needs a wise old shoulder to lean on."

She shook her head. "We're the bad guys now. I don't want the same look I got from that girl in the trailer. It's worse too, because we've spent time together. I can't go in there as Carl Hausen's spy."

"Well, it's your shitshow, honey, I'm just here for the paycheck. But it sounds to me like you can say and do anything you want. Old Carl doesn't need to know everything you find out. And besides, if you like the girl and you'd help her out anyway ..." He finished the rest of the drink as the waitress brought the next one. "Would you like to order some food?" she asked.

"Absolutely," Paul said. "If ever there was a moment for putrefied cheese sticks ..."

⊹⊷⊜⊶⊹

Her whole face looked broken, eyes swollen from crying.

Lydia had stood outside the apartment door for ten minutes before ringing the bell. A small, older woman with a kind face answered; her resemblance to Cherise told Lydia who she was. After a few moments of introduction, Cherise called from the kitchen to let her in, and she did, and Lydia hugged her, her body shaking with sobs.

There were sandwiches and bowls of salad and macaroni on the counter. Washed dishes and coffee cups drying on the rack. The apartment was small, warm, smartly finished in midcentury style—HausenHome's sophisticated NordicEdge line—with a few flea market bargains throw around.

Cherise positioned herself on a chair, looking out the sliding glass door toward the small patio while Lydia and Cherise's mother, Marion, spoke quietly.

"What do you think will happen with the ad campaign?" Marion asked. "She's been so excited by that."

"I don't know yet. I haven't been given any instructions. It's a lot of good work, and Cherise is wonderful in it. What I do know is they hired a crisis management company called Chandler/Perkins. They handle things like oil spills and sexual assault cases … I'm actually waiting to be told what to do. So far I don't know anything."

"Well," Marion said. She looked at Cherise, looked back at Lydia. Her look said it: maybe you could talk to her for a while now. "I might go out and get some fresh air," she said. To Cherise, "Honey, would that be okay?"

"Sure, mama," she mumbled, not looking at them.

"Alright then," Marion said, "I'll be back soon," and she left quietly. Lydia moved to the small dining table in front of the kitchen, facing Cherise's turned back. She sat and waited. After a while, Cherise sighed. "I got your messages. Thanks."

"Of course. I am so sorry. I don't know what to say. I'm in shock." Cherise nodded, not really paying attention. "What do you … what do you think you want to do?" Lydia asked.

A shrug.

"Have they told you anything yet? The police or anyone?"

Cherise shook her head. They sat in silence a long time. In Lydia's mind, questions floated like a lazy balloon on a summer afternoon—what to do next, what she was doing there. Whether she should be there at all.

"It doesn't feel right," Lydia said. Cherise turned to her. "In fact, something feels very wrong here." The look on Cherise's face told her: it was too much to consider right now. Still in shock. Something made Lydia move closer, slide her chair next to Cherise, reach out and take her hand. "This doesn't make any sense," Lydia said. Cherise nodded, then moved closer, wrapped her arms around Lydia, and cried.

⊶━◉ ◉━⊷

Later, back in the hotel, Lydia lay on the bed with a moist facecloth over her eyes, hands behind her head. Thinking about the conversation. How the ground had moved under her, under all of them.

After she had cried a good long time, Cherise said, through tears, "I don't know what to do. I don't know what to do."

"Your mother is here," Lydia said. "She'll take care of you."

"She doesn't know what to do either." Lydia could see it, too. Cherise felt so alone.

"I don't want to overstep my place."

"What do I do?" Cherise sobbed, overwhelmed again.

"We'll figure it out," and she found her arms around her again. "We'll figure it out."

Later, when Lydia recounted the conversation to Paul, he paced the floor in front of the bed.

"Are you going to tell her you're Benedict Arnold? Or Arnold Palmer? Or eggs benedict, or whatever it is you are, you *turncoat?*"

She stared at him through the thick rims, recounting the rest of the conversation.

Once Cherise cried herself out again and sat up, and Lydia brought her iced tea and Kleenexes, they got to talking.

"So what do I do?" Cherise asked. "What would you do? You have a business, you know what you're doing. I can't believe this. I can't believe what's happening. I don't know what to do."

"You have to let the police do their job. They'll find out what happened. Have you talked with them?"

"Yeah. A couple of times. They came and took the whole apartment apart.

They wanted to be sure he wasn't a drug addict or something." She wiped her eyes. "He wasn't, you know. By the way." Lydia could see the hurt and indignation, even under the sadness.

"What has it been, two days? They have to send the lab work to Denver, it probably takes some time to get the results. Is there a police officer who's your point of contact?"

Cherise got the card off the kitchen counter. "He asked me a lot of questions. He was trying to be nice, but you could tell they were the questions they ask if they think you're guilty or you did something bad. *How was your relationship? Did you have any fights?*"

Lydia could see the pain.

"Before we talk any further, Cherise, I have to tell you something. And you'll have to tell me what you'd like me to do, alright?" She said she would. "It seems that Mr. Hausen himself is aware of everything that's going on here, and he's very concerned. Personally. He asked Paul and I to look around on his behalf to make sure there isn't anything the police haven't seen or overlooked. It sounds like he wants his own accounting of what's gone on."

Cherise looked at her, tried to clear her eyes. "He wants you to be his spy?"

Lydia nodded. Cherise sat back. "It didn't come with any more direction than that," Lydia said. "I'm not quite sure what he's looking for. And I have the sense that he may not know either. I don't know the man, but I think it is what he says it is. He wants to know what happened."

"So, that's why you're here?" Cherise moved another few inches away.

"No. I'm here because I care about you. That's why I'm telling you this straight out. Cherise, look, I took this job because I needed it. At this point, I've earned my pay and I've given my client everything they wanted. This thing, this request from on high, is something else. I feel ... like I said before, something feels very wrong. If you want me to stay away, I will. If not, will you still talk to me? I promise I will tell you everything I find out."

Cherise looked through Lydia carefully. She hadn't been wrong about people too many times in the past. "For now," she said.

Back in the hotel, Paul said, "Oh ho, so you're workin' both sides of the street, are you?"

"I think it's an open-ended assignment," she said, enunciating carefully. "If things get too complicated, I will bow out gracefully."

"Uh huh? And then Arthur Corn Nuts and his agency buddies will just welcome you back with open arms, fresh off your job piloting the Hindenburg, huh? That's a great plan."

"I'm sorry, I have no witty riposte."

"Yes," he said, and plopped onto the chair, equally deflated. "We have no bananas."

18

Myron instructed Adele to provide Lydia whatever assistance she needed. Lydia had no idea if Adele was clued in to what the job was about; all she knew was Adele smiled very wide and intense while handing over the information she asked for, which included the fulfillment center's organizational chart. Now Lydia sat at the table in the suite she had moved into, across the hotel from the single room adjoining Paul's. He had been assigned a nicer single as well, but not a suite, which he complained about loudly. They used her suite as their base, deciding the Conference Room of Death was too close to the situation, and likely bugged.

Lydia studied the chart most of the morning, made notes of people she'd already met and her thoughts about them. Then she let her mind, and eyes, wander, as she perused its straight and dotted lines, its hexagons and ovals, traced the relationships and responsibilities with her finger.

"Will you talk to these people?" she said, and turned the chart to Paul, sitting across from her. A row of boxes near the bottom of the fold-out page, each marked *Picking*. Eight boxes, all the same size, not connected to each other but to the single rectangle above it, *Picking Supervisor*. She pointed to the lower line of boxes. "These folks were closest to Darnell and they might know him and his routine. See what they say."

"I thought we were going on these outings together."

"Let's try it this way first. I don't want to come across like the goon squad right away. Besides, your pleasing demeanor will unlock doors I'd have no way of opening."

"Happy to oblige," he said, and took off with his marching orders.

He made his way to the center, passed through security with his badge, put on the idiotic orange vest and white hat, and found the row of pickers. The first one: a skinny guy named Rodney Hammersmith. Very white skin, fair amount of acne, looked like he'd never seen the sun. Freckles, runny nose, wiped it with the palm of his hand straight upward, pushing over his forehead and into his hair, which was then pasted back, by what, Paul did not want to consider.

"Yeah, they told me you were coming," Rodney yelled, over the noise. "Hold on," and typed something into his handheld; logged off, stepped out of the working area, and did his compulsory look left and right. "Got hit by a klingon once," he said. "They tell you to look both ways but no one does and then you get run over." Paul nodded like he gave a shit, and led Rodney to the conference room he and Lydia booked for their use.

After they talked a bit, went through the name and job description, Paul scanned the page of questions Lydia had provided. She said to use his own judgment. They weren't looking for anything in particular, she said, just fishing. So, in a hard and flat tone, Paul said: "They handled everything well on the day of the accident."

"Uhm, yeah?" Rodney said.

"Everything went smoothly and everyone was informed of what happened." Again, without intonation.

"Yeah?" he said, slower.

"You were very happy with the day's outcome and how the situation was resolved."

Rodney looked around the room, maybe for a hidden camera. "Are you telling me or asking me?"

"What do *you* think?"

"Well, is this some kind of a questionnaire or something? They just told me to tell you what I know."

"That's right. And what do you know?"

"About what?"

"You tell me."

Rodney laughed nervously, went to stand up. "Look, they just told me to answer whatever questions you have. I'm happy to do that. But I don't ..."

"Ah, siddown, will ya," Paul said, trying to sound authoritative, but not succeeding. Rodney stifled a laugh. "Did you know Darnell? *Knew* Darnell?"

"Yeah."

"Ever think he was a girl?"

"What?"

"You know. Darnell. When I saw his name, at first I thought he was a girl."

"Well, I didn't see his name first, I saw him. And I didn't think he was a girl."

"What did you think?"

"I thought he was a guy."

"No, what did you think of *him*?"

"Darnell? Great. He was a great guy."

"Why?"

"Why did I think that or why was he a great guy?"

"Listen buddy, I'm askin' the questions here, so why do you just answer 'em, huh?" Rodney looked confused. "Why did you think he was a great guy?"

"Oh. 'Cause he was. Really nice and easygoing. You couldn't rattle him. Like he's always in a good mood and he's glad to see you. At least that's what he seemed like to me."

"How often did you see him?"

"We worked a lot of shifts together. You don't get time to shoot the shit here, there's no breaks. I mean there are, but you run out to get your drinks, go to the bathroom, then you gotta get back on the floor. But Darnell always said hi. A couple of times we talked in the parking lot before we clocked in."

"Got any enemies?"

"Huh?"

"Did … he … have … any … enemies?" Paul enunciated, absolutely reveling in the role of inquisitor.

"What do you think, someone killed him? I thought they said it was an accident or something."

Paul stared through him.

"No, I don't think he had any enemies," Rodney said. "It's a fulfillment center, man. We send out chairs and wrenches. No one has time to get to know anyone. By the end of your shift, you're so tired you just want to go home and sleep."

"So you liked him?"

"Sure. He was just … this guy who seemed to send out peaceful vibes. I liked it when he worked next to me, because I could almost tell he was over there and it sort of made me feel more easy about all the stress you have to put up with."

"Did you notice anything weird about him? Anything suspicious, anything that worried you?"

"Are you guys working with the police? 'Cause they asked all the same questions."

"We're not working with the police. This is off the record. Just for internal purposes."

"Well then, no."

"No, what?"

"I didn't notice anything suspicious or I worried about."

"Are you saying that because I said this was off the record?"

"No, I'm saying it 'cause it's true. Darnell was a great guy. Cherise is a great girl. I'm really sorry for her."

"So, you know they were together?"

"Well, yeah, everyone does. It's not a secret."

"You don't find that suspicious? Two people working at the same place involved with each other?"

"No. There's no rules against that. Lots of people who work here go out, or hook up or whatever. I mean, what else is there to do, you know?"

Paul did know.

"You know," Rodney said, "you're not very good at this. And you talk like some old movie. Do you have any other questions? I have to get back to work."

"No more questions," Paul said. "Just don't leave town without letting us know, alright?"

"You're a weirdo," he said, and walked out.

⊷═◉═⊷

They compared notes in the suite that night.

"Great guy, great guy, great guy," Paul said, slapping each page on the table. "And great guy. Of all the guys to go and die, it could have been some creepy bastard. But no, it had to be a great guy."

"Anything stick in your mind? Any comment, observation?"

"No. Just that they all knew he and Cherise were together. Everyone liked them. Not a bad word to say about either one. Though Cherise has a hot temper, I'm told. She flies off the handle. Cools right down, but she has a hair trigger."

"Huh."

"And what about you, Jessica Fletcher? Turn over any rocks?"

"Nothing to speak of." She scanned the notes she had taken during her own interview that afternoon; while Paul was busy roughing up the pickers, she had moved quietly to the man listed as their supervisor, Walter Mulbacher. She'd knocked on his office door unannounced.

"We're just ... we're so sorry for Darnell and his family," he said, after they introduced themselves and talked through a few items. "I can't tell you how upset we are."

"I'm sure. Did you know Darnell very well? Were you friends?"

"Well, no. You're not really friends with your employees here. I mean, we're all pretty busy and people come and go at all hours. My interactions with everyone are more about their numbers and keeping everyone on target."

"Oh really? Can you show me?"

Walt turned one of his desk monitors so Lydia could see. As she came around to his side, she looked down. He seemed very bunched up; shirt stuffed into pants, pants stuffed between his legs, tie stuffed into shirt. Everything stuffed tightly into something else.

"So this shows each picker and their turnover rate," he said, pointing to a line of bar graphs. "How close they get to the benchmark, where the gaps are, who's not performing. This lets you see the individuals and this view lets you see the team. Then you can compare it with other shifts, then everyone on your team. On my team. So I get a snapshot every morning of how we're doing."

"I see," she said, sitting back down across from him. Numbers, charts, software and data had the effect of short-circuiting her brain. It provoked a slight feeling of nausea. "So, you know what everyone is doing, and how they're doing it."

"That's what they pay me for," he said, smiling. He had a nice face, she thought. A sweet face. But pinched. There were people who wanted to work in high tech, in the world of logistics and automation, and a lot of those people were very smart. In her work she had met some very high-flying tech entrepreneurs, and the speed at which they talked, exchanged ideas, often amazed her. Then there were descending levels of tech folks, moving down the ladder of competence and bullshit. She encountered many who talked the talk but couldn't actually perform at the level of the sharpies. Then, steps below, were people like Walt. Not a shark, but a regular working guy who wanted in on the excitement of the tech bros, but were happy being handed the system already built and told to run it. It's a good position, too; you actually use the tools rather than create them, you get a feeling of accomplishment, and you make things happen in the real world.

"Did you ever have problems with Darnell?" she asked.

"What do you mean problems?"

"I don't know. Anything come to mind? Personality clashes, performance issues …"

"No. He's a great guy. Was a great guy. Did everything you asked him to. No complaints."

Despite Walt's outward calm, she felt a slight tension forming in her lower back; she thought of the famous Man-Ray photo of a woman with the f-holes of a cello stenciled there. She shifted in her chair. "So, you weren't friends, on the outside?" she asked again.

"No. I mean, I knew he and Cherise were a couple. They asked for shifts together and I tried to do it. But the software makes the schedules and you only have so much leeway. I couldn't always … accommodate them."

"Did they have problems with the schedule you set up?"

"Who, Cherise and Darnell?"

"Yes," Lydia said coolly, "that's who we're talking about."

"No. Well, I mean, yes, sometimes, if they wanted to be together."

"Is that standard? Do people ask to be scheduled together?"

"Well, they did. She did, I mean, Cherise. Sometimes."

"Really? Why?"

"I don't know. She just did."

"They live fairly close by, I believe, in one of the apartment buildings. It's not as though they had to drive a long distance to get to work. Any reason she'd want to be on the same shift?"

He shrugged again. "She just asked. I tried to do it when I could. But, you know, the software. You have to do what it tells you. You can't override it or they notice."

"Who notices?"

"Performance."

"What's that?"

"Corporate. They watch all the numbers, all the data. If things aren't on target, you get warnings and flags. You have to bring the numbers up to target."

"And do you?"

"Yeah, usually. I guess that's why I'm still here," he said, and laughed.

"You'll have to excuse me, since I'm not as familiar with the language and the technology as you are. Is Performance a person?"

"It's a division. I don't know where they are. I guess it's people. But, like, no one calls you on the phone or sends you an email or anything. You just open the dashboard and you see red where the performance characteristics are falling short of target. You have to close that gap and eliminate the red. Kind of like a game. It's probably some combination of people and software, but you only see it on your dashboard. All I know is, you can't let the red sit there and do nothing."

"What happens if you do?"

"Well, then my boss comes down and gives me hell. It's only happened a couple of times. And if you don't fix it, they don't give you a lot of chances. They get rid of people who don't perform."

"And you perform?"

"I'm still here," he said, and did the chummy laugh again.

"How do you communicate the ... what do you call them, the targets? ... to your employees?"

"Benchmarks," he said. "In our department it's called pick rates. How many picks an hour we have to hit. Usually I call a meeting so I can tell them face-to-face. I like to be a human about it, you know, not just turn up the numbers without telling anyone."

"Can they do that? Turn up the numbers without telling anyone?"

"Probably, but it's not nice. I talked to HR. She said it's better to do it face-to-face. I mean, if you just turn up the rate and make people work harder, it's like some kind of a machine. And I don't want to be like that."

"Of course not. That's very admirable. And how are the pick rates going? When they announced the takeover bid."

"They upped it. They wanted to show performance. You know, you were here. Everyone had to be on deck. We still are."

Lydia realized she had taken as much time as she planned; not going too deep into any one area, just getting a flavor. "Thank you again, Walt," she said, and shook his hand. Clammy and sweaty. "I appreciate your time."

Back at the suite, Paul scowled. "That doesn't sound very enlightening."

"We're not after anything here. Just nosing around."

"Well, it's hard to know what to ask if you don't know what you're looking for."

"I know," she said. "Old Carl doesn't know everything. He might be sending us off on a wild goose chase. It's his money."

"Yeah, well, don't send me out with another sheet of dumb questions if you don't know what you're looking for."

She seemed to lose focus, her gaze falling into the middle distance. "It will all work out," she said, dreamily. "And by the way, the consensus is you're about as subtle as Daffy Duck. The next time you go, why don't you just put on a French maid's outfit and chew on a carrot?"

"Well, thanks a lot. You know what I'm like. You didn't have to send me down there to make an asshole of myself."

"I do know what you're like, and you didn't," she said slowly. "Because now no one takes you seriously. And people are much less guarded around someone they don't take seriously."

He shook his head. "Naughty minx."

19

CHERISE CALLED THAT evening, just after nine.

"They want to talk to me. They have some information."

"Who?" Lydia asked.

"The police. They're on their way. Can you come over?"

"I don't think I should. If they're going to share their findings, it's probably for your ears only."

"I thought you wanted to find out what was going on." she said, and paused. "I thought you were my friend." Lydia picked it up. She needed someone sharper on her side.

"Yes, alright, I'm on my way," and in twenty minutes, she was.

It was the same detective who had led the investigation over the last several days, a man from the sheriff's department named Oscar Ryerson. He brought a patrol officer with him and a public information officer, and a thick manila folder. When Lydia arrived, they were gathered around the low coffee table, Cherise, Marion, and the three officers. Ryerson stopped talking and looked up when she came in. "Ms. Calligan, you're with Hausen, aren't you? This information is for Ms. Watson and her mother."

"I asked her to come," Cherise said. "She's helping me."

"Are you sure?" Ryerson asked. "In these situations, your interests and the interests of the employer don't always, uhm, line up. Wouldn't you rather have this information for yourself?"

"Are you gonna give it all in the press conference in the morning?" Cherise asked. He nodded. "Well then, she can hear it tonight."

Ryerson nodded, re-opened the folder and continued what he had been saying. He slid the report back toward Cherise. "The coroner is classifying this as death from natural causes. They're calling it …" he read carefully, "… new onset diabetes mellitus, uhm … hyperglycemia and keto … acidosis."

"He wasn't diabetic," Cherise said, emphatically, like she'd said it before Lydia arrived.

Ryerson scanned the report. "Subject ... uhm, Darnell ... collapsed about 1:18pm ... EMTs arrived 1:29 ... subject unresponsive ... resuscitation measures undertaken ... no signs of life ... autopsy results completed at the county lab in Denver ... uhm, vitreous humor ... that's the fluid in the eye, I believe, they use it for analysis ... glucose concentration 980, uhm MGL's per DL ... acetone detected in the blood ... diabetic keto ... acidosis ... indicative type I diabetes, undiagnosed." He put the report down, nothing more to read from. "I'm very sorry, Ms. Watson," he said. "The department grieves with you for your loss."

Cherise slumped forward, hands together, staring at the table. "But he went to Care. I sent him ..."

"I'm sorry," Ryerson said again.

"He's only 23. You don't die of something when you're 23."

Ryerson nodded solemnly; handed her two stapled pages and returned the rest to his briefcase. She took the pages without looking at them.

"What does this mean?" Marion asked. "Is there more investigation? What happens next?"

"I'll release the results tomorrow at the press conference," he said. "I've shared it with the district attorney's office. It's up to them to determine if there's any further action necessary."

Cherise looked at the pages in her hand. "Natural causes," she said, to herself, to her hands. "This is most unnatural thing I ever heard in my life."

⊷━◉ ◉━⊶

After the officers left, Marion made coffee and they gathered at the small kitchen table.

"I feel like I'm falling down a well," Cherise said. Marion took her hand, kissed it. "He wasn't that sick," Cherise said. "He's only 23. I sent him to Care. Isn't that what you're supposed to do?"

"They examined him there?" Lydia asked.

"Yes. The last couple of months. When things started, I made him go."

"What things?"

"Headaches, swollen feet, getting really thirsty. All these symptoms that didn't seem ... I mean, they went away ..."

"How many times in total, did he go?"

"I don't know. Ten maybe."

"You sent Darnell to Care ten times?" Lydia was surprised at the calmness of her tone. "And what did they say?"

"Take ibuprofen. Or NSAIDS ... uhm, inflammable reducers."

"Did they give you a prescription? Or send you to another doctor?"

"They don't have a doctor. Mama and I talked about it. It's only a nurse's aide or someone from the pharmacy. If it's an emergency they call the EMTs."

"And they didn't think this was serious?"

Cherise shook her head. "Everyone knows all they have is band-aids. But they saw him. I told them. They wrote things on reports." She hunched forward, staring dully at her hands. Lydia realized she was hunkered forward as well. She looked at Marion, who shifted her gaze to Cherise. Something at the bottom of her look, and she and Lydia both felt it, a sediment they both knew was there. And Paul's sarcastic voice in her ear: *Who are you worried about, you or her?* Whatever it was, her heart broke for Cherise. How alone she was in this strange, manufactured town, with nothing around them except dry, empty miles.

The next morning, Ryerson held his press conference and reported the cause of death.

At the regular morning check-in, Chandler/Perkins ate up the good news like sharks to bloody meat. No liability on the company's part. Afterward, Lydia made her way down a long hallway, past storage closets, utility rooms, doors with slats that seemed to blow hot and cold air, until she found a white door with the word "Care" on a small black plate, the same as the other doors on the hallway with names like M208-B. If you didn't know exactly where to go, you would miss it. She knocked and went in.

A single room, antiseptic white like everything else, a chair, a folding screen, a small desk, a mini-fridge on the floor, with a padlock, and a storage cabinet on the wall, also with a padlock. A young guy on one of the chairs, bent forward,

Fulfillment City

earbuds in, watching a video on his phone. He wore what looked like high school clothes under a white lab coat. When he saw Lydia, he took out the earbuds.

"Hi, yeah, what can I do for you?"

"Is this Care?" she asked.

"Yeah."

She introduced herself, explained what she was doing, asked the young man if they could speak. His name was Antonio. "Yeah, sure," he said, disinterested.

"You heard about the situation with the young man who passed away?"

"Oh, yeah, that was so bad."

"Did you take care of him?"

"No, I only started here two days ago."

"I see. Are there other people who might have cared for him I could speak to?"

"I don't know," he said. "I'm only in four hours. Someone else comes in in the afternoon. I work at HealthSaver the rest of the time."

"The drugstore?" He nodded. "Are you a medical assistant?"

He laughed. "Hell no."

"Are you a pharmacist?"

"No," he said, laughing more. He glanced at his phone, eager to get back to the game.

"Do you have any medical training at all?"

"Course not. I don't give shots or anything, I just do floor stock and check-outs. They just sent me here to fill in the extra hours."

"So, you're a stockboy? Sorry ... you stock the shelves?"

He nodded.

"What do they do when someone comes in with a medical problem? Do they have a protocol for diagnosis or triage?"

He looked blank. "All I know is they told me to cover the shift a couple of days ago." She was disarmed by his innocence and obliviousness of the situation.

"Do you know who was here before?"

"Nope, but hold on." Three cardboard boxes sat on the refrigerator, one opened. He pulled out a white paper bag and a small package from the bag, showed it to her. "They sent over a bunch of stuff and it all has this girl's name."

Marie Broward.

"And she's not here anymore?"

"I don't know. I'm only in ..."

"... four hours a day, got it. Okay Antonio, thank you very much for your time."

He went back to his phone.

⤙══◉ ◉══⤚

"Man, that so sucks," Reuben said, enjoying his day off, lazing in the bed. Paul knew Lydia was going into the center early, so he stayed in his room with Reuben for most of the morning. "Diabetes. Poor guy. And he didn't know?"

"Apparently," Paul said. "They held the press conference this morning. It's probably a load off the company's mind. No liability."

"But still. It sucks."

Paul had already pumped Reuben for all the information he needed, as well as anything else he felt like giving. Regarding the former, Paul found out that the foreman, or *Floor Supervisor*, on the org chart, coordinated the movement of each department's equipment and hardware. Reuben knew nothing about personnel or people, all he knew was equipment—when it was received, when it was dispatched. "I like it that way," he said. "I don't want to get involved in any politics."

"Are there politics?" Paul asked. "I thought everyone kept to themselves. It seems like no one even knows who anyone is."

"Well, mostly. But there's the top management, you know, the department heads and all. They get into some shit."

"Oh really? Like what?"

"Oh, no," he said. "You guys are the spies. I'm not giving you anything."

Paul dove under the sheets and grabbed him. "Not letting go til you talk." Reuben laughed, tried to push him off.

"Stop! Okay, okay." Paul let go. Reuben gave him a heavy-lidded look. "No, keep going."

"Freak," Paul said, and went down again.

Reuben put his hands behind his head, lay back on the pillow. "So, there's a couple times things got kind of weird. First ... well, you know McAllister, right? Everyone thinks he and Adele are together."

"Mmm-hmm," Paul said under the sheet, realizing, of course, there it was, in front of their eyes the whole time.

"He has a family and a wife and they come to company events and stuff. But if you ask me, Adele is just too perky to be working for a stiff like that without something going on. Some of the guys lay bets whether they're fucking or just handjobs and blowjobs. He seems like the kind of guy who thinks if they're not fucking then it's not sex. Like, if he has to go to confession or something."

"Ya?"

Reuben pushed in deeper. Paul grunted.

"So then, you heard about the guy who died last year, right? He was old. It was on loading, and I guess he had a heart condition. Everyone thought it was suicide by overtime. He had no kids, no wife. Lived in some trailer with a dog, and he basically worked himself to death. The only thing I heard was he had a life insurance policy, and all the money went to this girl in Fort Collins. Everyone figured she was a prostitute who was nice to him or something. But that was all before the center got really big and we had all these policies in place."

Paul was about to ask a follow-up question from down under when both their phones pinged at the same time. He surfaced and took a look, as did Reuben.

"Huh," Paul said. "All-hands 4pm."

"What does it mean?"

Paul shrugged; placed his hands against Reubens'.

"All the hands," Paul said, and kissed him.

⋆┝═◑ ◑═┥⋆

What all-the-hands was all about was repeating what the police reported during the press conference that morning. But more importantly, telling everyone to get back to work.

"Since they consider the matter closed," Myron said, "and no further investigation is pending, we have to turn our attention back to the business at hand … which is showing the world what a powerhouse Saltair Springs really is. Are we all together on this?" A smattering of applause at first, then the dark-suited corporate folks at the edges started hard clapping, and the others picked up the beat, picked it up into a loud, rhythmic cheer. "That's right!" Myron shouted over the applause. "We're back! *We're back!*"

"*Are* we back?" Paul leaned in to Lydia, them both standing behind the crowd gathered at the front.

"Nothing from on high," she said. "I consider the matter open until I'm told otherwise."

He shrugged. "Hey, by the way, did you know they had another death?" He conveyed the story, all the details Reuben supplied.

"Huh," she said. "I wonder what the mortality rate is for a place like this. I don't know if they're ahead of the curve or behind."

"How's Cherise doing?"

"Devastated. They're giving her a couple of weeks' leave. After that, I don't know."

"They're making this into a no-fault thing, aren't they? Absolving themselves of any responsibility."

"Oh yes." She knew the pre-existing condition explanation would deflect blame from the company, and Chandler/Perkins would milk it for all it was worth.

"You think she's gonna sue anyway? Or whats-his-name's family?"

"Darnell. I don't know."

"You think they'll send you on another mission of mercy to buy her off too?"

She thought about it. "Both sides of the street, young man."

"Yeah, well, you better be sure there isn't a bus barreling down the side you're standing on ..." She tilted her head, bracing for *old lady*, but he knew enough to stop there. She remained tilted, though, knowing he was right.

⤙▭◠▭⤚

"You know, I don't have a forwarding address for her."

An actual old lady had gone through her computer and the binder she kept on a shelf with the others behind her desk. "She just up and left," she said. "I don't know where she went."

Lydia found her way to HR to ask about Marie Broward, who had conveniently disappeared. "Do you hire the people who work in Care?" she asked.

"No," the old lady said, "they come from the drugstore ... the, uh, HealthSaver. Technically, that room is one of their walk-in clinics. It's their responsibility."

"So they might have records of visits and so forth?"

"Could be." The sign on the desk said Carol Ann. Lydia thanked her and was happy to leave. The old lady had little fans running everywhere that made the small office so chilly that she had to sit there bundled up in sweaters.

Lydia went to pick up lunch for Cherise and Marion at Taffy's, and as she walked back to the car, spotted McAllister and Adele sitting at a table, eating lunch together and laughing.

Outside Cherise's door, Lydia knocked, said, "Oysters on the half-shell." Marion opened, finger to lips, nodded toward Cherise on the phone. She was listening to a call, squinting, trying to jump in but not able. All she got out was, Yes, uh huh, okay, uhhhhm and bye. Lydia unpacked the lunch in the kitchen.

"What did she say?" Marion asked.

"She wants to do it this week. On Sunday," Cherise said.

"Oh dear. So soon. Can I come with you?"

"Of course, mama. God, it sounded like a convention over there, there were so many people in the background. I could barely hear a word."

"How did she sound?"

"I can't tell. Darnell didn't talk about her much. All I know is she wasn't around. Now she's acting like he was her little baby and she's so upset she can hardly talk."

"Is this ... are you talking about the funeral?" Lydia asked. She had arranged the plates of sandwiches at the table.

Cherise nodded. "I called his family last week. I didn't even know how to reach them. The police gave me his mother's number. She wants to do everything in Denver, where they live. She wants to put him ... bury him ... there ..." she trailed off. Marion took her hand. "Bury him in the ground," Cherise said. She thought of the ocean liner in California, the feeling of being stranded, marooned, inside a dark, hulking shell. Her stomach turned over. "What am I supposed to do, go there? Is that what you do? Go to a graveyard and stand by some piece of rock like it's the person?"

"I know, sweetie," Marion said, and took her in her arms again as she started to break into sobs.

Lydia was out of place. "Do you … need any help?" she asked.

Marion turned. "We're fine, but thank you for asking."

She nodded, backed slowly to the front door and let herself out.

20

"IT ISN'T RIGHT," Lydia said.

It was late on Friday. Paul checked his watch for the end of the day, tingling with anticipation of his evening with Reuben. "Say what?"

"We shouldn't be here. Cherise's mother is right. I have no business sticking my nose into this."

"Did she say that?"

"No, but it's pretty obvious. She thinks I'm a spy and a stooge and she doesn't want me around. And she's right. I'm telling McAllister first thing on Monday. This is between the company and the families, and I'm just asking for trouble."

Cherise and Marion had left for the funeral the day before. Cherise's father flew into the Denver airport, where they picked him up, then drove together to the Spragg home to meet Darnell's family. Of course, Lydia didn't ask if she should go. Obviously, no one connected to the company had any place at the funeral, no matter what Lydia felt.

"Whatever you want," Paul said—who was, at the same time, having his own second thoughts about leaving. In truth, he had begun to enjoy Reuben and their clandestine nighttime get-togethers. The easy exit he had been hoping for was turning out to be not so easy, and more important, not kind. He decided he would have to mention to Reuben what Lydia was thinking, and the chance they would leave next week. The regret passed over him like a cloud; certainly, he wondered, this couldn't be actual *feelings?* What the fuck was he supposed to do with that?

⊶⊷

The funeral was bad.

Wanda Spragg was a big, round, loud woman, who threw her arms around Cherise as though they were the closest of relatives. She burst into uncontrollable sobs, holding Cherise for dear life. Clutched in this stranger's grip, trying to soothe her, Cherise looked around at the guests in this house, standing there watching them, shaking their heads at his mother's inconsolable sorrow. Over Wanda's shoulder, through the window, Cherise spotted his two brothers alone in the back yard. They were bigger now than in the photo Darnell had kept on their refrigerator. After the handshakes and introductions, she excused herself and went out to talk to them. They were sitting on an old swing set, the seats' thick cloth almost worn through. It looked like no one ever came out here. Fresh brush marks in the dirt showed the yard had been hastily cleaned up; a blue tarp at the far edge, tied over what looked like stacks of flattened cardboard boxes. Cherise sat on the empty swing next to the boys.

"You know who I am?"

The older one, Jamal, nodded. "He told us about you."

She smiled. Introductions already made. "He told me about you, too. He sure ..." and she wanted to say *loves you guys*, avoiding the sting. But it sounded too weird, and she had to get used to saying it. "... loved you guys."

They both nodded, looking at the ground, kicking the sand. Small clouds of dust rose around their feet.

"Your mama's pretty broken up about this, huh?"

The younger one, Keiyon, had Darnell's beautiful eyes. He nodded.

"He talked about you guys a lot."

"Yeah," said Jamal. He was taller than his brother and slim and serious looking. "He wanted us to come and visit. When he had a break."

"How are you doing with all this?" she asked. They nodded together, again, scraping their feet forward and back. "I don't remember ..." Cherise said, "I don't recall ... Darnell talking a whole lot about your mama. I thought they didn't get along."

The boys looked at each other, unsure what they could say.

"No," Jamal said, quietly. "She told him to go away."

Cherise had put a few pieces together from things Darnell mentioned in passing: when he was in high school, his mother met a man in Las Vegas and she stayed there with him. Darnell had to watch over the house and his brothers.

When she came back with the guy, she told Darnell he was in the way and to get out.

"He took care of you guys, didn't he?" Cherise asked.

They nodded. Silence from both. Cherise felt they were being quiet not to incur the wrath from inside. Even though she never met them, didn't know them at all, she stepped closer and found them moving into her arms, embracing her in the empty yard.

They broke apart when Cherise's father opened the back door and asked her to join them inside.

"You coming?" she asked the boys. They shook their heads, quickly. A sign, she figured, of what was about to come.

The kitchen door was closed to the rest of the house while the large gathering continued out in the livingroom. A small table was set with several chairs, Wanda seated in the center with two men on either side, Cherise's parents at the ends. One of the men next to Wanda stood, indicated the empty chair facing them. Cherise looked at her parents. They didn't seem to know what was happening. The men wanted Cherise to sit facing them and Wanda. When her parents saw the arrangement, they nodded to each other, smiled at the men, then slid their chairs from the ends to either side of their daughter. Thus faced off, the man to Wanda's left leaned forward and began.

On Monday, Cherise relayed the conversation to Lydia.

"Basically, they said this was an atrocious miscarriage of justice, and a crime, and we shouldn't accept the police and the coroner's report." She was reading from pages of notes she had taken. "These lawyers found Darnell's mother and they said they're gonna make this into a huge thing ... sue the company, sue everyone in sight ... and they want me to go in with them." Cherise slid the business card across the table. *Harrison, Cordray and Wynn.* "As in, we always win."

"They said that?" Lydia asked.

Cherise nodded. "So I asked them, I said which one of you is the Wynn guy? He said he was a senior partner, this guy," Cherise indicated the card, "something Gallagher. I guess Harrison, Cordray and Wynn don't actually make housecalls."

"What will you do?"

"I don't know," Cherise said, slumped in her chair, looking defeated. "These guys looked like injury lawyers from TV, like they want to get famous off of this.

I don't think his mother has any idea who they are or what they're about. They said we had to sign with them right there, and my father said he wanted his lawyers to look at the papers, but they wouldn't let him, and then Darnell's mother got huffy and they had to sit her down and told her to keep her cool. I think that's the only reason she invited us, to get us to sign."

Lydia looked at Marion. "Bit of a steam engine," Marion said, nodding.

"They had this whole houseful of people I didn't know. I don't think his mother knew them either," Cherise said, "never mind no friends of Darnell's. It felt like they brought them in by bus or something. Then on Sunday, at the funeral, his mother wouldn't even talk to us. Some of Darnell's friends were there, and we were all sitting in the back, behind these people in the audience. They had cameras and lights set up for the sermon, and they were shooting it like a TV show, with speeches and interviews. When we were leaving some of the reporters figured out who I was and they chased us. We had to run to the car to get out of there."

Marion nodded. "There were none of the people you would expect to be stepping into an issue like this," she said. "You know, the reverends and politicians and respected people who know what they're talking about. My husband thinks this is too gray a situation for them, a workplace mishap, which is why the ambulance chasers descended on it. It was uncomfortable. They seem intent on making it into a media circus. My husband's gone home and he's consulting with his own lawyer now."

"What do *you* want to do?" Lydia asked Cherise. Before she could answer, Marion sat forward and put her hand on Cherise's arm, tilted her head in Lydia's direction.

"Well, his mother's a piece of work," Cherise said. "She never cared about him before, and now all he is to her is a payout. But the lawyers are right. We shouldn't believe anything the company says, and they probably have influence over the cops. And besides all that, a perfectly healthy guy died, and why did that happen?"

"So you want to join their legal action?"

Cherise looked at Marion, who looked at Lydia.

"My father said I shouldn't talk to you. He said you're a spy and you're gonna tell them everything I'm doing."

Lydia sat back in the chair, tightened her belt. Let out a long sigh. "I agree with him entirely," she said. "And I was going to tell you as much this morning."

Marion sat back in relief.

"Except for one thing," Lydia went on. "Could I speak to you privately? There's something I need to tell you."

Cherise looked at Marion, who didn't like this at all, but Cherise shrugged and went with Lydia into the bedroom and closed the door.

The previous Sunday, Lydia said, while Cherise was in Denver, she had spent the day resting in the hotel, watching news shows, when her phone buzzed. It was an unidentified number and she answered. On the other end was a rather soft voice.

"Lydia, it's Carl Hausen, how are you?"

She pulled the facecloth off her forehead and sat up.

"I'm well, sir, how are you?"

"Just fine, thank you. I want to speak with you directly, if that's alright. I appreciate your taking on the task Myron McAllister asked you to look into for me."

"Of course, sir."

"I know it's an awkward position to put you in, but the word around is you're sharp. In my experience I've found that a fresh pair of eyes will pick up things the others won't see. And since you're not on my payroll, I can rely on you for an honest accounting."

"Thank you for saying that, Mr. Hausen," she had said, "but I beg to differ. We're all on your payroll. The agencies as well, the folks who sent me here. They all want ... we all want ... your business very much."

"Well, that's what I mean. I'm the client they want to keep happy. And I'll tell you something, Lydia, I think happiness is overrated. What I like is information, and I like to be satisfied that I'm getting the information I need. If that translates into happiness, that's okay, but it's not what I'm looking for. The people on my payroll tell me what they think I want to hear because they think it'll make me happy."

"And you don't want to be happy?" she asked, warily.

"I want to know what I need to know. And I'm thinking you're someone who can find that out that for me."

Lydia felt slightly off balance, not just being on the phone with old Carl directly, but with the soft, emphatic way he spoke. She couldn't quite formulate a picture of who this man was. "If you don't mind my asking, Mr. Hausen ... why me? I'm sure there are many qualified security companies or private investigators you could call in."

"Because my understanding is you're someone who can see things from the outside in. And that's what I need right now, the perspective of an outsider. Something is not right over there, Lydia. I can tell, but no one seems to be able to weed it out. And that is a liability for my business at this moment. So I hope you'll continue looking into this matter, personally."

"Of course, sir."

"Thank you, Lydia. I'll make it worth your while. Just give me the effort, alright?"

"Yes, sir."

And the line went dead.

"What did he sound like?" Cherise asked.

"Odd. More than a little disquieting. But I'm telling you this because I think he really wants the truth about what went on here. And I want you to know what he said to me so you can make an informed decision about whether you want me around or not."

Cherise took this in in silence, then they returned to the living room and Marion's scowl. "Ms. Calligan, are you going to tell the company about Mrs. Spragg asking Cherise to join her lawsuit?"

"Mrs. Watson, I'm sure they know that already. They probably have a 747 full of lawyers on their way here right now. But, no, I'm not telling them anything. What I just told Cherise, and what I can tell you, is that I don't believe they're asking me to spy on *you*. And I have no intention of doing that. I think it's something else entirely."

"Well, I'm sorry, Ms. Calligan, but I am just not comfortable with you around my child. Mr. Watson and I would prefer that you leave us alone."

Lydia understood, and stood.

"They wanted justice," Cherise said, softly. Lydia and Marion both turned to her. "The lawyers and Darnell's mother and all the people in that house. They all said I should get justice. They were all angry. The only ones who weren't were his brothers. They were just sad. Those two, and me, we lost something … someone …" Marion took her hand.

Lydia said, "Cherise, you can get your own lawyers. If your father's doesn't work out, I know some very honest, very good people I can refer you to."

"Yeah, wonderful, great. And then what'll I have, money?"

"Well, money's not so bad …"

Her face crumbled. "But still, I won't know what happened. And I'll look at the money and it'll make me throw up because that's what I'll have instead of him, or the truth …"

They sat at the table then, the three of them, a triangle of points equidistant from each other.

After a long, moment, Lydia said, "I already advised the company to pay someone off who was only trying to tell the truth. And that backfired on me, spectacularly. So, my judgment is not what it used to be. As your father said, the smartest thing would be to leave this situation behind, go home, and let lawyers take care of it. And get the justice you deserve."

Cherise looked at Marion, who clearly agreed.

"But you're staying?" Cherise asked Lydia.

"Well, the prince of darkness asked me to. How can a girl resist?"

Cherise laughed for the first time, just a bit. Then she put her head in her hands and looked down at the table.

And then the volleys began. Chandler/Perkins whacking down the story, Harrison, Cordray and Wynn bringing it back to life, Cherise and Lydia watching from the stands. First round, Chandler/Perkins: opinion pieces, straight news coverage, you name it, they quashed the story, turned it around even, as Lydia suspected they would. With the selection of photos they released, a new narrative began to emerge. Darnell was overweight, out of shape, in poor health. Brought it on himself. The images didn't even look like him. Then a video appeared, of Cherise being harassed by someone with a cell phone in the supermarket parking lot. "I don't want to talk to you," she is heard saying, and when the photographer doesn't stop peppering her with questions, she yells, "I told you, I don't want to talk to you!" and tries to whack them with the car door as she gets in. "Oh! Jeez!" the cameraman yells, leaping back and laughing, "Wow!" and Cherise and Marion driving away quickly. The implication of course, Jesus, there's a hothead. The company issues a response to the video. *We condemn anyone harassing our employees.* But still, the video is out there.

"Spin doctors," Lydia said, after watching a segment on the evening news. "They whittled it right down to the angle they want. At this rate, I give it two weeks before it fades completely from view."

"Great," Paul said. "And are *we* fading completely from view? I thought you said we were out of here."

She had not told Paul about the call from Carl. Not sure why. She felt it was necessary to tell Cherise, but for some reason, she didn't want that direct connection known by anyone else. And since she cancelled their early departure the week before, Paul had been able to continue falling into whatever it was that was happening with Reuben.

"I'd like you to find something out for me, if you wouldn't mind," Lydia said. "Get any details you can about the fellow who died last year. What his name was, how it happened, anything you can scrounge up."

"Can't you just ask McAllister or HR?"

"I did. Adele, to start with. The answer I got was chilly. It wasn't relevant to the matter at hand and that's not what I should be asking about. That coming from McAllister himself."

"So there's something there."

She brushed him away. "Off with you, young man. Go forth and be irritating."

Reuben had said the old guy was on loading, so Paul started there. The current loading chief was a guy named Christopher, who looked like a wiry teamster with a mohawk. He wore his dirty jeans jacket with the sleeves torn off to better display the daggers, rifles, machine guns, throwing stars, and other weapons of death splayed across both arms. He was terrifyingly lean in a way that suggested anything but healthy living: veins in arms, temples and eyes throbbing, he looked like he could burst at any moment.

"Don't know!" he shouted, as he continued his own loading. The trucks idled loudly and they had to shout to be heard. "I wasn't here last year. I know the guy's name was Ben or Bert or something. He was, like 62. Shouldn't have been on loading. Don't know why they put him here. Accident waiting to happen. Death wish is what I heard. Fuck him. If that's how he wanted to go."

"Is there anyone here who was working last year who might have known him?" Paul yelled.

"No! I hired all new people. Healthy people who aren't gonna drop dead and drag my fuckin' numbers down."

"Okay, thank you!" he shouted, moving away from the fumes, the truck and the crazy. Before he got too far, Christopher shouted, "Ask Walt! He was loading manager then. He's on picking now."

When he knocked on Walt's door, he saw the look on his face, and his thoughts, fairly clearly: what does this idiot want, and, I can handle this clown. Thus prepared, Paul did not disappoint. "Ehhh, what's up, doc?" he began.

"How can I help you, Mr. uhm, …"

Paul maneuvered his narrow hips into the chair opposite. Crossed his legs. "Just Paul. So. Sounds like all the trouble with Darnell is over. Poor guy. What was it, diabetes?"

Walt nodded, solemnly.

"Well," Paul, said, slipping into Cary Grant, "that's what you get for hiring someone *with a disease*."

Walt narrowed his eyes. "What does that mean? I didn't know that. No one did. Not even Darnell, as I far as I heard."

"Yes, well, be that as it may. Wags tell me there was another *expiration* here, about a year ago. Bert or Ben or something. On the loading dock."

Walt had no reaction at all, not even a twitch, but Paul detected a reflex far below that pre-empted any movement. Paul was such a good liar, he appreciated another when he saw it.

"That was unfortunate," Walt said. "Bernie something. I just started, I didn't know anyone yet. He was one of the first hires when the center opened. Before I got to know him or even talk to him, yes, there was a very unfortunate event."

"People seem to drop like flies around this place."

Walt stared evenly. "Actually, this is one of the safest facilities you'll find. There's always a certain number of injuries and losses every year at centers like this across the world. We don't deviate from the industry standards at all. In fact, as I said, our numbers are consistently in the top ten percent for safety, on a comparative scale."

"Well, go-*lly*, you sure do sound like you know a lot."

"I've been in logistics a long time," Walt said, dryly.

"So, how's *picking* compared to *loading*?"

Walt was unclear on the emphasis. "It's very interesting. You have more ability to adjust and improve. There's a lot of science and technology involved. But I understand you've spoken to all my pickers already, so you know what it's like."

"I do indeed. So. Nothing more you can tell me about old Barney?"

"Bernie," he said. "You'll find out more than I know in his personnel file. He was old and he shouldn't have been on the dock. I was too new to get to it fast enough. I feel bad about it, but it didn't have anything to do with me. Talk to HR if you need more information."

"HR," Paul said. "Well, *that* sounds awfully official. I may just do that."

Walt lowered his chin to give Kathy's scowl of disapproval.

When Paul found his way to HR, he was told the files on that incident had been removed and weren't available. In the suite that evening, he reported what he found.

"The files were removed," Lydia repeated. "Well, that's convenient. And she looked for them?"

"Yeah. And I stood there for half an hour while the old bag meandered her way through every goddamn file cabinet in the whole place. About froze my ass off, too. I thought old people keep things too hot."

"It's Colorado, dear, everything is cold. So, things come back to Walt. That's interesting. What did you think of him?"

"Scrunched. Secretive … sneaky … can't think of another alliteration …"

"Suspicious."

"You think there's something there?"

She shrugged. "All we're doing is looking at the pieces … for patterns. See if any belong to each other." He waited for more. "A dotted line is still a line."

⇥➔◉ ◉←⇤

Lydia brought out a pitcher of iced tea, poured Cherise and herself a glass and sat down across from her at the kitchen table. Marion was still irritated by her presence but for the time being put up with her, and modestly excused herself from the apartment when Lydia came by. This afternoon, Cherise had been sleeping on the sofa and still looked bleary after waking up.

"What is grief?" she asked, out of nowhere.

"You're asking *me*?"

"When I was a kid, at my school, they had Charlie Brown posters on the wall, and these little kids were always saying *good grief*, and I never knew what it meant. Is there such a thing as good grief?"

"Well ... grief means processing the loss of something ... big ... that's hard to take. But good grief, I don't know. I think in the Charlie Brown world it was a way of saying Heavens or Goodness. Grief, itself, is something you have to go through. It's painful, but necessary."

"How do you do it?"

"Why are you asking me?"

"You look like you lost something big yourself. The way you are. You seem kind of ..." and stopped.

"Go on. Kind of what?"

"I don't want to be rude."

"You won't be. I'd like to hear."

"Well, kind of like you fell into someplace bad and haven't come back to this world."

Lydia smiled. "I'm continually impressed by your powers of observation. And your optimism."

"I don't think I'm that optimistic anymore."

"It'll come back, I promise. And you're right. I did fall into someplace bad."

"What was it?"

"What that was ... I still haven't processed ... all of it."

"Well, you have to talk for a while 'cause I am sick of talking and sick of crying. I feel like I have cried myself out." She waited a beat. "So?"

Lydia let out a long sigh. "Something bad happened because I didn't think it was important. I may have mentioned it to you before. And because of it, someone died."

Cherise raised her eyebrows.

"There was a well-known campaign I created for a client in California. About berries. And the ads were cute … I thought they were cute … and for a long time everyone else did too. The ad featured a little boy with a cute lisp, and we came up with this slogan, about the berries … *de berry vest* … and boy, those berries sold. For decades. But in the last version, the boy we cast was Black, and he did the line with the same lisp … and people felt insulted. They said it was demeaning. I thought I knew better and I advised my client to ignore the chatter and keep running the spots. And then there were protests, and counter protests, and this horrible event where some man who had nothing to do with any of it showed up to one of the protests and shot a woman and killed her."

"Oh God. Did they catch him?"

"Yes. He was schizophrenic, just some unhinged person with a gun. Incompetent to stand trial. But it doesn't make a difference. A woman is dead."

"So … this little kid was Black. And you made him look like an idiot."

"All the kids lisped," Lydia said, surprised by the defensiveness in her tone. "That was the whole campaign."

"But people told you it was offensive."

Lydia shrugged.

"And you didn't listen to them."

She nodded. "I thought I knew better."

"Uh huh," Cherise said, and she followed her thoughts until they connected. "And this woman," she said, "the one who got killed … she was Black, too?"

Lydia maintained a studied non-reaction.

"Huh," Cherise said. "So, what is this for you, a guilt job or something? You think helping me out will soothe your conscience?"

"I don't think anything at all. That much is clear. I don't know anything anymore."

Cherise looked the woman over carefully, using whatever penetrating x-rays Darnell said she had. But no image came into focus. "You know," she said, "I'm not crazy being anybody's charity case, *Lydia*. I got a lot to figure out here."

"I know. I'm just trying to be honest with you."

"Are you? Or are you really not getting things? Like when people tell you they're insulted and you don't listen?"

"What am I not getting here?"

Cherise sat up. "Well, did it occur to you that the prince of darkness might have some other reason for asking you to be his spy? Like maybe he wants some kind of information he can use in case Darnell's mother's lawyers really get something on his company? Or if I hire my own lawyers and they want something they can use against me? Did that occur to you? That he might be using you?"

"I think I have it under control."

"Do you? 'Cause that's what you say, but do you know what you're really doing? You still look pretty spooked to me. You said you got all freaked out because that girl got killed, so you closed your business and went into this whole overcoat routine. Is that true? Because that all doesn't add up to me."

Lydia took in a long breath. "You're right. There were a lot of other things that came to a head. I don't quite know what they all are."

"Well, that's what I mean. Here you are, on this side hustle, for the guy who owns the company that kinda killed my boyfriend, and you think you got the whole thing under control?"

Lydia shrugged. "You're right about everything."

And now Cherise had to take the measure of this woman. Who she was, what she was doing here, how much she could trust her. How much she was using Cherise. For some reason, it made her crack up.

"So now I got to worry about you too?" Cherise said. "Whether you're some kind of spy sent here to report everything I say to your good buddy … with his log cabin and his damn rifles and his Confederate flag, out in Utah, or where ever the hell he lives?" She felt herself smile for the first time in a while. Lydia wanted to smile as well, but her eyes were wet.

"I wouldn't hurt you, Cherise."

"I hear you. But you sure you can tell us apart? I mean, you can tell one Black girl from another, right?"

Now Lydia did smile, but flushed deep red. Which gave Cherise a really good laugh. "Oh lord," she said, shaking her head, "What am I going to do here?"

21

"HEY!"

Paul jumped, knocking his coffee over the papers on the table where he'd propped his feet. Behind him, someone whipped open the conference room door. "Jesus, what?" Paul yelled

It was meth head Christopher, still sweating. He slapped a folder onto the table. "You wanted this," he shouted, even in the quiet of the conference room. "Stuff about that guy you asked for. They found the file." A manila folder, frayed at the edges. *Bernard LaPierre* in pencil on the tab. Christopher walked out without another word. Paul gathered up the papers and read through the folder. Standard scheduling reports, hours worked, time in, time out, basic hiring information. Other notes handwritten, also in pencil on sheets marked Addenda. He read those, read them again. That evening, in Lydia's suite, he pushed the papers across the table.

"So, get a load of the last page. February through April. HR notations about Bernie's meeting with his supervisor. Five times. And look who the supervisor is."

She searched for the name. "Mulbacher. Yes. He was in charge of loading at that time."

"But five different events. He said he didn't get to know him and implied he didn't know what was going on because he just got hired. That's not true. He met with this guy five times. And look at the notes. *Stressed. Overtired. Concern about injury.* This old guy told him repeatedly he had problems. And nothing in here about resolution or response. Five times the guy said he was in trouble, and stuffed-up Walt let him dangle."

"Do we see a specific action? Do we see responsibility here?"

"Well, for one thing, the guy's not telling the truth. He said he didn't know him and he did. He said his time there didn't overlap, and it did. And he's a liar, anyway. I can tell." They both said, at the same time, *"He's hiding something."*

"I knew you would say that," Lydia said.

⊷⟴ ⟴⊷

Meanwhile, back on Wall Street, the campaign to take over Country Goods resumed in full force. HausenHome executives began appearing on business shows and interviews, assuring the markets of the company's strength, its ability to deliver on the takeover and beyond. But Harrison, Cordray and Wynn were doing their job too; they connected Maria Carvey with a growing online movement of YouTubers, bloggers and influencers, who repeated the stories of cruel treatment at Saltair Springs. Dozens of videos, shot with clandestine cellphones showed the unpleasant conditions so many workers described.

Arthur called Lydia that morning, asked if she thought another visit to the trailer might be in order.

"I think that would be the worst thing to do," she said. "I gained her trust once, then she felt betrayed. I have no standing. That's a movement we're going to have to let play out by itself. If Chandler/Perkins has a better idea, that's what they're getting paid for."

"Understood," he said. "How is your other assignment going? Anything to report?"

Lydia took the call off speaker, picked up the phone. Slowly, as it traveled from cradle to ear, she formulated her concern and what she could and would and did not want to say to Arthur. He had been her friend, her protector, and was chiefly responsible for extending a helping hand when she needed it. She was in his debt. But there was a price to be paid by her, and all of them, for the boost.

"Arthur, I'm at a loss here. The overlord of home furnishings asked me to sniff around his own plant, for something he doesn't seem to know. I've been rebuffed by people who appear to be hiding things and I've uncovered a couple of curious and possibly troublesome connections. I don't quite know why I've been asked to do this and I don't like not knowing what's going on. Am I being led down the proverbial home and garden path?"

"I wish I had some intelligence for you, but I don't. What I can tell you is, Hausen is paying its bills and renewing their contracts, and all the firms on the payroll are just as happy as can be."

There's that word, Lydia thought, right on schedule, the one Carl doesn't care about. Arthur continued: "Whatever you're doing there seems to be keeping the money flowing here. It would be against my better judgment to tell you to stop. I have nothing concrete to base that on, just a sense of how pleased the client is."

"Arthur, I finished the job you hired me for. They have all the assets and messaging and everything I can provide. I don't want to be the fall guy for something I have no idea about."

"Lydia," he said, coolly, "we all count on your best judgment."

"I understand," she said, and they ended the call on that pleasant note.

After they were done, Reuben rolled off and lay on his back, exhausted. Catching his breath, Paul said, "Can I ask you a gossip and innuendo question?"

"I don't know anything," Reuben said. "All I know is hardware. Doesn't lie, doesn't cheat, just depreciates."

"Well, I *depreciate* that, but still. Do you know Walter Mulbacher?"

"I know who he is, but not to talk to or anything."

"He's the picking supervisor. He was Darnell's boss, the guy who died."

"Oh yeah, his office is the one off the floor. He looks kind of like a squirrel, all bunched up in there with his nuts."

"That's the one. So, anything? Rumors, hearsay, tasty little nuggets?"

"Well," he said, and rolled over, sat up on his arms. "Something happened a few months ago. I'm not sure exactly because, you know, I don't want to know. But security showed up one day. They escorted him out of his office, and took all the computers, equipment, everything. I only know because they asked for an inventory of his stuff. I didn't have it, I only know about floor equipment. But the next day, everything was back, and he was back, and no one said a word. We thought maybe he got some computer virus or a security intrusion."

"And?"

"What?"

"Bunched up in there with his nuts. What did you mean by that?"

"Nothing. It was just a thing to say."

"No it wasn't." Paul said it the way he drilled his exes when he sensed the whiff of a lie.

"Well …"

"Ya, well?"

"Well. I overheard one of the pickers talking one time. They thought it was porn. He was watching videos in there and the firewall picked it up and he got in trouble."

"But no one knows for sure?"

"Well, he was back the next day and no one said anything. If it's a personnel matter, it's none of my business."

⤙⟶⊙⟵⤚

Meanwhile, Wanda Spragg and Harrison, Cordray and Wynn arrived in Saltair Springs to launch the next strategy, a press conference in the parking lot of the Midway Hotel. Lydia watched out her window. They were making the case now against the sheriff's conclusions, pushing back on Chandler/Perkins' narrative—which provoked its own storm of online pushback, including a thread about how careless and irresponsible Cherise had to have been. Which coincided with, or provoked, her own shift in grief from shock to recrimination.

"I knew it," she said, over the morning donuts. "I should have said fuck it to the center, we're driving to a real doctor in a real town. They're right, those people. It was my fault."

"Oh, baby doll, no," Marion said, and took her hand. "It was a freak situation. No one could have known."

"She's right," Lydia said, "this was not your responsibility to diagnose. All that talk about fault is just Chandler/Perkins trying to deflect responsibility. It's a spin strategy and it's not real."

"I hated that little cage," Cherise said. "Every day, I wanted him transferred to another position. I knew it was too much."

Marion shook her head. "My lord, all this work they make you kids do … climbing up and down those walls, running around those machines. It scares me to death. What was it again poor Darnell had to do?"

"I told you, mama. He filled orders. You stand in this little box and the screen tells you what to pick, and some klingon ... this robot on wheels ... brings a tray of stuff and you have to find the piece from the number on the screen and throw it in a bin, then the robot brings another tray and the screen gives you another number and you have to do it again. And they keep track of the seconds, how long it takes you to do each one. You get a warning if you're too slow, if you don't hit your benchmark."

Marion shook her head.

"They increased the benchmarks as well," Lydia said. "When they announced this takeover deal. They wanted to show how productive the center could be. What was the last benchmark they set?"

Cherise sighed. "Ninety-eight."

"Is that a lot?" Marion asked.

Cherise shrugged. "Who cares?"

After breakfast, Lydia walked out to the patio and called Paul.

"Are you up?"

"Barely."

"Do me a favor. Today some time, go over and ask our squirrely friend what the pick rate was for the week Darnell died. If it was a range, find out the range."

"Why do you ask?"

"Why not ask?"

And Paul did, as irritating as he could, and relayed the number back to Lydia in the afternoon.

"Ninety, you said?"

"Yes. He said there wasn't a range. They started Monday of that week at ninety and ended at ninety. They upped it a couple of times in the weeks before, but not that week."

"I see," she said. "Thank you."

⤛▬◉ ◉▬⤜

She wasn't sure why she did it, just that the thought entered her head. She watched herself as she stuffed a couple of sweaters into her overnight bag and put on the rain bonnet from the bottom of her purse—another of the clear plastic ribbons

Paul said made her look like an idiot—and walked casually past Walt Mulbacher's office with the bag and the bonnet.

"Knock, knock. Just wanted to say thank you for all your help."

"Oh," he said, straightening up from the monitors. "Are you and Mr., uh, Paul, leaving?"

"Yes sir. Our work is done. It's been very interesting meeting you all. We really enjoyed it."

"Us too. Despite the circumstances. Do you know when the videos will be on the air, or online, or where ever?"

"I'm afraid I don't," she said, then quieter, confiding in him, "they don't tell us. We just provide the assets and someone else puts them out there. But I think what we gave them is wonderful, and we have you to thank for that."

"Of course. Anytime."

"I wanted to tell you, one of the big agencies in San Francisco was very impressed with the footage we sent them. They couldn't believe the volume of merchandise you move here, especially given the size of your operation. I mentioned that you had been in logistics and you really knew how to make the system sing." He smiled, face flushing. "Just astonishing," she said. "That week when they first announced the takeover bid, you all were performing at quite a high level. Tell me, how much merchandise were you moving?" And he told her. "Astonishing," she said again. "Now, you said there was some metric, a something rate per hour ..."

"Picks."

"Right, picks. And to move that much inventory, do you have to ... is the pick rate ... related to that somehow?" And he said it was, and explained how. "And what kind of a ... pick rate ... did you have to have to hit that number?" And he told her that, too.

"Ninety," she said. "My goodness, that sounds like a lot. And you don't have to look at some computer or something to remember?"

"I know it," he said. "That was an important week. The benchmark was ninety."

"And that was for everyone? All your folks had to hit that goal?"

The flush wasn't as red as a moment earlier.

"Yes," he said. "Have a good trip. Need to get back to work now. Nice to have met you," and he leaned behind the monitor so his face disappeared from her view.

Back at the suite, she tossed the overnight bag on the bed, yanked off the bonnet. Pondered how to phrase the question. When she did, at Cherise's apartment later, it came out as, "How can you be sure the pick rate Darnell had to hit during that week was ninety-eight?"

"Because I know it was," Cherise said. "He told me."

"Could he have been mistaken?"

"No, why would he tell me a number that was higher than it was? We both worked in picking, we know how it works."

"Do they keep records of things like that?"

"I don't know, maybe in the logs. But it changes all the time. They have software and algorithms that make those things go up and down."

"But as far as you know, all the days of that week … up until the incident … Darnell's benchmark was ninety-eight?"

"Yes," she said, annoyed. "I told you."

Later, in bed, Reuben stared at the ceiling. "Everyone had to work faster that week. We had that all-hands. That was the order. All departments had to speed it up."

"Right," Paul said, "but how come one individual gets a different benchmark than everyone else? Doesn't that seem odd?"

"I don't know that much about that department. But if it's like any other, there's all kinds of variables the software uses to set each individual's target. So maybe it took something into account and assigned Darnell one number and other people different numbers."

"I asked around. That's not how it's done. It's not by the person, it's by the department. Everyone has the same goal. And I checked, it *was* ninety that week. For everyone. Except Darnell."

"I think you're chasing your tail."

"Possibly," Paul said, and smiled at him. "In that case, can I chase *yours*?"

22

DESPITE EVERYTHING ELSE, it was just against her nature to do nothing.

Her father and his lawyers were doing things, talking among themselves, and they told her to sit tight. Lydia asked her questions and told her very little besides, basically, to sit tight. Her mother wanted so badly to help, but all she could do was cook and tidy the apartment, and tell her, in not so many words ...

And by now Cherise felt like she would explode. She'd sat in the apartment and cried, moped, stared out the window long enough, and grief, whether it was good or bad, needed some action. So she got in her car and drove away.

She hadn't looked carefully at Wanda's house a few weeks earlier because everything had been so chaotic: the awful gathering on Saturday, the funeral Sunday, hustling into the car and driving back on Monday. But now the street was empty and she had a chance to look more carefully. The houses in this neighborhood were stately and severe, like Victorians, but smaller, and all done in hard brick and stone. This part of Denver felt like a nineteenth-century industrial city, tough and serious and close to the ground.

She forgot which house it was and parked in front of the wrong one. Walking toward the right number, she looked into the backyard from the corner. The back porch was stacked with boxes now. Or rather, empty boxes. Small ones, big ones. Some flattened, others torn open. The swing set still there, lonely and abandoned.

She walked up the front steps. On the porch, more boxes. Delivered today, unopened, from different stores. No HausenHome—she checked—but big box stores, online stores. This woman did like to shop.

She rang the bell.

The door opened and Keiyon peered through the screen. "Hi."

"Hi back," she said.

Solemn though they were, she detected some excitement behind his eyes.

"How you doing?" she asked.

He shrugged.

"Your momma home?"

Shook his head.

"Can I come in?"

He nodded, pushed open the handle. "How come you're here?" he asked. The house was dark and quiet. Smelled of dust.

"I want to talk to your momma. I figured I might as well do it in person. You know when she'll be back?"

He shrugged again.

"Your brother here?"

Shook his head again.

On the TV in the livingroom a video game, paused. An open bag of chips on the floor in front of the TV.

"That what you do in the afternoons?"

He nodded.

"Not much of a talker, are you?"

He smiled, shook his head.

"Like your brother."

He shrugged.

"OK if I come in and wait for her? You can play your games, I won't bother you."

He nodded, very excited.

"Show me what you're playing," she said, and he did. He told her what game it was, and how he was doing it; what his tricks were, who the other players were. She sat behind him on the sofa while he lay on the floor in front of the TV, holding the controller.

After a while she felt hungry but didn't want to dig into his chips. "You got any water, anything to eat in there?" She nodded toward the kitchen.

"Mmm-mmm," he said. "You can look."

She did, and saw a lot of things. She stepped through the house slowly, moving into the hallway, peering into a bedroom. Boxes. Some opened, some still sealed. She picked them up to examine them, the descriptions on the receipts hard to make sense of.

Incense waterfall. *Look like real rock, many color choices, water tricklingly soothingly while aromatic incense fill your home with peace and tranquility.*

Negative ion generator. *Far surpasses all other ionic generators, eliminates 30 million negative ions per second.*

Shiatsu foot warmer and massager. *Improves blood flow, circulation, deep kneading tissue and heat for men, women, gift, plantar fasciitis.*

She stepped into the bathroom.

Long reach comfort wiping tool. *Wiping aid for limited mobility, elderly, pregnancy, disabled, arthritis, shoulder pain, surgery.*

Back to the kitchen. Small appliances that all seemed to do only one thing, like slice an egg, make a personal-sized pizza, create a star-shaped taco bowl; some used, some still in their boxes. One item in a bright red and pink bottle lying sideways on the counter, the top flipped open. Cotton candy flavoring extract. *Multi-purpose flavoring drops for baking, weight management, beverages.*

"You got any *food* in this house?" she called. Keiyon stared at the screen, shrugged. She filled a glass with tap water and drank. Scoured the pantry and refrigerator. Walked back into the livingroom. Keiyon leaning forward, staring at the TV. Such a little slip of a kid.

"You hungry?" she asked.

He nodded, "There's some chips."

"You want something else?"

He shrugged. She realized that meant yes; she already understood some of the language of this family. Back in the kitchen she found a stale loaf of bread and American cheese slices, put them together in a fry pan, pressed down with another pan and brought the finished sandwiches to the livingroom.

"Thanks," he said and chewed into his. "Mmmwow, this is good."

She ate hers quietly on the sofa, one leg crossed over the other, watching him play.

"Where do you eat mostly? School?"

He nodded, not breaking his concentration. "Momma doesn't like to cook."

"No, really?"

The bag of chips was almost empty but she could smell it from where she sat, and she knew the smell of stale chips.

"That your dinner?"

He shrugged. "Momma might get a pizza or something."

"Your momma come home every night?"

He shrugged again. These Spragg boys. Won't say a bad thing about anyone.

After a while, she slid onto the floor next to him. He smiled at her while he played. She turned, looked at his profile. The resemblance. She couldn't say anything to him. Couldn't ask any more about the quiet in here, the emptiness. The person who was supposed to care for him. She wished she could wrap her arms around him and take him back to their home.

The front door kicked open. Someone carrying in the boxes from the porch and dropping them on the floor.

"Keiyon, where you ..." Wanda started, then saw Cherise. "Oh. What are you doing here?"

"Hi Mrs. Spragg, I hope you don't mind. I wanted to talk with you."

"No," she said, "that's fine," and wiped the dust from the boxes off her coat, brushed her arms and legs. Buying some time. "Sure, that's nice, uh ..."

"Cherise."

"Yeah, I know. Let me get myself settled here, then we can talk. You doing ok there, little man?" Keiyon nodded, didn't take his eyes off the screen.

Wanda disappeared into the bathroom to wash her hands. She smoothed her hair and came back out. "You want coffee or something?" After it was made, they sat at the small table in the kitchen. It was the same table they'd sat at weeks earlier with the lawyers, but it had been positioned near the back of the kitchen then, close to the door. That spot was now stacked with empty boxes to be tossed into the yard.

"So, what do you want?" Wanda asked, seated across from her. "You come to sign the papers?"

"Well, that's what I want to talk to you about. I have some questions about your lawyers. Where'd you find those guys? I mean, do you trust them?"

Wanda opened her mouth to reply but thought better of it. She put her hands in her lap, demurely, and smiled. "Honey," she said, "they're lawyers. It's not your problem. All you gotta do is sign the papers and let them do their job."

"And what are they gonna do?"

"They're gonna get justice is what they're gonna do. They killed my son, that company you work for. They killed a perfectly healthy boy. Hell, they killed your boyfriend, Cherise. You ought to be madder than all of us. You sign that paper and those boys'll make sure that company gets what coming to *them*."

"I'm just not sure."

Wanda repositioned herself in the chair. "What aren't you sure about?"

"They're making this into a media circus, Mrs. Spragg. I mean, with all these press conferences and making all kinds of statements and accusations ..."

"Honey, that's how it works. That's what you got to do. I'm sorry if you have no appetite for it, but we got to get some compensation here. For my son and your ... I don't know what, maybe, your future husband?"

She nodded. It was possible.

"So you see," she said, maintaining the patient smile. "You had the most to lose. They owe you, girl. Big time." Then, quieter, "We could use that money, too. Look around you. That boy in the other room, the other one ... that's money their brother would want them to have."

Cherise did look. All these boxes. Always the boxes.

"You know," Cherise said, "that company has a lot of money. They hired this fancy crisis management firm to smack down the stuff your lawyers are saying. And it's starting to backfire, if you want to know the truth. They're trying to deflect the blame onto me and Darnell. Those people are really slick, and you got these ... I don't know, injury lawyers or something, who seem like they're out of their depth ..."

Wanda's eyebrows began to knit. "They're perfectly fine."

"My parents aren't sure they doing what's in your ... what's in *our* best interests ... they're talking to some people they know ..."

"*What?*" Wanda said. "You're gonna get your own lawsuit? Aw hell, girl, that'll ruin everything."

Cherise held up a hand. "I'm not saying that. I don't know what we're doing yet."

"Those lawyers are perfectly fine," Wanda said, the smile drooping. "What I don't appreciate is someone coming in here and making judgments about what I'm doing for my own flesh and blood. He was *my* son ..."

"I know," Cherise said, "and he was *my* boyfriend. And I loved him and I don't want to see him made into some kind of a clown in a reality show ..."

And now the smile was gone. Cherise knew immediately they were a bad match: two people with two fuses too short. It struck her funny, though, and logical, why Darnell was so comfortable around her. He was used to it.

"Who do you think you are?" Wanda said, leaning forward. "Far as I'm concerned, you're just some girl he was fuckin' around with. I didn't have to cut you in on this at all. I only did because the lawyers said all the interested parties should go in on it together. *They* said that, not me."

"Because it'll get a bigger settlement?"

"Well, duh. What do you think this is all about?"

Cherise put her hands on the table. Looked at her hands on the table.

"You lost your son, Mrs. Spragg. He was a really good guy."

"I know that, *Cherise.* That's why we're doing this."

Oh well, Cherise thought. Got to rip off the band-aid eventually. "This whole thing is so not what Darnell would have wanted," she said. "I mean, did you even know your own son?"

"What do you ...? Of course I knew my son! I loved my boy."

"Really? You never called him. You never saw him. You went to Las Vegas and left him taking care of his brothers. You kicked him out when you came back 'cause you didn't want him around your new man ..."

Wanda slammed the table with her full weight. It shuddered, the coffee cups jumped, splashed everywhere. She stood and smashed it again. "Who are you to come in here and talk to me like that? Who the fuck do you think you are? I lost a child! I was being nice to cut you in, and now you say this shit to me? You get the fuck out. Just get the fuck out of here right now," and she pointed, hard, toward the door. Out the corner of her eye, Cherise watched Keiyon, pretending to be glued to the TV.

"Alright," she said, and stood. "But I want you to think ..."

"I'm not taking any more out of you. You want to be out of the case? Well you are. So, get out and don't come back. And don't be calling me all crying and apologizing. I was trying to be nice to you, and you go and throw your nasty attitude in my face? You are out. *Out!*"

As Cherise moved toward the door, to Keiyon she said, "See you later ..."

"*Out!*" Wanda screamed.

He didn't move. She waved, made her way through the front door to the porch. The heavy wood door slammed and shook the patio with the impact. She took a moment to take a long breath then started walking slowly toward the car.

Back in Saltair Springs, Marion shook her head. "Oh, dear, I wish you hadn't gone there alone."

"I wanted to, momma. I figured she'd be like that. I didn't want you to sit through it."

"Well, I'm sorry you had to. It doesn't sound like it was productive at all."

"No," she said. "But at least now I have some idea who buys all that crap we send out. My god, you should have seen that place. It looked like ... well, it looked like a fulfillment center."

"And you don't think she's watching over those boys very well?"

She shook her head. "Darnell told me a little."

"What do you want to do, dear?"

And that was the question.

"What can I do?" Cherise asked, almost to herself. "It feels so strange. Like all these parts are moving and I have no control over any of them."

Marion clasped her hand on the table. "Maybe it's time to come home, honey, and leave all this behind." Cherise shrugged. "Well then, at least get that strange woman out of here. I really doubt whether you should trust her at all."

"I know, momma. We talked. She's using me for her own purposes, I know that. Maybe I ought to do the same." She thought about what Wanda said. "Maybe that's how it works."

All Marion could do was shake her head.

23

THROUGH THE SLIDING glass doors of her suite, Lydia pondered the wide blue sky, the stucco-colored houses and tiled rooftops. The sameness of it all. The randomness.

Sometimes awful things happen to innocent people.

A driver blasts a car through a busy intersection at 100 miles an hour because, his lawyer says, the driver had mental problems. The driver doesn't die because he had the foresight to lease a new Mercedes, and a new Mercedes protects the driver, who suffers almost no injuries at all. But the new Mercedes kills six other people who happened to be passing through the intersection at that moment in their own cars, none of which protected them the way the Mercedes protected the driver.

In some heavily guarded building somewhere, a man makes a decision—on a whim, random and personal, perhaps irrational—and thousands of people in South America or the Middle East or eastern Europe lose everything—their lives, their families, their homes—and become wandering souls in a hostile, violent world, searching for a place to be safe.

Inside this hotel, Lydia was safe. The town around this hotel was safe, from bombs and terrorists, from armies with orders to kill her and destroy her home. The giant box in the middle of this town provides jobs and money for the people to buy food, pay their rent, feel safe. And that giant box receives things from trucks that receive them from boats that receive them from factories where they were made, all over the world, and all the people in this town, in one way or another, are involved in sending those things to other people in America who want them, who feel those things will make their lives better and fulfill their wishes and desires. Make them feel safe. There's safety in money transferring hands, one to another, and in maintaining the production line necessary to ensure those transactions take place. So, what is random and what is deliberate? People do things that hurt other people, and they do it with intention. Other times, just meaningless; a fool gets into a car and kills many others, emerging unscathed. Darnell had an undiagnosed illness, and one day, like a bubble in a bathtub, it simply burst, for no reason at all. It was random.

Soon enough, Paul arrived with breakfast—two muffins and two fancy coffees. He found Lydia transfixed, staring at the sky through the glass door. By now, he could now identify her various grades of stupor, from complete dissociation to mild amusement. This one he correctly identified as big thought just coming to the surface.

"I wonder if old Carl is playing me for a stooge," she said.

"Beg pardon?"

"Cherise said it. What if I'm not the picture of cheerful recuperation I think I am? What if, instead, I come across like a bright but lost old codger, and Carl saw it, and he's using it for his own ends? Sending me out to find evidence to use against Cherise and give Chandler/Perkins more ammunition for the hatchet job? I mean, I vanquished Maria Carvey for him with a single blow."

"Yeeks, that's awfully diabolical. You think he would really do that?"

She turned and focused her eyes on him. "I cannot believe *you* are the less cynical one in this conversation."

"Well, so far, have you given him anything?"

"No."

"Have you found out anything you're not telling him?"

"No."

"Then whatever is going on, it's still a draw. No harm done."

"I guess so," she said, and turned to look back at the tiled rooftops. "No harm done." And she slipped back into the daydream. Paul craned his neck to see what she was looking at. "What?" he asked.

"Just a tiny thing," she said to the window, dreamily. "Like a rattle under the hood. It isn't loud and you want to ignore it, but you know it's something."

⤙═◦ ◦═⤚

Saltair Springs was strangely quiet at night. The center, which operated around the clock, was located on the railway line, the one concession its planners made to the world that existed before it. The building itself blocked the sound of the train from the residential part of the city. All one would hear is the plaintive whistle from a distance. The cracked, single-lane road that once led into the old town had been replaced by three lanes of thick, reinforced blacktop, to accommodate the caravan of trucks moving in and out at all hours. But that road, too, circumnavigated the residential neighborhood. You could, ironically, sleep with the windows open, as Cherise was doing tonight, the breeze gently blowing the soft plastic blinds against the frame. As she lay in bed alone, she still felt his presence in the sheets, in the indent in the mattress. When her mother had arrived, she tried to strip and remake the bed, but Cherise stopped her, didn't have to say why. So the sheets hadn't been changed. She knew, when she took the sheets up, there would be the slight discoloration from his body's warmth and moisture. She had joked with him about it. "Look what you did to my hundred-dollar mattress pad," and smacked him across the chest. "Ya big sweaty man."

He only smiled. "You can take it off my side."

"And have you mess up the mattress too? No sir. You take more showers, that's what you're gonna do." And because he didn't, she still had this sliver of joy, the shape and size of the place he carved in her life.

Marion had started, ever so gently, to try and make her feel better. She brought up how young Cherise was. How the world was full of people and she had only begun to discover them. A single glance told her that was a bad direction to pursue, and she backed off. But yet, in the middle of the night, grabbing at something to hold onto, a rope to keep from falling into the ship's empty hull, Cherise thought about it. She *was* young. This was her first serious relationship. You really have until you're thirty to get your shit together. Everything holds up pretty well until then, you can mess up and start over many times. But then sadness washed over, like the billowing smoke that precedes the explosion, and engulfed her as the force of the blast arrived. Why does something else get to decide what she does and doesn't have? Why is she the one who has to take it and agree to try again? In their bed, she surrendered to it, and sobbed as hard as she had every night since the shock of his sudden disappearance had worn off.

"You alright honey?" Marion called from the sofa in the living room.

"I'm fine," she called back.

She closed her eyes and turned on her side, smelled the smell of him, and remembered.

It was weird because there was nothing said or done that made it. No conversation where her skin got tingly, no syrupy walks through sunsets, nothing romantic at all. They met at a crappy restaurant and went on a couple of dates, and it was just there, the two of them together. Like a handshake, two parts that fit together. Because it never happened before, she wasn't sure what it was. One of her friends in Atlanta once told her she was *jagged*. She said it that way—sharp and rough around the edges. *Jagged*. What she meant, and Cherise knew, was that she was oddly shaped—not physically, but as a person. Very smart in some places, not at all in others; quick to judge, quick to calm down; good at listening and talking, bad at staying emotionally connected over any period of time. Weird, rough edges that make it hard to form a bond with regularly shaped people. But Darnell had soft, malleable edges that absorbed her jagged ones. Her edges didn't bother him at all. She thought of the one fun event the company sponsored, about nine months earlier. They'd decided to do some "team building," so they gave a big picnic at the Croft Playing Field, the sports complex near the supermarket. They hired an events company to bring in games and rides, a portable Ferris wheel, Skee-ball, and hot dog stands. And it worked: people got into it, running excitedly from one ride to another, kids eating ice cream and clutching their red tickets for prizes and rides. Everyone was there. McAllister and all the department heads gave speeches. They weren't long, just the kind of rah-rah bullshit they say at company events. But when the sun set and cooled the air, there was this smell, this sense of rightness, and hope, that everything seemed to be in its place, at least for her. When Darnell grabbed her hand and ran, pulling her toward the tilt-a-whirl, she laughed, a full-throated, unselfconscious laugh; the thing she always wished she could do, but was *too high strung, too reserved, too wound up*, whatever her teachers or mother or friends said. For once, a handsome guy reached out and took her hand and pulled her along, and they ran, across the field, past the people, waving and smiling. At McAllister, at their department head, the new guys on picking, the HR lady, the crazy bruisers on loading, the guy who ran the forklift into the wall on his first day. It was the first party of the first part of her real life, and even though she knew they were working in this weirdo town in the middle of nowhere, it was only the beginning. They would have time, and a life. By some stroke of luck, she had found it.

"You look sad," Darnell said, across from her in the seat on the Ferris wheel, high up and stopped, waiting while they loaded the seats below.

"I'm not." She didn't know how to talk to him, to say what she felt. "You mean a lot to me," was the best she could come up with. He took her hand. Looked at her with those eyes. "You're the best one ever," he said. And she cried and laughed at the same time. She felt like the person within herself who, with him, she could be.

The pillow saturated with tears now, she ran her hand over the shape in the mattress. Took a long breath to savor whatever was left, whatever he had left for her. The awful sense of emptiness. The opposite of what was here before.

24

AND NOW, PAUL felt, things began to swing the other way. Reuben's clinginess had reached his breaking point. Reuben started asking the kind of teasy, casual questions people ask when they're trying to burrow their way in, trying to create domesticity. *How did the big meeting with Bob go, hon?* Well, Paul said, to himself, he did not like domesticity. And anyone who thought they could burrow their way into him had another thing coming. More and more, Paul was unsettled by these discomforting flip-flops where Reuben was concerned. He had planned that clean break at the beginning—the reliable Bugs Bunny *so long suckah!*—but then began having actual feelings, followed by the stomach-churning shock of attachment. Which was now flipping into existential terror: he realized he needed to escape on the next plane.

"OK, when are we out of here?" he asked Lydia, the next morning in her suite.

"Uh oh, what happened? You get the little lady in the family way?"

"Hardy har. I mean it. I'm not doing anything useful here. You're on the fence about this whole thing anyway. I don't like hanging around getting paid to do nothing."

"What are you going to do at home, *not* get paid to do nothing? Don't look a gift horse in the house ... or the mouse ... or ... what is the word?"

"*Mouth.* See. You're cracking up too. Time to get out of frontier town and back to civilization."

"Well, something certainly touched a nerve this morning. What, pray tell, could have brought this on?"

He felt irritable and exposed. He didn't like whatever this was so close to the surface, and that she could see it and poke it so easily.

"Never mind me," he said, "what about you? You say you're worried about Cherise? Well, look who's talking. From the woman who hasn't taken off *this ...*"

and he stepped up to her and angrily untied the belt on the trench coat, yanked open the buttons and shook the lapels, "… godforsaken, stupid piece of *shit* for two whole years. I mean, what the fuck is with you? Do you sleep in this thing?"

She was startled by the sudden hostility. She closed the flaps again, buttoned the buttons slowly. "Good lord," she said, "just let me deal with things my own way."

"That's fine. Unless you're playing nursemaid to some kid who doesn't need it. You're not her mommy."

"She trusts me," Lydia said, not convincingly.

"You know what? I think you're *projecting*. You see this poor, sad kid, and you want to nurse her back to health. Well, guess what? She's fine. She's young and she'll get over it. And even if she doesn't, it's none of your business. She has a mother. Let *her* deal with it. But you, lady … who hasn't taken her coat off in two years … you need to heal thyself. And get us the fuck out of here."

Despite the outburst, she couldn't argue with anything he said, the little prick. She could never understand how someone so touchy, selfish and callow could stumble over the right thing as often as he did. In fact, she had come to the same conclusion: getting out would be the smart thing to do. The pragmatic thing. Her motivation was cloudy, her intent unknown even to herself. She was being paid by a client to do a job and she was no longer sure her calibration of right and wrong was entirely restored, or even, how reliable it had been in the past. She couldn't keep making the same mistakes. And once again, someone else's life was involved. She would have to tell Cherise she had no place in this business and would make her exit as soon as possible.

"This is the hardest thing I've had to say in years," she said to Paul, and he waited with eyebrows raised. "You're right."

And so, that evening, Paul pondered how to bring it up to Reuben. After shuffling through various approaches, he decided to go with tormented interior conflict. That was usually a winner.

"You've been so quiet," Reuben said, after a dramatic length of silence.

Paul shrugged, staring gloomily into the corner. "Is it what Lydia said?" Reuben asked. "What was it? A rattle under the hood?"

Paul shrugged again.

"She sure likes her analogies." Reuben hoped his smile would pry open the can, but it didn't. "But what is it really? You've hardly said a word."

"Well," Paul said. On occasion, in client presentations when he hadn't prepared, he just started talking and let the word salad fall where it may. Sometimes it worked, sometimes it didn't. He decided to give it a shot tonight. "Lydia says there's nothing more to find out. It's all a big nothing. So, we're packing it in. I don't think we'll be here past Thursday."

"Oh," Reuben said, stunned, and sat up in the bed. "I didn't know ... I thought ... well, I thought you said it was kind of an open-ended thing."

"Yeah, I did too. But it looks like it's only dead ends. So, unfortunately, I'll be gone by the end of the week."

Reuben looked down at his bent knees under the sheet. He leaned forward and hugged them. "Will you be back?"

"Oh, sure. At some point. And like I said, you're welcome in SF anytime you like."

"Could we ... make a plan? You know, to visit?"

"Things will be so crazy when I get back. Tell you what, I'll call you when I get into the city and we can figure it out."

"Thursday," Reuben said. "Wow. I didn't know. Okay. Wow."

The guillotine thus dispatched, Paul kissed him. "But we have all the time til then to celebrate." And as the wave of relief flooded over him, he ruffled Reuben's soft curls. Looked into his handsome brown eyes. He might miss those curls, and all the naïve, unsophisticated sexiness Reuben seemed to radiate. Reuben was the opposite of guys in the city, who calculated every move and gesture. Even though Paul continued to score high with those guys, he knew his charming crinkles would soon turn to bags, the yes's to no's, and he should begin to consider the possibility of some nice guy in the sticks with boundless trust. Someone who would treat him like the rare treasure he wanted to be. But looking at Reuben's sad face right now, all he could think about was what he would stuff in his bag first.

"Let's get some dinner," he said cheerily, and kissed Reuben again.

⇥━◯ ◯━⇤

When she walked into Cherise's apartment the next morning with the box from Donut Wagon, the air was heavy with tension, like the scent of burning from a small electric motor running too fast. She looked from Marion to Cherise, who weren't looking at each other, each attending to some detail, wiping the countertop, arranging placemats. Lydia was tempted to ask, but figured she'd find out soon enough.

They took their usual places at the table, cracked open the box and dipped the donuts in coffee. All eating in silence. Cherise sighed, trying to be nonchalant. "I went over to Denver the other day." Lydia waited. Marion watched Cherise though trying not to. "I had a talk with Darnell's mother," she went on. "*That* woman's a piece of work." Lydia continued to chew softly. It felt as though Cherise and Marion each had something on their mind, but it wasn't the same thing, and it had been discussed and left uncomfortably unresolved.

Marion placed her hands gently but firmly on the table. "My husband is conferring with his attorneys. They're not at all interested in joining Mrs. Spragg's action. They feel the attorneys she's retained are using her for their own purposes. The goal here should be an appropriate and dignified response." Marion turned to Cherise—for approval, or to pick up the thread, Lydia wasn't sure. Cherise did neither, just chewed her donut, staring into space.

"That sounds like a reasonable approach," Lydia said, leaving the end a question. Marion watched the side of Cherise's head for the follow-up, the decision. Cherise took her time chewing, gathering her thoughts. Took a sip of coffee. Still staring at the medium space, at nothing.

"If we go back to Atlanta and leave everything here," she said, slowly, "the trail goes cold. They file papers and money changes hands. A *negotiated settlement*," she said, her contempt for the phrase. "But I was robbed of something. And I don't get it. And I don't know why."

"Well," Lydia said, "I think your father's approach is the right one." Marion sighed in relief. "I know it sounds like a compromise, Cherise, but that's how these things work."

Then Cherise did look up, her eyes unreadable. "Well, you ought to know."

Lydia sat back slightly.

"I mean, that's your whole strategy, isn't it?" Cherise said. "You compromise this to sell that. You look the other way and make the money. You sell out some client and a girl gets killed. And now you show up here, making nice with me but keeping one foot in the water and playing it right down the middle. Keep the compromise going."

Lydia sat fully back now, her back against the back of the chair.

Marion scowled at Cherise, put her hand on her shoulder. Cherise shrugged it off. "Momma, go take a walk."

"I don't think you need to ..." Marion started, but Cherise cut her off. "I said, go take a walk."

She nodded, left the table, and got her coat. When the door was closed and the apartment quiet, Lydia, who hadn't moved, leaned forward again and put her arms on the table. "You have more to say."

Cherise searched the table for the answer. The unresolved discussion.

"Everyone is telling me to leave it to the lawyers, listen to the lawyers, let someone else take care of it."

"I know," Lydia said, "I'm sorry. But that's the right thing to do." She put her hands over Cherise's.

"And you're saying that, too?"

"I am. And you're right, I have compromised too much. I don't know what they expect of me. And you might be right that they're using me for purposes I'm not aware of. Whatever it is, this could be a powder keg and I don't want it to blow up all over me. Or you. So you should do what you're told, and let the professionals take care of it."

Cherise looked right at her. "Did you hear a fuckin' word I said?"

"Yes, and I ..."

"Listen," she said. "Shut up and listen to me, alright? I can handle things myself. I always have. But this thing I can't do. Whether I like it or not, I'm the kid. I'm the girlfriend of the *deceased*. I'm the disgruntled employee causing problems. Everyone else has the power."

"I know, but ..."

"Shut *up*, would you?" She looked down at her hands, her fingers spread wide, willing them to do something. Then she looked up at Lydia directly. "So, now you listen to me. I don't know what your fuckin' problems are, but it sounds like you just gave up and dropped out and let everyone else make your decisions for you. Maybe you can afford to do that, but I can't. I need this figured out. If I could do it myself, I would. But I don't have the keys to the kingdom. Scary old Carl gave them to you. So … *Lydia* … get up and get working. If you don't give a shit about your life, that is not my problem, because I give a shit about mine. You said you're here because you needed to fix something, right? Then do it and stop *com-pro-mising*."

Lydia couldn't look away from the burning eyes.

25

PAUL SHOUTED AT her so loud the phone in the room rang, the front desk calling to ask if everything was alright.

"No it's not alright, and *fuck you very much!*" he screamed and slammed it down.

"Uh-oh," Lydia said, "no more extra coffee pods in *your* basket, young man."

"You said we were leaving!" he shouted again.

"And we will ... just as soon as I get a handle on some of these ..."

"You talked to Cherise, didn't you? This happened when you talked to that girl! What the fuck is wrong with you? Do you just say yes to everyone? You used to have a spine! You used to be decisive!"

"And I agree with you on everything," she said, hands splayed wide in case Paul broke out in a full tantrum and started throwing things. "And you don't have to stay. You are free as a bird. I will handle the rest of this myself."

That stopped his tirade.

"Oh," he said. "Wait, do I still get paid if I go home?"

"Uh, no. Paychecks mean butts in chairs."

"Aw, fuck you," he moaned. "Get out of my room."

"It's my room."

"Aw ... *fuck!*" he shouted, and started past her toward the door. "Then I want a suite ..."

"No."

"Fuck!" he shouted from the hall and slammed the door behind him.

⊷══◉ ◉══⊷

Lydia watched the parking lot through a small window in the security office. When she saw him approaching his car, she skittered out quickly.

"Excuse me … Mr. Mulbacher," she said, as he opened the car door.

He looked up, surprised. "I thought you left."

"We had a few loose ends to tie up."

He scanned the lot for anyone watching, anyone coming.

"It's only me," she said, calmly. "But, you know, I had just one more question, if you wouldn't mind."

His eyebrows raised.

"Well, I checked," she said, "and I didn't know there were so many organizations in the supply chain industry, in warehousing and fulfillment … it's just fascinating, I must say."

"Yes?"

"And it was such interesting reading. As I understand it, there are standards … numbers, I mean … pick rates set according to all sorts of variables, the equipment available, the demand …"

"Yeah, I know all that. What's your question?"

"It seems the rate assigned to Darnell during the week they announced the takeover bid, the week he passed away, was higher than the rate assigned to the other pickers. And that is unusual. Pick rates seems to be standard across the unit."

He blinked a few times. She thought about what Paul said; takes one to know one.

"I don't know where you got that information but it's not right. I already told you. Everyone was the same."

"You're sure of that?" She wanted to say, *you're sure you want to stick with that answer*, but you have to leave some space for them to wriggle out of.

"Yes," he said, firm.

She nodded and thanked him. He got into the car.

"One more thing …" she said, but he closed the door with her hand on the rim. She shouted, and he opened it, startled. "Oh my God, I'm sorry, are you alright?"

"Yeah." She pulled her hand out, stuck the fingers in her mouth. "Ow, yes, it's fine." She shook her hand, looked at the finger. A bruise, nothing more. "It's fine, really." He nodded, then he pulled the door shut carefully and took off.

Back at Care, Antonio was on duty again. Lydia showed him her finger, now swollen. He stared at it, blank, clearly no idea what to do.

She asked for an ice pack and disinfectant. He opened the supply cabinet and let her choose what she wanted. She pulled out a box of cloth bandages, a bottle of iodine, a bottle of alcohol, and some cotton wipes. She realized she couldn't carry them all at once—Antonio seemed paralyzed, watching but not helping—so she put the roll of bandages in her mouth, picked up the other supplies in both hands and moved them to a table to work. The room was so small she bumped the desk as she leaned over, knocking everything off it. "Oops, sorry." She shuffled a few feet over, the roll of cotton still in her mouth. It felt like a scene in a movie, people stuffed in a phone booth trying courteously to pass around each other.

Antonio leaned down to pick up the stuff on the floor while Lydia put down the supplies and cut the bandage. A piece of paper had fallen under the refrigerator. "Don't miss that one," she said, and he reached in to pull it out. "What is that?" she asked.

"The stub from my check," he said, standing back up.

"They still do checks? Wow, even I know about direct deposit." She held the cotton in her mouth while she stretched it out with one hand and cut it with the other.

"They do that," he said fanning himself with it, looking for the wastebasket, "but they give you a paper anyway. The receipt I guess."

"Ah." She rolled the cotton over her finger. "That looks like it's from HausenHome."

"Well, ya," he said, like *duh*. "That's where we are."

"I thought you were paid by the drugstore … HealthSaver?"

"I am when I'm there, but you get paid by Hausen for the hours you're here."

"Oh. Would that girl … Marie … was she paid the same way?"

"I don't know. Ask HR. They do all that stuff."

She finished wrapping the bandage and sealed it with white medical tape. It looked like the end of a torch to be set on fire. "Not very good, is it?"

He shook his head no.

In his room, Paul looked up at it. He was lying on the sofa, watching TV, eating microwave popcorn. "What happened? Lose your finger in a bet?"

"Car door. I was trying to wheedle some information about this discrepancy in pick rates. That's what I get for being surreptitious."

"Hey, workman's comp. Get that claim in before it heals."

"But you are right about Walter," she said. "He is a liar. He's sticking with the pick rate being the same for everyone. Cherise says it was different."

He looked back at the TV. "Is it important? You might be making something out of nothing. I've already been told I'm chasing my tail."

"And a lovely tail it is. But it shouldn't be there."

"Huh?" he said, turning his hips and looking back.

"It's a tiny detail but it's nagging. Like a run in a stocking. If you leave it, the whole thing will unravel."

He shrugged, uninterested in her latest analogy. He thought of sharing it with Reuben for a good laugh, except now he couldn't, hiding out as it were, not answering calls or messages, on the pretext of having left town already.

In the afternoon, Lydia went back to Cherise's apartment, where she found her, as well, lying on the sofa, staring at the ceiling.

"Have you had lunch?" Lydia asked. Cherise said no, so Lydia prepared sandwiches, poured them lemonades. Handed Cherise the plate with the sandwich, where she remained, on the sofa, Lydia taking the chair next to the table. With her upright, Cherise horizontal, she felt the vaguely therapeutic positioning gave her license to ask.

"Cherise, tell me something. What's your relationship with Walt Mulbacher?"

"Walt? Why, are you thinking he did something?"

"I don't know," she said, biting into her sandwich. "There's some things that don't add up. Anything come to mind about him? Any conflicts or disagreements you might have had?"

"Well, Walt's a … I don't know what to say … I don't want to sound … never mind."

"Go ahead, say it. It's just you and me."

"Well, Walt's like a guy … like one of these guys … I don't think he's ever been out of Colorado … and I think he has some ideas about people."

Suddenly, Lydia understood the classic shrink setup. She'd just never been the one in the chair before. Lying on the sofa, Cherise could stare out the window and not see her at all; Lydia couldn't see Cherise's face, and from the tone of her voice, she could feel how much easier it was for her to speak, to free associate.

"Ideas like?" Lydia probed.

"Well … I don't think he's racist or anything. And I know when you say that, you know, people think … you've seen there's not a whole lot of Black faces around here. And I think people … well, they don't know how to act."

Lydia chewed her sandwich, thoughtfully. "You know, I think you're trying to say something but I don't know what it is."

"I think he saw Darnell and he had some idea of what he was like. And then he stuck with that and wouldn't change his mind."

"The idea he would have had was …?"

"That he was … I don't know … lazy or something. I don't mean to put him down. Walt, I mean. He was just doing his job."

"And what was his job?"

"Well, you know. To hit the numbers. We all have to. I mean, I'm like an overachiever. You give me an assignment and I'm all over it. Walt loved me, he said I was his secret weapon. But Darnell. I think he thought … I just think he didn't like him. Like he didn't do his job. And there was some kind of … well, not racist, but more like what my grandparents used to say. *Prejudiced*."

"Do you think that affected his working relationship with Darnell?"

"Look, he's a nice guy. I don't want to get him in trouble."

"You're not getting anyone in trouble." Now Cherise did sit up, turn and look at Lydia, like, are you kidding? "Just go ahead and say it," Lydia said.

She lay down again. "Well, I thought he kind of kicked him around, treated him like he was lazy or something. And he wasn't. He hit every benchmark they set for him. He hardly ever got warnings. Whatever they threw at him, he did. He was just easygoing. He didn't make a big deal out of it. Like, when the boss said jump, he didn't jump high enough. Like he wanted him to act more … I don't know … more *yes, sir*. And it seemed to get under his skin."

"Whose skin?"

She thought for a moment. "Well, I was gonna say Walt's, but that's not right, exactly. I mean. It's kind of weird. He seemed to like us. He knew how hard we worked for him. But then, other times, he was just like … I don't know … more pressure, more work, you're not good enough, you're not trying hard enough. Like he was two people, almost."

"Do you remember any other times when he put pressure on you?"

"Not me. I overachieved."

"Right. Darnell then."

She had to think. "He made him take a lot of hours. Like, twelve and four-teen hour shifts. He said he had to take them or they'd let him go. He said his rate was too low and he had to make it up with the extra hours. I was on float, so I didn't know what was going on with that team. I asked him once, and he said it was the software, that he didn't make the schedules, it just came out that way. And I was worried about it, because he started to get the swollen feet and headaches. That's when we started going to Care. And then overnight shifts, and that was really tough. He didn't sleep enough, so I asked Walt to put us on shifts at the same time. He said he'd try, and he did, sometimes, but a lot we weren't. I don't know. Walt's a nice guy. He really is. But it felt like they were pushing him … Darnell I mean … like, out of spite or something."

"Could he have had something against Darnell personally? Did he do any-thing to cause any discord between them?"

"Are you kidding? Darnell? Nothing bothered him. But like I said, some-times he had it out for him, other times they were best buddies." She took her phone from the table, thumbed through photos, and showed Lydia. "Look, here's them together." In the photo, Walt looked pleased, standing next to Darnell, who was a good half foot taller, his arm around Darnell's shoulder, their heads leaning close.

"When was this?" Lydia asked.

"Last summer. They had this big carnival thing, with rides and stuff."

"May I look?"

Cherise handed her the phone. Lydia flipped through. Lots of pictures of Cherise and others, standing in groups, smiling, lifting plastic cups. Some of Darnell playing a bowling game on grass, trying to knock over pins with a large ball. A Ferris wheel. Friends of theirs, smiling, raising glasses to the camera. Walt with Darnell and other people. One of Walt with two women, the HR lady and one she didn't recognize.

"Who's this?"

"Walt's wife," Cherise said. "I forget her name."

Lydia handed the phone back. "So, you had the sense that Walt was stressing Darnell out with too much work, and you thought he thought Darnell was lazy, but also, that you were friends and they liked each other?"

"Yeah. So that's why I didn't want to say anything. I don't know what I'm saying."

"Did you ask anyone else if their schedules were as punishing as Darnell's?" She shook her head. "Why not?"

"Well, I didn't want to be a complainer. Like they're treating us worse … treating Darnell … I didn't want to get in trouble or a bad reputation. I mean, this company is all there is. If they throw you out, you're gone."

"You never spoke to Walt about it in private?"

"No. We're not friends like that. He's our boss. He does everything by the book."

"I see."

Cherise sat up. "What?"

"I don't know," she said. "But, thank you."

When she left Cherise, she went back to the center; placed her briefcase and files back on the table in the conference room, put on the hardhat and walked the whole place, with no purpose or intention. Just walked and looked. It was the first time she had done this alone, without an agenda or peering through a camera lens.

She followed the belts that carried the merchandise, watched the patterns, the routing it took from one place to another. It was all planned, nothing random about any of this. She had been told many times, this was one of the most successful centers of its kind. Everything had to be thought out. She watched the force, the energy, that propelled the boxes, the pressure that built up to create that propulsion, that inertia.

Inertia, she thought. Funny word. Comes from inert, but it's the opposite; only something that's not inert has inertia. It's the opposite of the thing you think it would be.

26

ENGINEERING A DISAPPEARANCE takes as much skill as engineering a creation. And the videos and comments and postings began to fall away. Harrison, Cordray and Wynn were stumped. The surge of support they felt seemed to dissipate, the interview requests, callbacks, agreements for TV spots diminish. It seemed the public just got tired of the story. What happened to some guy in some building in some state wasn't that important anymore. Maria Carvey accepted the loss of momentum as inevitable; the people who pledged support drifted off like ghosts. The only ones who still watched the story carefully were the ten dedicated agents in a war room at Chandler/Perkins in New York, who had been working with technology teams and social media specialists to surgically target and remove offending posts, mentions and threads. They covered the surface with a blanket that smothered the sharp edges of the story. While the legal case continued, the court of public opinion seemed to have moved on. And HausenHome's investment bankers moved back into high gear, reaching from all directions to embrace and digest Country Goods.

⊶⊷

"Oh my, that is quite a list," said Carol Ann from HR.

"Can you pull this information together?" Lydia asked.

She tilted her head back to read through the half-glasses, then forward to read over them entirely. As she did, Lydia looked around the room. The only humanity in the whole place, this small office on the Executive Level at the opposite end from McAllister's. There were actual living plants here and stuffed gnomes sitting contentedly on bookshelves; an electric kettle for tea, an upholstered chair with a needlepoint pillow. It felt genuine and homey, Lydia thought, probably because this is where they welcome you in or kick you out. Warm in every way, except for the fans.

"Sorry Carol Ann, if you don't mind my asking, but aren't you cold in here?"

Carol Ann gathered her sweater tighter around her neck. "Am I ever! You know what it is? There's something wrong with the heating or the AC on the floor below. It exhausts some kind of fumes up here. It was making me dizzy and they said they would fix it but they haven't. So until they do, I have to ventilate the room myself and keep the air moving."

"Aha. Sorry."

"That's what I get for coming back to work. Twenty-five years, and I could have been happily retired in my vegetable garden with my dogs. But no."

Lydia nodded sympathetically.

"I think I can get this for you," Carol Ann said. "Give me a day or so?"

"That would be fine. I'll stop by tomorrow."

"This is all about Walt Mulbacher," she said in her cautionary HR voice.

"Yes it is."

"Oh, dear. I assume … confidential?"

"Oh yes."

⊶═◉ ◉═⊷

Walt lay on the bed with the TV on, strumming his fingers over his chest. Kathy hummed in the bathroom through frothy toothpaste and electric toothbrush. Funny, he noticed, she hummed on key with the electric frequency.

He thought about telling her the ad agency lady had been buzzing around, asking him questions that didn't seem related to her job. Kathy would ask why and Walt would say, honestly, he didn't know. But he also knew there were things he would tell Kathy and things he wouldn't. Work things. Things he didn't want to say. He debated bringing it up in the lazy minutes before they got into bed, before the news, but decided not to. She would only tell him to get tough with this lady, or go to his supervisor and tell him. In either case, he felt an unspoken resistance, words or reasons he did not venture to explore. The discomfort in his stomach disappeared when he shifted his focus to the TV and the top story: newborn penguins at a zoo in San Diego. That was newsworthy, he thought; they really were un-believably cute. Standing up, falling down, standing up again, their mother pushing them along the ice with her nose. Yes, he decided. He would just deal with this lady himself.

→═◦ ◦═←

Paul was surprised when he walked into her suite: the trench coat was off, presumably hung in a closet somewhere. Seeing her now, unencumbered, was the Lydia of old. He did his exaggerated Cary Grant double-take. "Don't tell me you listened to something *I* said?"

"Just getting down to business. And here's the business." She tapped the pages on the table. "In the last eight months, Darnell Spragg had, in the aggregate, more hours than any other picker, more of those hours during overnight shifts, more inconsistency in his benchmarks, and on average, higher than anyone else's. He was working that kid much harder than the rest of the team, and hiding it from everyone, probably including Darnell."

"Mulbacher?"

She nodded.

"But is that a crime?" he asked. "He did have an underlying medical condition."

"The world is not random. There is intent. That has to count for something. Shit doesn't just happen."

He sat down slowly. He could see how serious she was now. "Why would he do that?" he asked.

"Because he didn't like him."

Paul looked over the papers. Scowled. "You think this is really what old Carl was looking for? It doesn't sound like it's gonna make anybody very happy."

"Well, that's fine, because old Carl doesn't want to be happy."

"Say what?"

"He told me. Late night mystery call a few weeks ago. He said he doesn't want to be happy. He wants to know what he needs to know."

"You didn't tell me," Paul said, surprised at the omission.

"I'm sorry. I had no reason for not telling you." She thought, even by saying that, there must have been one, but she couldn't summon it up. "In any case

… to answer your question … this *is* what old Carl was looking for. He knows something is wrong in his house and this is it."

"Mister stuffypants?"

She nodded firmly.

"You're sure? You just graduated to taking your coat off. Maybe you shouldn't be wielding a terrible swift sword just yet. I mean, to start with, why? What's the motivation?"

"In simplest terms, he didn't like him. Cherise knows it, but she doesn't see it, or she's too nice to say. He's a racist … or prejudiced, or whatever word they use now. He didn't like him."

Paul squinted one eye. "You know, as a commie pinko, left-wing homo, I'm all in on that one. But are you sure you can make it stick?"

"You said it yourself. He's a liar and he's hiding something. It's time for people to pay for what they do. There has to be justice."

"What are you going to do?"

She looked up at him with determination he had not seen in two years.

"I'm going to nail that little weasel to the wall."

27

ONCE UPON A time, she relished battles. Taking on a Goliath and winning: CEOs who thought they could bamboozle the little lady; account execs who wanted a taste in exchange for a new piece of business. She had almost forgotten the sensation, the thrill, and for the first time in a long time, felt the desire to reclaim that power and come back to the world. She had been good at it, too. She knew the rhythm and pattern, the way to get through defensive shields to the center, to the soft core. She took deep breaths and felt the confidence fill her like oxygen.

She knocked firmly and opened the door without waiting. He looked up, sighed, rolled back from his desk and laced his fingers behind his head.

"Ms. Calligan," he said, calmly.

"Mr. Mulbacher," she said, just as calm.

"What do you want now?"

"You don't seem surprised to see me."

"You've been playing games all week. I expected it." He indicated the chair squeezed between the front of his desk and the wall. "Please."

She closed the door firmly, made sure he heard it click. Lowered the plastic blinds and stood with her back to the door. "You've got quite a setup here, don't you?"

He shook his head. "What does that mean?"

"Big supervisor with the office and the monitors. Everything *data driven*, worked out to the smallest degree. Software, algorithms. Mumbo-jumbo to hide behind."

"I honestly have no idea what you're talking about."

"What's the thrill? I mean, enlighten me. What's so exciting? Is it just the fun, pushing buttons and pulling levers in your little man cave?"

He rolled back slightly from the desk to show how untethered he was.

"I'm sorry? What on earth are you talking about?"

She stepped closer to him. Looming was easy here because the office was so small. Her height and bearing worked to her advantage, looking down at him.

"You make all these people run around, you move all this equipment, you make all these things happen. And you do it from behind these screens and monitors with no one really knowing what it is you're doing. You're so good at it, no one bothers themselves to keep track."

He feigned confusion. Spread his arms, tried to smile. The good guy.

She stepped closer, looked down at his crotch, the shirt and sweater tucked—stuffed, really—into the pants. Made sure he knew what she was looking at, then raised her eyes to his. His cheeks flushed.

"What are you really doing in here?" she asked, in the soft, mellifluous voice.

"I'm doing my job. Besides, I don't understand why I'm getting the third degree from an *ad agency* we hired to make commercials. Isn't that what you're here for? Why are you even asking me these things?"

"That is what I'm here for, Walter. We like to tell a story that's true. Sounds better, looks better. Sells more product. But what you've been telling me isn't the truth. And I'm curious why."

"Ah, this is bullshit. I've had it." He picked up his phone.

"Don't waste the effort. Call McAllister directly."

He did, and spoke to Adele. Told her what was happening and listened, nodded. Hung up.

"Surprise," she sang. "You have to talk to me."

His eyes searched the space in front of him for a moment, for an explanation. *Confidence*, someone must have told him. She could see him girding his loins, the voice—wife, shrink, friend?—telling him to be a man. Those voices are the most fun to whittle away at. She settled into the chair across from him, her weight pressing it against the closed door.

"Why, Walter?" she asked, calmly.

"Why what?"

"Why the subterfuge? Why the hiding? Why the skulking around behind systems and reports? If you want to do something, why not be a man and just do it?"

And that did do it. A good little flinch there. Good place to start drilling. What was amazing to her were the tells. The little things people do that reveal the weak spots. We're trained to ignore them, or if we don't, not to provoke them or hurt anyone's feelings. It's cruel to do so. We're all so nice. But Lydia had been on the outside for a while, she had been on the street. Someone handed her a lifeline back but seemed to know that she had seen something, been through something, that would penetrate the defenses of nice people and slice right through them.

"I am totally in the dark about what you're asking," Walter said.

"Are you?" She leaned slowly, smoothly, closer to him. "You like to make things happen. You like to make ... what did you call it ... output ... a success. And you like to hurt people."

He sat back. "I do no such thing."

"Oh Walter. You don't have to hide from me. I'm on your side. I make the ads that tell everyone what a good job you're doing. That's *my* job. That's what I'm paid for. So give me some credit for knowing my own client. All this equipment, all those graphs and charts on your screen. You use it to do your job, but you also use it to hurt people. And that's the part I'm foggy on. I would like to know why. I really would."

"Lady, you are cracked. You got a ..." and he stopped, she saw him put it together. The reflex Paul mentioned, the skillfulness to mask it. "I just don't know what you're asking about," he said. "Please get out of my office." He stood. His body language would have prompted anyone else to stand as well, but she wouldn't budge.

"No, Walter, I don't think so. I think you need to tell me about this. Get it off your chest, for one thing. It's got to be a burden to carry around. It must feel terrible."

"No idea what you're talking about." Eyes darting to the door. Good, she thought. We're moving to denial. Face turning red, but not red enough.

"Give it a shot," she said. "Give it a guess."

"Is this about Darnell?"

"What do *you* think, Walter?"

"Oh my god. Lady. Come on." He sat again. "The police were all over this thing, they did a thorough investigation. You know as well as I do, that guy had underlying medical problems. Even he didn't know about them. There's no liability on the company's part. There was nothing any of us could have done. It was very sad, but it was no one's fault, least of all mine. Jesus."

"That is the conclusion they came to Walter, you're right. There is no liability here, in the eyes of the law. But you know who's not satisfied? You know who smells something isn't right?" She leaned forward over his desk. "Guess."

A thin lacquer of bravado over real fear. Good.

"Carl Hausen," she said slowly. "He knows how things work. He knows what you do. He knows what you do better than you do. And he's the one who wants to know. And I'm his proxy, Walter. What I know and see, he knows and sees. For all intents and purposes, you're talking to Carl Hausen right now. So tell me. Why do it?"

"I don't know what you're talking about." He grimaced. Kind of funny, and she smiled. Who was he doing? Clint Eastwood, John Wayne? The tough guy sneer didn't work on his chubby features. He held his hands in an odd sort of posture now, just above his lap, fingers straight out, as though willing them not to do something. An image popped into her mind. She had a nephew, a small child, and when he was scared, he used to grab his crotch for security. That's what it was. He wanted to grab his ding-dong and hold onto it, but he couldn't, not with her sitting in front of him. Pointing the way in.

"Okay, Walter. Then maybe you can shed some light on something else for me. Tell me … why did they take your computers away and escort you out of the building last October?"

A nice deep pulse on the Adams apple.

"That was a security problem. We had a trojan in the system. It originated from an email sent to my computer."

"Oooof," she said, smiling and shook her head. "No it wasn't. I haven't seen the whole report, but you and I know what it was." She held it only a brief moment. "Titties and pussies, Walter. Titties and pussies at work." Shook her finger at him, tsk-tsk'ed. "What happened? Someone find you in here with the lights off and the naughties on?"

"No."

"Had to blow off some steam in the middle of the day? Knick-knack paddywhack, give yourself a bone?"

"*No.*"

Peeling the layers away.

"I think yes, Walter. And it's pointless to lie. Everyone knows. You know how I know? Because the people on the floor told me. Everyone knows what you do in here. They can smell it on you. They laugh at you." His face began to collapse in on itself. "What gets you off? Pretty girls? Asian girls? Underage girls? What do you look for, Walter? They all wonder out there. They place bets on what you're watching in here that makes your little pickle go *pop*."

The mouse backed into a corner now. She'd get nothing further in this direction, time to come at it from another angle. She pulled the papers from her briefcase, placed them on his desk.

"Ok, Walter, then perhaps you can explain some of this to me. I went through your records. I looked very carefully at what you've been doing in here. These show a pattern of pressure you put on Darnell. The hours you gave him. The strange shifts you made him take. The uneven benchmarks. You know the system very well. You made it look random. The police didn't pick up on it because you're so good. Like you said, there's no liability here, the company's not at risk. But Mister Hausen knows when his system is being misused and he wants to know why. And so do I. And that's all there is to it, Walter. We just want to know why."

He shook his head, eyes welling up. Stared at his hands, his fingers, opening and closing, squeezing nothing. "There's nothing wrong with what I did. It's all by the book. You can't find anything that says I did wrong."

"Oh, but I can. No one checks your work, Walter, because you're the expert here. I know how much they rely on you. And you deliver. But I've looked over all the logs and examined all your little tricks and tweaks. I've been watching you, Walter. You treated one employee very differently than you treated all the rest. And when I show these reports to everyone—and I will—they'll see it too."

"I only did what the software said," he said, willing his mouth not to turn down and tremble.

"You and I both know that isn't true, Walter. No monitors to hide behind. I see you and I know what you've been doing. With your dirty little hands. Tell me the truth, Walter. Tell the truth, for once."

He looked at her, pleading not to go there.

"Your dirty little hands."

He looked down at his lap and whispered something.

"I'm sorry?" Lydia said.

"I didn't mean to."

She took a long breath in. Let it out. "Go on."

"I ... we ... have to work," he said, and began to sob quietly. "We have to be good. I have to be strong. I have to be a man and make things happen."

"And how do you make things happen, Walter? By hurting people?"

He shook his head, tears dripping onto his open hands. "Nooo. I didn't mean to. It was an accident. It was work. It was for the company. If you're strong and hit your goals, then everyone is happy. Everyone knows you can do things. I did it by the book. I did what they told me to. I didn't know there was anything wrong with him. I couldn't ... I felt so ... I didn't mean for that to happen ... I liked Darnell, I really did."

"Then why did you punish him?"

He looked up again. His mouth screwed into a grimace, his hand a tightened fist. "You have to be strong. You have to make people do what they have to do. You can't be a fat, lazy ass. A good manager makes his people do what they have to."

"Was Darnell a fat, lazy ass?"

He nodded.

"Are *you* a fat, lazy ass?"

He sobbed, nodded, looked down at his hands in his lap.

"Did you hate him?"

"No," he cried. "I liked him. I just ... I have to be strong. They all told me." And he let it go completely, the dam breaking as he sobbed and sobbed.

She took another long breath then stood for a moment, watched his shoulders heaving. "Well, Walter," she said, "you have to live with it. Being strong means taking responsibility for what you did. We're all responsible for our actions."

She leaned forward, collected the papers from his desk and put them back in her folder. Before she opened the door, she turned. "Just so you know. I did something wrong and someone died too. There's no going back."

Then she turned the knob and left Walter alone.

28

AN HOUR LATER, lying on the bed in the suite, she realized she didn't know how to reach Carl Hausen. She tried calling back the number he called from before, but it went to voicemail. She said she had some information for him and hung up. Then she let out a long held breath and waited for the feeling of satisfaction one gets after a job is complete. A little came. Just a bit. Probably after she relayed what she learned and the information was in someone else's hands, that relief would come. She was sure of it.

⊷⟾◉⟽⊶

"He *confessed?*"

Lydia nodded. Cherise's jaw dropped.

"He said that to you?"

She nodded again.

"Walt ..." Cherise said, her head tilting to the right. "Why ...?"

"He's a sad little man who doesn't think much of himself. There are lot of people like him."

"But, did he mean to ...?"

"No, no. It was just an accident, an awful, terrible accident. Or a coincidence." It seemed to give Lydia pause for a moment. "No matter what, though, I am so, so sorry."

"And you told Carl Hausen all this?"

"I'm going to. When he calls me back."

Marion sat forward at the table. "But this is very serious, Ms. Calligan. You're telling us this man acted willfully and maliciously to hurt poor Darnell? And he told you he did?" She nodded. "Well, that changes everything, I have to say. Cherise, honey, I think we need to tell your father, and see what his lawyer wants to do."

"That's a good idea, Mrs. Watson."

Marion looked at Lydia, more confused than before. "But Ms. Calligan, don't you *work* for the company? Don't they pay your agency for your work?"

"They do, Mrs. Watson. But I told Cherise I would tell her everything I found out. And if it wasn't for her, and a good kick in the ass, we wouldn't have found out at all."

"Mightn't this put you on thin ice with your employer?"

"I suppose. But I can't seem to manage ... compromise ... and keep my balance any more."

"Well, it seems to me this changes everything."

Lydia shrugged. "Not being a lawyer, I don't know how these things work. I imagine without a clear line, cause and effect could be hard to prove. But it might give you more leverage in a settlement for wrongful death, if you go that route. Which of course it was." She looked at Cherise. "This should never have happened to you. Or Darnell."

But Cherise hadn't been listening to either of them, her mind elsewhere.

"I don't know," she said. "Walt. It doesn't ... I don't know, it doesn't add up to me."

"I know it doesn't," Lydia said. "Because you're young and you're trusting and you don't know there are people like this in the world. I'm sorry you have to find out this way."

"And it was an accident?" she asked again, trying to reassure herself.

"A terrible one. I'm so sorry."

Cherise looked at the space in front of her, where the answer had been placed. "Huh."

⋅⊷═◉═⊷⋅

Later on, after Lydia told Paul, she waited for the sense of relief again.

"So, you happy?" he asked. "We out of here now?"

She sat at the table in the suite, trench coat draped over the back of the chair, staring straight ahead. She'd laid her glasses on the table and Paul was startled by the darkness of the circles under her eyes. "Hello?" he said, snapping in her face. "You get what you wanted?"

"I guess so," she sighed.

"You guess so? Is that a yes or a no? Are we on the next plane or what?"

A longer sigh. Then, "Yes."

"Finally. Thank God. You have no idea how badly I need a Zuni margarita."

"Well, you'll get everything that's coming to you, I'm sure." She rubbed her eyes and tried to rouse herself. "But first we have a few loose ends to tie up. I have to tell old Carl what I found out. As if that's going to do him any good."

"You going to tell Cherise?" he asked, joking.

"I already did."

He stopped abruptly. "Oh, that's wonderful. That's just superb. You told the victim's girlfriend before you told the man who hired you? The man who pays your salary and all the agencies depending on you?"

She nodded.

"Well, God bless you, darling. Boy oh boy, if they thought you had a death wish before, they ain't seen nuthin' yet. Would you mind paying me now? I don't want to be standing anywhere near you with that target painted on your back."

"It's the best I can do," she said to herself and stood. "The best I can do." She looked at him. He shrugged, not sure what she wanted. She shrugged; didn't know either. She picked up the folders from the table. "Do me a favor, take these back to HR, will you?"

"Nuh-uh," he said, "you. That old bag bit my head off when I went up asking for them."

"Oh, poor you, scared of a little old lady. You were probably nasty and deserved it."

"Yeah, well." They both knew it was true. "Still. You bring 'em back."

"Fine," she said. "Baby."

⋆⇥▬◉▭⇤⋆

Lydia knocked first, then walked into HR. Carol Ann sat behind her desk, turned to the side, typing at a computer on a small stand. She looked up and took off her glasses and smiled. "Those all for me?"

Lydia nodded and placed the folders on her desk. "Thank you so much for gathering all that information."

"Find what you needed?"

"Oh yes."

Fatigue swept over her again and she had to sit down. Maybe all the stairs, though more probably the earlier events of the day. Possibly the fumes that vented into this office.

"That's why I take the elevator," Carol Ann said. "This place is bigger than it looks. You end up walking a lot more than you think you do."

Lydia nodded. Tried to regain her breath. She felt cold, and realized she had come without her coat. She'd left it at the hotel, draped over the chair. Wrapping her arms around herself, trying to warm up, she looked around the room, at the bookshelves with ivy overflowing and draping down, pictures in frames of smiling people. Carol Ann and an older man, her twinkling blue eyes as warm in the photo as they were at this moment. Lydia took in the smile, the kindness. Looking back at Carol Ann, she noticed the fine lines and wrinkles, which made her look older than she probably was. When she rose to put the files in the cabinet behind her, Lydia realized how tall she was, almost as tall as Lydia herself. She was wrapped in a long brown knitted sweater, the kind of cardigan that hangs almost to the floor. You'd need something like that if you worked in here all the time. After one final, big breath, Lydia said, "You have a lot of responsibility. You're the only HR person for the whole facility?"

Carol Ann smiled as she sat back down. "I am. And I love it. Keeps me busy. Helps me draw on my old skills."

"Ah. You used to do something like this?"

"Oh, no, nothing like this. I was retired. And very happy. But my partner passed away and I was alone, so I needed to do something."

"I'm sorry. How long ago was that?"

"About a year. Sweet old fellow." She indicated the picture on the desk, herself smiling with a sad-faced older man, deep bags under his eyes. "Poor Howie. He had a hard time."

Lydia nodded, sympathetically. "Are you from the area? Did you grow up here?"

"No, no. I lived in Denver most of my life."

"Ah, a city girl."

"Always!" Carol Ann said, and laughed.

"So, big change coming out to cow country?"

"Yes, it was. But my husband and I wanted the quieter life. We bought a ranch with a lot of land. Just ideal, just what we were looking for. But after he passed, the ranch was a lot for one person to handle."

"Oh, dear, yes, that sounds like it would be."

Lydia felt her eyes scanning the room and landing on another photo on a shelf behind the desk; a younger Carol Ann with another older, sad-faced man. Huh, she thought. Must be the husband.

"But I love the kids," Carol Ann said. "All the energy that's going on here. It's so exciting."

"You like to help them?"

"I do. I have to interview every one and give them their startup paperwork. Line up their training. A lot of kids never had a job like this before, so they come up and ask lots of questions."

"You interact with people on the floor a lot?"

"They have so many procedures and protocols nowadays! There's whole notebooks full of rules you have to follow." She indicated the bookcase that took up half the wall and the rows of dark blue binders along one shelf; on the spines, *National Reference of Human Resource Standards.* "They change all the time, too. What you can say, what you can't say, what you can do, what you can't ... and everyone counts on me to keep up with it so nobody gets in trouble!" Lydia noticed the supplements stuffed carefully into the bindings.

It was so pleasant up here. Away from the banging and roaring and hydraulic whining everywhere on the main floor. Only the vague sound of humming from the machines below. Lydia felt comfortable; the plants, the odd items on the desk, the bookshelves. Idiosyncratic, like Lydia herself. Carol Ann seemed smart and efficient, a normal person in this madhouse. She might be the kind of person Lydia would like to hire at some point for her own business. She felt a trust and connection between the two of them. So much, in fact, now that it was all over, to drop some of her guard. She nodded at the file cabinet. "Did you ever have problems with Walter?"

"Oh, yes, well," Carol Ann said, and lowered her eyes. "I'm not supposed to talk about it ... but since you asked for the information, it seems you put two and two together ... there were a few issues ... I think that's all I can say."

Lydia remembered the photos Cherise showed on her phone. Pictures of them all at some outdoor event. Darnell and Walt and his wife, and next to her, Carol Ann. The blue eyes made her remember.

"Did you ever have words with him?" Lydia asked.

"Well, there were a few. Yes, he had some infractions. But I'm sure you figured that all out by now."

Lydia shook her head. "These boys. What are we going to do with them?" Carol Ann smiled, understanding. "What people get away with nowadays," Lydia said. "You should hear some of the things they do in San Francisco. Things I've had to put up with."

"I can just imagine."

Perhaps it was the air in the room, or the fatigue, but she felt herself letting go, speaking freely. Just listening to herself talk. "I mean, the rudeness and the pushiness. Everyone wanting their way. It's so much nicer here. People seem kinder and more honest."

"I think so," Carol Ann said.

"I'll bet that's on account of you. You've probably set the tone for good behavior, running things the way you do."

"I try," she said. "Not always succeeding, but I try!"

"Do you have much by way of disciplinary problems?"

"Oh, nooooo," she said, scowling. "People here work so hard. My lord, the number of hours they work. Those kids have so much energy."

"They do. But you have a lot to manage yourself. You must be very organized."

"I am."

"Do you oversee the Care office as well?"

Carol Ann furrowed her brow as if not recognizing the word. "Oh that?" she said. "Oh no, that's a big pain in the neck."

"How so?"

"Well, they didn't want a fully staffed infirmary ... something to do with expenses ... so the company made this deal with HealthSaver to put one of their instant clinics in here. We don't really touch it. If there's anything serious, they call emergency services and have the EMTs deal with it."

"Do you have to do any administration for that or that's all on HealthSaver?"

"Oh, I can't recall the exact relationship. I think the materials belong to them and the staffer is one of ours. So the hours the staffer is onsite, they're our employee and we pay them. I guess they did it that way because it was easier than us being billed by HealthSaver."

"Oh, me. That does sound complicated. Do you have to sign their time cards?"

"The payroll company does that, all I do is approve the hours."

"My lord, you are a marvel."

"Not always marvel-ous, let me tell you."

"Frustrations?" Lydia asked.

"Oh, like you wouldn't believe," Carol Ann said, and looked skyward.

"Huh. Do you ever ... review the medical reports the staffers write when someone goes in?" Carol Ann tilted her head, smiling evenly. Lydia felt a tiny blip in her chest, like a muscle spasm. "To Care," Lydia said. "The, uh, clinic."

"Oh, I suppose I could. But I have so much work of my own, I don't have time to look at every paper that comes up from down there."

"Ah." Lydia took a breath. "It's been so fascinating to see how one of these operations works, from the inside out. You know, I go online and order things all the time, but I never gave a thought to how it was packaged or delivered. It's really quite amazing. You all do such an incredible job. A lot of the credit goes to you."

"Oh, no. The geniuses have it all worked out, we just follow the manuals."

"But you, I mean. You're different. You seem like the only person here with any real world experience. That must be why they come to you and seek out your advice. You must be very good with people."

"I try."

"I have my own business, in San Francisco," Lydia said. "Well, I used to. I closed it a few years ago. I had some hard times and I couldn't maintain the frantic pace."

"Oh, I'm very sorry."

"Personal problems. But the people. Oh! What I really couldn't take were the lazy ones. You probably know what I'm talking about. I had so many people on my payroll who thought of it like some kind of a gravy train. Working for some high-class ad agency, then they'd take three-hour lunches and talk with their friends ... honestly, sometimes it was like running a kindergarten."

Carol Ann nodded, listening.

"The worst ones are the men," Lydia said, and leaned forward, taking Carol Ann into her confidence. "These young guys. They think you're there to work for them. I don't want to call it sexist or anything, but it seems to be in the DNA. Like this fellow Paul, you may have seen him. He's working with me here. Another one of them. Thinks I'm here to take his notes and keep track of his schedule. The good-looking ones are the worst."

"Oh, I know what you mean."

"It's the entitlement I can't abide. I mean, I've had to work every minute of my adult life. I don't get a break. Nobody is coming in and saving my backside. And these guys come along, they think you're their mother! Even though it's my agency, with my name on the door, they've got their feet up on the desk like it's their own livingroom."

Carol Ann watched with a blank expression.

"I think they're weak, is what it is," Lydia said. "This whole macho act and the bravado and all. But underneath, they're just weak."

Nodding.

"I don't know why more people don't see it."

The twinkling eyes.

"It makes me sick, if you want to know the truth. You seem trustworthy, so I hope you don't mind me venting my spleen."

"I understand you," Carol Ann said. "It's no different here."

"Really?"

She shook her head.

"Some of them make me sick," Lydia said.

"Well, that's a bit much ..."

"It's true. The things they do. I figured out what happened with Walt, by the way. Why he got called out in October. You know what it was."

Carol Ann shrugged.

"You have a good heart to keep him on," Lydia said. "That's so disgusting. How do you deal with stuff like that, day in and day out?"

"Walt just needed some talking to. He's a lost soul, that one."

"You spoke to him a lot?"

"Well, I had to!" she laughed. "Goodness me, he wouldn't move out of his own way otherwise."

"Lazy?"

"Well … sad. A bit pathetic, honestly. He needed motivation he didn't have on his own."

"You know, I got that sense. But his numbers were good. You must have done a very good job with him."

"Oh, I knew him. I talked to Kathy."

"Kathy?"

"His wife."

"Ah."

"And she clued me in. He just needed motivation, that's all."

"Sounds like he needed more than that. I saw him in there, all hunched up in his little office. I'm curious, what do you say? How do you motivate someone like that? I could use the advice, for the sack of lazy bones waiting for me back at home."

"Well," Carol Ann said. "You have to start with patience, that's all. Find out what people are like, and listen to them."

Lydia watched her face. She seemed like such a kind person. You always hope for kindness, for understanding. Especially from old people. That's what they're supposed to do for you. To be for you. Lydia always hoped for people to be just like you wanted them to be. She thought, perhaps, by hoping so much, Carol Ann would understand, and would be that person. That she would see how much Lydia was hoping.

"And sometimes," Carol Ann said, "you have to take them by the scruff of the neck and make 'em do it. I hate to say it, but it's true."

"I can bet."

"Just shake 'em and give them a little discipline."

"That one, for sure," Lydia said. "Lazy ass."

The tiniest shrug of agreement. "You know what he was watching?" Carol Ann asked. "Videos of women who beat men up. Dressed in all these crazy outfits. The men are all tied up on a bed or a, what do you call it, a rack. The women hit them and call them all sorts of names."

"How did you know?"

"We have this software. It tracks everything on the network. It gives you a log so you can see everything the employee is watching."

"Oh my lord!"

Carol Ann nodded. "Hundreds of 'em. I understand he does the same thing at home."

"Kathy?"

She nodded again.

"Poor thing," Lydia said.

"Can you imagine?"

"Did he know? I mean, that you knew?"

"Well, I had to make it clear what we knew. Why we pulled him out of work."

"But they can fire you for something like that."

"Oh yes. But Walt's a decent fellow underneath. And he's a good worker. He's one of the best in the industry. We really wanted to keep him. At least that's what I was told."

"So, you handled the situation? That must have been tricky."

"Oh no," Carol Ann said, "you just have to get to know these people. Learn what makes them tick."

"What do you think makes *him* tick?"

"He certainly needed some guidance. And direction. Very good at his job but not a decisive person. He needed to be prodded."

"That makes sense. How do you do it?"

"Well, you sit them down and you tell them, look, you need to make this work. You need to stand up and be counted as a man. They need a kick in the ass … pardon my French … a lot of them. A lot of the time."

Lydia had forgotten how cold it was in the room until she felt a chill at the base of her spine. It made her straighten her back ever so slightly, radiating out to the nerves in her hands. "You had to meet with him a lot?"

Carol Ann shrugged. "He definitely needed motivation, that one."

"What do you say to someone like that? I'm so curious."

"Well, I said to him, I said, Walter, you have this group of people looking up to you. You're their leader and you have to take on that role. You can't sit in your office hiding behind a computer all day. And truth be told, you can't go sticking your hands in your pants like some kind of a pervert, or do you know what will happen? You'll turn into one."

"You told him that?"

"Darn right. Dirty behavior on company property. On company equipment. You can't have that. I told him so. And oho, believe you me, he heard it."

"He did?"

She nodded. "And I asked him what the benchmarks were, and if he was hitting them, and he wasn't. So I had to get tough with him."

"You had to."

"But he *was* lazy. *Is* lazy. That's just his nature. Kathy told me. So, you get on someone like that, you just get into their head, and you tell them, now listen, you *move* that lazy ass of yours, and you hit that number. You can't whine or bellyache or blubber your way out of it. Shit or get off the pot, I always say."

"How did he take it?"

"Oh, he was a little pansy. Not a queer, not like that, just a little pushover. I found out. You get on him and you tell him. I said, you have a choice here. You can be a pathetic little baby or you can do what I'm telling you and get it done. And it worked. He hit those numbers, month after month. But I had to stay on top of him."

Lydia found herself smiling, and nodding confidently. Job well done, her manner conveyed. She felt the camaraderie between them; they bonded over sad, pathetic Walt. Because Lydia had zeroed in on him too. She tried to recall exactly how. Was it when she discovered he had been running the loading dock and lied about knowing that old guy Bernie? Paul had gone looking for the files. He went to HR, but they were gone. Then the crazy meth head brought them to Paul and told him they had been found. That was it.

"Well, anyway," Lydia said, "he had a lot to get motivated with that crew. Now, come on, you have to admit, some of the people on his team are absolutely hopeless. The scrawny one, with the pimples? I'm surprised that one hasn't run over his own foot with a forklift."

"They have, you know."

"Really?"

She nodded. "They get into all kinds of scrapes. We don't report it. Unless it's something serious. They're all kids down there, most of them. This is the first real job many of them ever had."

Lydia gave it her folksiest, *yep, don't I know it* nod. "Tough about that young man, though," she said. "Darnell. I feel bad for his family. But truth be told, he really didn't take care of himself. He was in bad shape. Overweight. And the girlfriend couldn't have been doing him any favors. Now that one's a real loose cannon."

"I wouldn't know about that," Carol Ann said. "That wasn't on my radar."

"They were a little too forward, if you ask me. A bit … pushy. Asking for scheduling changes. A lot of accommodation to their own comings and goings. I wouldn't have blamed Walt for trying to keep him in line."

"Well, it's all done by software down there. Doesn't have anything to do with me."

Lydia sat back in her chair. "A lot of them are just childish now," she said. "You're right, they don't want to work hard, so you have to find ways of motivating them. Just like the girlfriend. And since we were featuring her in the spots, it made things more difficult. I can tell you, she gave me a very hard time. Didn't want to do this, didn't want to do that. Honestly," she said, quieter, "I had to bend backwards and forwards to give that girl what she wanted. Just a little too entitled, if you ask me."

Carol Ann pulled back slightly. "Well, they all do work very hard."

"Maybe," Lydia said, and grimaced. "They're spoiled. Those two especially. Carrying on all the time. Do you know how many times she bothered Walt about adjusting her schedule this way and that? As if the company works for *her?*"

"He told me."

"So I honestly don't blame him a bit, now that this is all over. I mean, come on. People work for the employer, not the other way around."

"He did need some help in that area."

"Walt?"

"Yes. He told me about the two of them and the scheduling she was asking for. I told him. I said, Walt, you have to stick to the manual and whatever the software tells you. Don't bend the rules for these kids or anyone else. You can be a good manager, but you also have to follow the rules. Like you say, we're all here to work, not to parade our dalliances in everybody's face."

"Well, I'll tell you, those two took advantage of the system. But good."

A demure, quizzical expression from Carol Ann.

"They were getting together," Lydia said. "Nuzzling around when they were supposed to be clocked in. They had a whole system going on."

"But that's not possible," Carol Ann said, sitting up. "Everyone is tracked. Their time is accounted for and locations are monitored."

Lydia smirked. "Walt knew about it. He looked the other way."

"But I told him," she said. "I told him to stay on top of those two."

"I watched them. While we were making the spots. She dropped her guard once or twice. They had Walt wrapped around their finger. You're right, he's not a very strong individual. The girl is a hard worker so maybe that's why he let her get away with it. Falsifying hours, giving them prime shifts, treating them like they're royalty or something."

"I told him specifically," Carol Ann said. Her eyes wandered, searching for something. Lydia became aware of the door behind her, if it was open or closed. It was open.

"You know, he was a lot more clever than he let on," Lydia said. "*Darnell*. Trying to get a lot of free medical care out of the company."

"Oh, well, I made sure that wouldn't happen. I knew what *that* customer was up to. I told Walt, I said, you stay on top of that kid, don't you let up. He's a game player, I can tell."

Lydia reached back and gently pulled the door closed. Carol Ann nodded at it. "Keep that open, we need the air."

"What was he up to?" Lydia asked.

"Oh, playing Mister Lovey-dovey all the time. Giving us all that stinkeye. Like he was so special. Sauntering around here like he didn't have a care in the world. Like he wasn't supposed to be doing a job, like the rest of us."

"That is infuriating, I agree with you. How was he … what did you say? Mister Lovey-dovey?"

"Oh just … the two of them. The way they acted. Kissing and smooching and running around like children."

"Ah. Right. And there was that event last fall. A picnic or something?"

"The fair, yes. We rented all kinds of carnival rides and games. The company went all out on that one."

"You were there?"

"Of course! I had to help run the damn thing."

"And you saw those two? Behaving like children."

"Disgraceful. Gimpy eyes and their hands all over each other. Pawing each other. They just had ..." and she stopped. "I can't recall it now," she said, brushing it away. "They're all the same down there. They all work very hard."

"But those two did get special treatment. Why do you think Walt gave it to them?"

"I couldn't tell you."

"They demanded a lot more than they were entitled to, don't you think?"

"I don't know," she said, slightly agitated now. "It has nothing to do with me. Open that door, would you please?"

"But it has everything to do with you," Lydia said. "You're the only human resources person in the whole building. Everything else is machines and fork lifts and software. They have a lot of managers down there, but only one person watching over all the people. And that's you. So you must be very good at it."

"Like I said, I needed to work. No one else had the expertise they were looking for."

Lydia nodded, gave her the confident smile again. And the strange sensation of moving inside herself, like falling down a slide. Inertia. The opposite of the thing you think it would be.

"What did you do before this?" she asked.

"Eh?"

"Before you retired."

Carol Ann's face had become still. The twinkle and warmth had evaporated some time while they were talking.

"I worked for the coroner's office," she said, without intonation.

"In Denver?"

She nodded.

"Were you a technician?"

"No, the administrator. I ran the office."

"For twenty-five years," Lydia said, impressed. "You ran the city of Denver coroner's office for twenty-five years?"

"The whole county."

"So ... you would see all the reports. And work with the police. You would know what they look for."

She nodded.

"What forensics and doctors look for."

She made no move.

"And what they miss."

Carol Ann sat straighter behind her desk. "Open the door," she said.

"In a minute."

Lydia reached for the lapels of her trenchcoat, then remembered it wasn't there. She felt so cold. Perhaps that's why it took a few moments for the next thought to arrive. "So, if you *had* seen the reports from Care, you would have known what they meant, even if no one else did."

"I don't see the reports," Carol Ann said. "I don't know what you're talking about."

And now Lydia could really feel the effect of the air venting into this room. It made you slightly dizzy, but also calm. Allowed your mind to wander, imagine, associate.

It all made sense, of course. Smart and efficient. "Walter pushes the buttons and pulls the levers," she said. And she thought of Carl Hausen. He was smart too. Funny she still had no read on him. Was he a good person, a bad person? Once upon a time she had such good instincts about people, but now she couldn't tell. He was opaque, behind that pasty, childlike skin. But he knew something was wrong over here. He asked her to look into something that no one else could see.

A quick flash of light drew Lydia's attention back. Carol Ann's face had changed; her lower jaw thrust out, cradling the upper, like a claw. Lydia remembered what the crepey skin reminded her of now. Papier-mâché. A mask of fragile material which, when moistened, will sag and droop. As she watched Carol Ann watching her, she realized they really were alike. They both wore a mask of bravado covering something else. And as Carol Ann's mask lost its shape, revealing the bitterness and disappointment beneath, Lydia felt as if she were looking in a mirror. As she studied it, she asked, no one in particular, "What was it? What could it have been? Racism? Is that it? Because they were Black?"

"I heard what you tried to get me to say," Carol Ann said. "I'm no racist, *you're* a racist."

Lydia nodded. Fair enough.

Whatever happened to Lydia three years earlier had torn her mask off too. But when that happened, the only person she wanted to hurt was herself. Staring at this reflection now, she saw how it could be aimed at others as well. "But what did they have?" she wondered out loud. "They were just kids." She thought of that carnival and the picture of the people lined up in it, and Carol Ann standing next to Kathy. She could imagine the afternoon, almost placing herself in the scene. Cherise and Darnell running past, their laughter and happiness so open and free. And these blue, hopeful eyes staring out through the holes in a mask. Watching them, following them, taking them in. Their joy would be too painful to bear. Lydia could understand. She remembered what Paul said about her. That she was making a fool of herself, hurting no one but herself. Just to see how much pain she could inflict.

"Was that it?" Lydia asked. "You saw the reports. You knew he was sick. Was it just for the fun? For the cruelty? To see what would happen?"

"That kid had diabetes," she said, her voice grave and flat. "There's no crime here."

The flash of light again, and Lydia realized it came from the reflection off a metal letter opener in Carol Ann's lap. She must have palmed it from the desk drawer while they were talking. She held it in her left hand now, as she stood up slowly.

They regarded each other with even gazes. How alike they were. Lydia sat at a desk too. She had control over people and stories. She could make people believe whatever she was paid to make them believe. It's all crafted so beautifully. There is no crime here.

And yet. She had been hired to find something out for Carl, and she had done her job. But there was something else still. Something she needed for herself.

"But why?" she asked.

Carol Ann stared down at her.

"Because they had everything," she said. "And I have nothing."

And looking into this well of hurt and disappointment, Lydia understood. Unbearable emptiness, so painful the only thing you can do is lash out—at yourself, at others. Something charm and wit can only mask for so long.

Lydia took a long, final breath and stood up.

"Thank you," she said. They both knew she meant it.

Then she turned around and reached for the door. If the letter opener got to her neck before her hand got to the knob, then so be it. But the door opened and she walked out. Carol Ann remained standing at her desk, a frozen apparition, her hand clutched tightly at her side.

29

"AND YOU LEFT her there like that?"

Paul's eyes were saucers.

"Well, what was I supposed to do?" Lydia said. "There was nothing there. Nothing can be proven. As far as anyone is concerned, it was just two old broads getting high on glue."

"But oh my god," Paul said, flopping onto the chair. "The old bag."

Lydia nodded slowly. Exhaled several more times. "The old bag."

They sat for a few minutes unspeaking.

"Boy, that is one wacky distribution center," he said. "What are you going to do?"

"Well, at this point, I think discretion is the better part of ... value. I'll let our benefactor know what I heard and what I think, and let him decide how he wants to handle it. I'm not sure what I would tell the police even if I called them."

"Well, Jesus Christ, you almost got spachocked. I think that qualifies."

Even she was momentarily stumped on that one. "I think the word you're looking for is *spatchcocked*."

"Yeah," he said. "That."

"Aha, yes. Very good. To prepare a chicken by cutting down the backbone and spreading it open. From an old English expression, I believe, dispatching the cock. Something you're more familiar with than I. But that aside, I think giving old Carl the whole story, up to the minute, would be a better idea than me just calling in the keystone cops."

At which point her cellphone rang. She looked at it, showed Paul the number and nodded. Answered and set it on the table.

"Lydia," Carl said.

"Mr. Hausen," she said, nodding, her eyes scanning the corners of the room for the microphone.

"We on speaker?" he asked.

"My associate Paul is with me. No one else."

"Oh," he said. "Yes."

"Sir," Paul said, and saluted the phone

"I understand you have some information for me."

And she relayed the conversation, and everything she found out up to that time, and he listened. When she was finished, a moment of silence—they weren't sure if he was thinking or put his phone on mute—then, "Thank you."

"Of course," she said.

"Have you shared this with anyone else? Myron or anyone?"

Paul met Lydia's eyes.

"Mr. Hausen, I told the young man's girlfriend everything I learned, except this afternoon's latest event."

"You told the girl everything else? Everything you just told me?"

She closed her eyes. "I gained her trust by assuring her that I would tell her what I found out. I felt that was necessary to get you the information you needed."

This time they could hear the breathing on the other end. The sound of a sniffle. He might have had a cold, perhaps wiping his nose.

"You like math, Lydia?" he asked.

"Not particularly."

"I do. In school, I was fascinated by logarithms. I liked the idea of value expanding with increasing proportionality. It's a very positive view of things. Gives you hope."

"If you say so."

"One of the things logarithms help me calculate is risk. And you know what increases proportionally, the longer it goes on?"

"What, sir?"

"A lie. And what it costs you. Something most people don't take into account. Nine times out of ten, the longer a lie goes on, the greater the impact of the fallout. Don't know why people don't look at the numbers. When you lose, you lose bigger than if you hadn't lied at all."

"That's an interesting way of looking at it."

"So, I tell you what. I'll overlook the fact that you told someone else something you should have told me first. And you know I'm right. But I'll also tell you that I like it when I give someone a tough job and they do it. If that's what you had to do, then that's what you had to do."

Paul sat back and crossed his arms, mouthed, *You lucky SOB*.

"And we'll see what trouble that gets us into," he went on. "Cost of doing business I suppose."

"Glad to be of service," she said. "Now, if the matter has been resolved to your satisfaction, I hope you don't mind if my associate and I bow out at this point. This was a detour neither of us expected."

"Sure," he said. "Before you go, though."

Paul and Lydia stopped in their tracks.

"My understanding is you've had a tough time of it the last couple of years, Lydia."

"Nothing that wasn't my own fault."

"Well, I tell you what. With our takeover of Country Goods right around the corner, my advertising budget is gonna skyrocket. I'd like to bring your agency on with the big ones from New York. Good healthy retainer. A year at least, to start. That should give you a nest egg to get your shop up and running again. That work for you?"

Silence.

"Lydia?"

Paul leaned over the phone. "She's speechless. I'll offer a qualified yes on her behalf."

"Well, I appreciate all your efforts," Carl said. "Pleased to have you join the team. I like how you figure things out. *A rattle under the hood*. That's good."

Lydia looked at Paul, who looked back at Lydia.

"Uh, yes," she said. "Thank you."

"We'll be in touch," he said, and hung up.

She sat back in the chair, relaxed into the cushion. "What do you know? All this time I was joking, but I guess the place really is bugged."

Paul stared, his mind working. "Oh no!" he shouted, smacked the top of his head. "Oh, no it isn't." Lydia raised an eyebrow. "*I'm* the one who got spatchcocked," he said.

"Eh?"

"What day did Carl call you first?"

She looked at her phone, scrolled through and told him the date. "Ya ha," Paul said. "The day *after* I told my sweet, simple country bumpkin you were backing out of the job. Old Carl knew everything we were doing all along."

She shook her head at him and had to laugh. "Sonny boy," she said, "the trouble you get us into."

30

IT WAS NICE to be on a plane again. The rumble of turbines pushing you forward, pushing the past behind. Paul could almost feel them moving at three hundred and sixty knots, or so said the map on the screen.

"So," he said to Lydia, "you gonna take the money?"

She looked at the pathetic Manhattan in his plastic cup. "You're not on an expense account, you know. You're paying for that yourself."

"I *know*," he said, irritated that she wouldn't.

"Let's see the reception we get. If I'm persona non grata, it might not be worth it."

"What are you talking about? Arthur and his buddies got a ton of new business thanks to you. Everyone is overjoyed. Isn't that enough to come back for?"

"We'll see," she said closing her eyes and leaning against the headrest. "Moral scruples. Among other things."

Paul downed his drink and grimaced. "Jet fuel. Yuck." He wiped his mouth. "What is *moral scruples*? What are you, Sister Mary Catherine?"

"What we just did. What I just did. To save my own ass."

"What? You gave them a great campaign and made some good money and, oh, by the way, uncovered some bad people doing some bad shit. Sounds all very scrupulous to me."

"Maybe," she sighed.

"What do you think is gonna happen back there?" She raised an eyebrow. "To the good, the bad and the very ugly," he said.

"Oh. I don't know. Cherise and her family have a lawyer they trust. They know everything the company knows. How they work it out between themselves is none of my business. Carl sees it as *a cost of doing business*, so I guess insurance will handle it." She thought about it and grunted.

"What?" Paul asked.

"*There is no crime here*. That's what she said. Got to hand it to her. Enough ambiguity to save their bacon. Although ..."

He waited.

"... on the subject of insurance," she went on. "She said her husband died, a couple of years ago. Alone, on a ranch, with no one around. Then her boyfriend. Same thing. She didn't seem all that broken up about either one. I wonder what the police might turn up, or the insurance companies, looking at those deaths a little more carefully. Considering they took the word of someone who worked with the police for twenty-five years."

"Nice old lady," he said.

"And poor Walter, getting it from all sides. I did the same thing the rest of them did. It's funny how some men almost hand you a guidebook to their weak spots."

"What are mine?"

"Too many to count."

"You feel guilty about using it?"

"On Walter? I feel bad for the guy, but what they did was terrible. And sad."

Paul lifted his arm and snapped his fingers toward the approaching flight attendant. Lydia ducked her head into her lap. "You did not just do that," she whispered.

"That's what they're here for!" he huffed, and ordered another Manhattan. When Lydia lifted her head, tears slid from under her dark glasses.

"Well, take it easy," Paul said, "I'll apologize if it means that much to you."

"It's not that," she said, and wiped her eyes. "I didn't like what I saw in the mirror back there." Paul craned his neck. Was she talking about the bathroom? "Back *there*," she said. "That hateful woman. You should have seen her face. Without the makeup. I don't want to turn into that. Not having anything at all. Living such a duplicitous life."

"Is that a possibility?"

"There's a lot of things I've been afraid to look at. I haven't been treating myself very nicely. You were right. Much as I hate to admit it."

"You want to say more?"

She thought about it. "No," she said. "I think that will just have to wait for the next book."

Paul didn't press. This was not the moment—twenty minutes from seatback trays up and stowed—so he just put his hand over hers on the armrest. She turned to look at him carefully. He was such a handsome guy. Under all that cynicism, the sweetness he worked so hard to keep hidden. Both of them with their protective shells.

He cleared his throat. "So, back to the question. You gonna take the money and open the agency again?"

The plane dipped slightly as they began their descent. She felt the pleasant, gentle pressure of her body against the seat.

"Time only moves forward."

Cherise wasn't sure what to do with the information Lydia gave her. Which is what she said to her lawyer directly. She told her father she would take over managing the case and now he waited for her decision on how she wanted to move forward. Compensation was one thing, she told him, but more important, she wanted something Darnell would be proud of and that he would be remembered for. As she pondered what that could be, she got into her car and drove back to Denver.

Both boys were at home when she rang the bell.

"Your momma here?" she asked.

"No," Jamal said. "You want to talk to her?"

"*No.* I want to talk to you. Can I come in?"

They found their way to the kitchen table. She brought a bag of cheese popcorn and they all ate for a bit.

"Your brother was a pretty good guy," she said, finally. "I really miss him."

They both nodded. Not looking at her, but she felt something warm and familiar.

"You know," she said, "your brother and I, we had something special. I don't know what it was, but it sure pissed some people off. And it doesn't feel right to just pack my suitcase and go back and forget him. So I was thinking … and it's okay if you don't want to, I don't want to come off like some crazy ex-girlfriend … if it would be okay to spend some time together. Like, on weekends or an after school or something. Maybe I could take you guys to a museum or a movie. Or just take a walk. I feel … well, I feel like I'm kind of related to you. I hope that doesn't sound weird."

They shook their heads.

"That'd be good," Keiyon said. His smile was just what she remembered.

"Okay then," she said, and took their hands.

"But what about momma? She's pretty mad at you."

"Don't worry," she said. "I'll take care of her. I know her better than she thinks I do."

They nodded. She felt their hands in her own, and she held onto them, warm and solid. They felt full.

www.ingramcontent.com/pod-product-compliance
Lightning Source LLC
Chambersburg PA
CBHW050330110726
47899CB00007B/2448